Ady, Black Sun

World Writing in French
A Winthrop-King Institute Series

Series Editors
Charles Forsdick (University of Liverpool)
and
Martin Munro (Florida State University)

Advisory Board Members
Jennifer Boum Make (Georgetown University)
Michelle Bumatay (Florida State University)
William Cloonan (Florida State University)
Michaël Ferrier (Chuo University)
Michaela Hulstyn (Stanford Univesity)
Khalid Lyamlahy (University of Chicago)
Helen Vassallo (University of Exeter)

There is a growing interest among Anglophone readers in literature in translation, including contemporary writing in French in its richness and diversity. The aim of this new series is to publish cutting-edge contemporary French-language fiction, travel writing, essays and other prose works translated for an English-speaking audience. Works selected will reflect the diversity, dynamism, originality, and relevance of new and recent writing in French from across the archipelagoes – literal and figurative – of the French-speaking world. The series will function as a vital reference point in the area of contemporary French-language prose in English translation. It will draw on the expertise of its editors and advisory board to seek out and make available for English-language readers a broad range of exciting new work originally published in French. This series is published in partnership with the Winthrop-King Institute, Florida State University.

Gisèle Pineau

Ady, Black Sun

Translated by Tiffane Levick
and Timothy Lomeli

Liverpool University Press

First published in English translation by Liverpool University Press 2025
Liverpool University Press
4 Cambridge Street
Liverpool
L69 7ZU

Originally published in French as *Ady, soleil noir*

British Library Cataloguing-in-Publication data
A British Library CIP record is available

ISBN 978-1-83624-261-1 hardback
ISBN 978-1-83624-264-2 paperback

Typeset by Carnegie Book Production, Lancaster

Translators' Note

Gisèle Pineau is a prolific writer who has published over thirty texts in French over the course of her career. Her writing is popular in the francophone world, demonstrated by the almost yearly re-edition and republication of her books *Exil selon Julia* and *Papillon dans la cité*. Despite her success, very few of her works have been translated into English. Our decision to propose *Ady, soleil noir* for the Winthrop-King and Liverpool University Press World Writing in French: New Archipelagoes series stems from this lacunae.

This novel in particular builds on archival research to offer a reconstruction of the life of Adrienne Fidelin, or Ady. Until recently, Ady had largely been erased from history, even though her trajectory is similar to Joséphine Baker's: she performed in revues and films, danced in troupes, and modeled for various magazines. In addition to her own artistic endeavors, Ady was also a muse for numerous surrealist creators, such as Picasso, Paul and Nusch Éluard, Lee Miller, and, of course, Man Ray, and contributed to preserving their work, particularly Man Ray's.

Despite her own career, and her involvement in the creation and preservation of some of the surrealists' art, Ady's name is largely absent from discussions on the surrealist movement. Often simply relegated to "muse" and thus not seen as an artist in her own right, Ady's identity has tended to be fetischized in both French- and English-speaking circles, especially given her position as a woman of color from the exoticized Guadeloupe archipelago.

Pineau's novel contributes to rectifying this treatment, and many of our decisions within the translation tie in with her aims. We sought to bring to the fore the complexity of Ady's identity, teasing out her position as a perceived foreigner in Hexagonal France. As such, we decided not to translate French proper nouns, for instance those indicating names of cabarets or streets, in order to remind readers of the Parisian and francophone settings. We have, however, adopted anglophone typographical norms, as we sought to normalize these settings and emphasize Ady's background. In this vein, we have included a glossary of terms that bear cultural significance, especially in relation to the Caribbean and to Ady's identity. The majority of the terms italicized in the translation are included in the glossary. In several instances, we decided to add a small amount of Guadeloupean Creole to further bring attention to Ady's background and reflect cultural norms. This is the case for the nicknames given to Ady's sisters, as well as the terms that refer to her parents (*papa*, which is incidentally the same word in French, and *manman*).

Additionally, given the specificity of the cultural context surrounding the usage of the French word *nègre* explained in the glossary, and in an effort to avoid using racially loaded terms in English, we have generally left it in French. In some instances, where there is an explicit contrast established between "Black" and "white," we have translated *nègre* using a noun preceded by the adjective Black, capitalized, as is common practice in postcolonial literature and theory. A number of other racial slurs have also been kept in French and explained in the glossary, so as to respect the different connotations of terms relating to specific geographic and cultural contexts.

Ady, soleil noir is not simply a biography. Pineau takes advantage of the genre to imagine critical moments and conversations, and her novel sheds light on many of the crucial discussions around French identity happening at the time, and on what it means to be French. About an important Guadeloupean woman, written by an important Guadeloupean woman, the narrative structure of this book allows Ady's story to be told from a Guadeloupean perspective. Our translation seeks to provide a version in English of Pineau's version of Ady's voice, that is in line with the intention to reclaim and revalorize Black identities present in the original novel. We hope our choices contribute to showing that Ady is *not*, as she contemplates, "nothing more than a Black doll without a soul."

Tiffane Levick and Timothy Lomeli, June 2024

Ady, Black Sun

Ady, soleil noir, novel by Gisèle Pineau (Philippe Rey, 2021)
Translated from the French by Tiffane Levick and Timothy Lomeli

In spite of my resolution not to get involved again, I had at this time made the acquaintance of a beautiful young mulatto dancer, Adrienne, from the French colony of Guadeloupe. We were in love, and were received by the others in the south with open arms.

Man Ray, *Self Portrait*[1]

1   Man Ray, *Self Portrait* (Boston: Atlantic Monthly Press, 1963), p. 293.

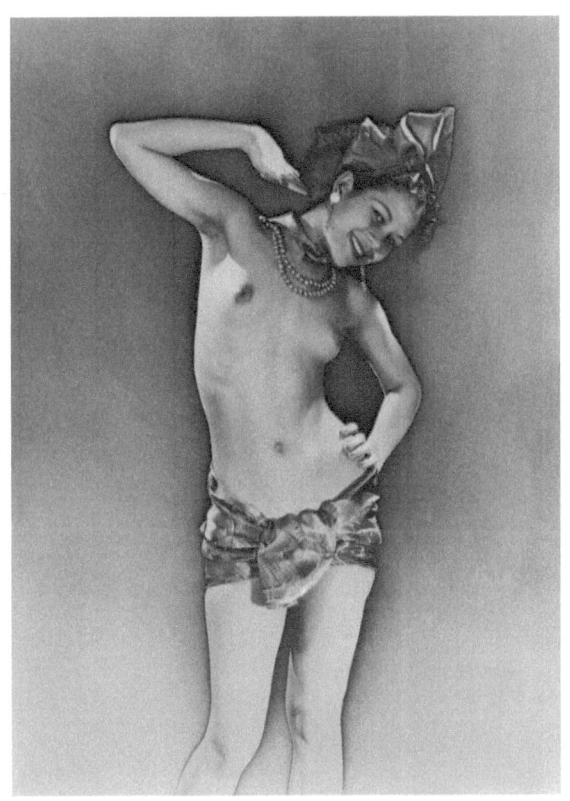

Ady, 1937. Banque d'Images, ADAGP / Art Resource, NY © Man Ray
2015 Trust / Artists
Rights Society (ARS), NY / ADAGP, Paris 2023.

I can picture him.

He's wearing black-framed glasses.

He's looking at a naked girl, café-au-lait skin, sugary sweet. Wearing only a pink ribbon in her hair.

Is that me?

It was a long time ago. A very long time ago.

Yes, that's me. In another life.

I'm naked. I'm smiling. Posing upon his request. He's taking photos of me.

It was a long time ago. A very long time ago.

I remember.

"My Little Black Sun ...." That's what he calls me.

I'm not even cold. Not even embarrassed about showing my small breasts and the brown tuft between my thighs.

Naked,

Black,

happy.

We're in love.

I'm his muse and we're having fun.

It was a very long time ago ...

I

Rally to my side my dances
my bad-nigger dances
the carcan-break dance
the prison-spring dance
the it-is-beautiful-good-
and-legitimate-to-be-a-nigger-dance
Rally to my side my dances and let the
sun bounce on the racket of my hands ...

Aimé Césaire
Notebook of a Return to the Native Land[1]

---

1 Aimé Césaire, *The Original 1939 Notebook of a Return to the Native Land*, bilingual edition, trans. and ed. by A. James Arnold and Clayton Eshleman (Middletown: Wesleyan University Press, 2013), p. 55.

33 Rue Blomet

That November evening in Paris seems so far away.

Winter 1934.

So far away, yet still so close. I can almost taste it.

I remember, I'm running to escape the great hands of the cold air trying to smother me. Quai de Javel. The darkness is inky between the glowing puddles from the streetlights and blinding flashes of car headlights.

All around, gusts of wind blow like icy blades of steel, like stinging lashes of a whip. I stumble and stagger along the icy sidewalk to escape the searing memories of my dear Guadeloupe – these raging demons are still chasing me.

That was yesterday.

Today, I am an old woman. Seventy-five years old.

My mind falters sometimes.

But the old memories are still there, still intact.

Yes, I can picture myself clearly on that sidewalk.

With the salt of the tears I shed on my pink-powdered cheeks, I race toward the place that looks so much like my island, my sweet lost homeland ...

I am nineteen years old. This is my fifth winter in France.

The chill still brings tears to my eyes.

I cry and sniff because of the cold.

I cry. I can't help it.

I already cried too much in Guadeloupe.

I stopped crying in 1930.

I will soon arrive at my destination. My heart knows it, it is already beating a little stronger. I'm running toward a warm promise, a sugary treat, the sweet desire for intoxication and abandon, for jubilation, giddiness and vice. Tonight, yet again, I will shake my body from head to toe to dislodge the terrible sorrow swarming inside me.

As round as a woman's breast, the temple coveted by all. It seems to be full of inebriating milk that makes you belch with pleasure and laugh at the bitter setbacks of life, at the canker of grief.

Paris is infatuated with this place. Lord, there is something burning here: the sand from the beaches of Grande-Terre at noon, the burn of rum in the guts on an empty stomach, the firm penis of a man in the middle of the night when the moon is a flambéed banana stuck to a chalkboard, up there in the sky.

I have stopped running. I soar toward the dance floor. I have big beautiful wings on my back and I am going to carve out a path through the sky to fly back there, back home, as soon as I walk through the door at 33 Blomet.

Back in those days in Paname, all you had to do is say "33" to any taxi driver and he immediately chimes in "Rue Blomet!" *Marrade* and *bamboche* guaranteed … There's also 33 Rue Vavin, with the Boule Blanche where Stellio performs …

Caribbean music is in vogue. Creole dancehalls and cabarets are springing up like tropical flowers growing in the asphalt. There's the Élan Noir at 124 Boulevard du Montparnasse, the Pélican Blanc not far from Place Denfert-Rochereau, the Jockey on Rue Campagne-Première, the Madinina Biguine on Rue de l'Arrivée, the Mikado on Boulevard de Rochechouart, the Tagada, Savane and Boule d'Or on Rue Plumet, the Magada Biguine, the Bal Tabarin …

It's like stepping across the sea. At least that's what it feels like to me. And it's not just me.

At 33 Rue Blomet, we're taken straight back home, to the other side of the Atlantic. When I say we, I mean the Caribbeans in Paris, naturally. We're a sign of the times, like all Black things the earth has to offer.

Oh, the Bal Colonial … It makes everything disappear – the foggy sky of the motherland, the soot-colored snow outside, the heavy coats, mousy gray wool jackets, hand-knitted gloves and hats. We are so hot all of a sudden. We dance the *biguine* better than back home. We Black people are seized with a raging fever from the island music that seeps through every pore of our body.

We can't help it; we have to cling to one another in this arena of madmen. We bump into one another, rub up against each other, swaying our hips. We shuffle our feet. We twist our arms and legs. We writhe furiously.

It's true, we show the world our way of warding off fate, of braving tough luck, escaping the mundanity of the day-to-day.

At 33 Rue Blomet, we bring white people onboard our *bamboula*. We're all tossed around in the tremendous rocking and rolling, intoxicated, transported to some wild place, one with no flags or shackles. Free, joyful, bewitched by the haunting sound of a clarinet or a saxophone, removed from reality, lustful, drunk with pain, joy and pleasure entwined. The war is over, the war to end all wars, they say. Memories of the 1928 hurricane are dead and buried, the 1929 stock market crash is a thing of the past, the Weiler lady who killed her engineer husband with three bullets from a revolver when they got home from the Bal Nègre is forgiven.

The sidewalk is crawling with giddy revelers, Black and white. They're chatting, smoking, joking around outside 33 Blomet. They look like a flock of bats – men wearing fedora or bowler hats and baggy coats. Frozen icy smiles, shivering chicks, with rabbit furs draped over their light colorful dresses making them look like the big stuffed animals from the fun fair.

The bellman has recognized me for six months now. I show up every Saturday night. I'm now a proud regular.

"Good evening, Miss Ady! How are things?" He bows to me comically under the string of red lights hanging in the doorway.

I pout like a Parisian and sigh, saying that I am waiting for spring to arrive, for the sun to return.

He raises an eyebrow. "For that to happen, princess, you'll need to hop on a cruise ship and head back home." He's also from Guadeloupe. And he has abandoned the Rue Cases-Nègres of his childhood and the sugarcane fields his schoolmaster promised him. He barely knows how to read, and yet, during the week, he works for a printer on Rue Montparnasse specializing in maps. He wears a gray smock and unpacks boxes, arranging things in alphabetical order and calibrating the colors. He hovers between ink and paper. In the workshop, they call him *"Y'a bon Banania."* Affectionately. It makes him smile. Why take offense? These white people are just a bunch of fools. At 33 Blomet, he dons a formal suit on Saturday and Sunday evenings, a scarlet livery uniform adorned with fringes, gold braids and buttons, black pants and patent shoes. BAL COLONIAL is embroidered on his hat in gold thread. The outfit gives him the panache of a *prince nègre*. At 33 Blomet, he is flattered if people say that he looks like Féral Benga, the famous Senegalese star of the Parisian music hall. He regains his standing.

All of a sudden I am no longer cold.

The taxi drivers are perched at the bar with their caps screwed onto their heads, sipping on amber punch. They look me up and down, cigarettes hanging out of their mouths. Smoke surrounds them in grayish clouds. One of them, aroused, fondles his crotch. Behind the bar, the barman wiping glasses gives me a jaded look. I return a knowing nod. Take off my woolen gloves, remove my coat and cloche hat. No, I am no longer cold. My heart is racing under my flower-patterned dress.

On the other side of the glass door, the music is pounding. The customers shimmy and embrace in the noisy, smoke-filled room. The atmosphere is frenzied on the balconies, in the stairwells, around the pillars and railings, on the benches and the dance floor. You can't be shy at the Bal Blomet. Butt cheeks are kneaded like dough and tits are fondled at tables cluttered with glasses and bottles. Rum and champagne flow freely. Ashtrays overflow with smoldering cigarette butts. Greedy mouths steal kisses here and there. My God, women's lips are divine! Red flowers, flaming hearts, sparkling rubies, juicy strawberries and cherries, pink butterflies that flit and flutter away. Léardée's orchestra is in overdrive, but the dancers still want more from Creol's Band. More music, please! More joy! More notes! More rhythm! More life!

Here in the middle of the 1930s, I think people need to feel alive more than ever. Enjoy life, have a good time – that's what matters. We are all survivors of the worst, all of us. We all want to live in the present. Dancing at the Bal Blomet is like being on the edge of a cliff with blinkers on. There is nothing around or behind you anymore. The past is dead and the future looks like a dream whose eye you don't want to catch.

My legs are tingling as I join the end of the queue of people stamping their feet and stammering in Creole. Laughter echoes all around. They are speaking English and Spanish, French tinged with accents from elsewhere. And the joy lodged in my heart swells and comes to life. I feel it flowing through my veins – it feels like a river.

I'm smiling.

Why am I smiling?

Because I'm overflowing with joy. Because I have a joyful nature. Because I am going to dance my life away to the strains of a *biguine*. Elegant Black men in jaunty suits stare at me voraciously. They stroke their thin ties and jig about like roosters in a cockpit.

These werewolves eager to take a bite out of me left their islands or the shores of French Guiana to board ocean liners or clapped-out banana boats. Lying in the third-class bunks in their cabins, they clung to great big dreams, not anticipating the harshness of winter. Before long, they had to learn to cover their Black skin with wool, wear big lace-up shoes with thick soles, run in snow and blizzards.

They toil over in Boulogne-Billancourt. Laborers at the Renault factory, metalworkers, fitters, welders. The gifted among them dabble in mechanics. Others assemble the bodies of beautiful cars they'll never be able to drive or afford. They live in workers' hostels, on the top floors of buildings or hotels, in shabby little rooms under the roof – until something better comes along – with Turkish toilets and washbasins on the landing. Rats, cockroaches, fleas, bedbugs, and moths on every floor.

Rumor has it that their ancestors were kings in Africa. At the Bal Blomet, these fallen princes with callused hands seek their revenge. They know that the white women are eager to shake their hips and swoon in pleasure. Distinguished bourgeois women from swanky Parisian neighborhoods sway to and fro and offer themselves up to them, clinging to their sweat-soaked shirts. It's quite a spectacle, these swarms of blonde dance partners falling into the men's arms, one after the other: limp, clammy, sweet, like ripe fruit. Good Lord! The smell of the *nègre* drives them crazy.

The girls from back home glare at me. It's not like this is some kind of catfight! And yet their eyes shoot me peculiar messages, apparently I should bite back my smile because I'm beneath them. They twist their painted lips and suck their teeth without really knowing why, perhaps to intimidate me, to afford themselves a sense of composure. Two or three *doudous* wearing madras and lace pose and *fè dyèz*. I recognize them – maids, laborers, nannies, errand girls, seamstresses in fashion houses. Some of them, adorned with cheap diamonds, hope to be noticed by a music-hall tycoon. They want to become showgirls, singers, actresses. To be famous like Joséphine Baker. Before long, they will soon be beaming as brightly as me, vying for the attention of wealthy and well-fed libidinous older gentlemen, eager to pamper them in exchange for a favor or two. For a single evening, they'll reign as the belles of the ball.

Joséphine Baker, the Black Venus ...

At heart, these Caribbean women are no less desirable than *la Négresse* from Missouri who arrived in Paris in the 1920s with her feet covered in corns and calluses, her big square teeth, cloche hat and Charleston, flamingo feathers, banana skirt belt. She was clever, Jo. Did what the whites wanted her to. Played the role of the wild woman, escaped from her unruly jungle, fallen from her baobab tree. *Adieu*, America, *vive la France*, where anything goes! *Bonjour*, Paris, where people let their hair down to *musique nègre*! It only took her one night to become the darling of Paname and dethrone the old Mistinguett ... La Baker is now rich. And the whole world admires her, everyone wants a piece of her. The girl fills her pockets by delighting audiences as she wiggles her butt in front of cardboard cut-out backdrops. They writhe with laughter when the Black beauty winces and rolls her eyes. She also climbs trees, her breasts bare, and crawls on all fours – exactly how they imagine people must move down in Africa, or over on our sugar islands, out in the savannahs and beneath the coconut trees, among the lions, giraffes, monkeys and panthers ... She amassed such wealth that, after the war, she was even able to acquire a *château*: Les Milandes ... All thanks to her exotic body and her wicked jiggle.

I take my four francs out of my purse. The tall *nègre* behind the counter exudes an air of self-assurance, Amazonian gold slipped onto almost every finger. Enormous signet rings, phenomenal bands set with precious stones. Black pants and tailcoat. Pink satin tie on an immaculate white shirt with a wing collar. He has declared himself master of ceremonies, the man who opens the door to heaven. He hands me my entrance ticket.

I'm still trembling a little from an excitement that I cannot and will not contain. An unbelievable urge grabs me by my guts. I need to dance. Need to be possessed by the music. Maybe there will be some nice men on the dance floor this evening – dukes, the Viscount of Noailles and his Lady, the Prince of Wales ... Who knows? Joséphine Baker will be there with Pepito, her dark Sicilian, and Chiquita, her salon cheetah. Maurice Chevalier has been to the Bal Blomet. So has the scandalous Kiki de Montparnasse. Even the Martiniquaise artist Léona Gabriel, who performed at the Olympia in '29.

Beautiful Léona, I remember her ...

I saw her singing island songs under the palm trees of the Guadeloupe pavilion. In 1931, at the International Colonial Exhibition in the Bois de Vincennes.

I was barely sixteen years old.

I had arrived in France six months prior with my three sisters and my little brother. It was my first spring. The Parisian sky was as blue as the sky back home. It was hot, like back home. Enthralled, we danced the *biguine* to Alexandre Stellio. We ate *boudin*, accras, fried fish. In one afternoon, we took a trip around the whole world and the French colonies. We went to the zoo, fed the monkeys. We even sailed on the Lac Daumesnil, aboard a pirogue from Indochina. I remember wandering along the aisles, lost in the crowd, among the pavilions from all over the world, the African huts and sacred temples of Asia. We went home exhausted at the end of the day, just after the fireworks. That night, in my bed, my head was filled with images of *la Grande France*, with new and foreign words: Djenné, Ouagadougou, Anchor, Bambara, *Toucouleur*, Guinea, Algeria, *indigène* ...

At 33 Blomet, too, there are all kinds of *indigènes* and oddballs ... Businessmen, bankers, surveyors, doctors. And schemers, lunatics, dirty old men of all stripes ... Defrocked priests, wingmen, ditzes, bores, pimps, socialites, showboats, panderers ...

My favorites are undoubtedly the artists, with all their little eccentricities. The writers drink punch while gawking at the island birds. The painters picture models behind a smokescreen. The Montparnos have their local haunts and their friends, their bottles, lady gigolos, flasks covered in rice powder. And then there are the muses hanging around – evanescent, mysterious. Tonight, the princess Aïcha Goblet is there, sitting alone with her drink. She seems detached from everything, enigmatic. Wearing her eternal turban, she looks at the world without seeing it.

I saw Aïcha again, years later ...

I think it was in the fall of '37. Man and I are sitting two tables away from her at La Coupole on Boulevard du Montparnasse. Man photographed her shortly after she arrived in Paris. He goes over to say hello and afterwards he tells me that she, a circus girl and a *métisse* from Martinique, was a famous model in the Roaring Twenties. She posed for men who would become famous painters: Modigliani, Fujita, Pascin – and Granowsky, her companion ... The latter, a Ukrainian, was nicknamed The Cowboy, because of his trademark Texan hat. He drank a lot, Cowboy the painter. Looking for a fight in the bars of the Parisian Wild West.

Man also loved fancy dress.

Back in those days, in the late '30s, there's always some kind of costume ball being held somewhere in Paris. Anyone who's anyone hurries there to partake in the drinking and the *bamboche*, to escape from reality, make unlikely acquaintances, perhaps forget about Hitler looming on the horizon ... Artists, aristocrats, writers, theater actors, dancers ... Man and I race to these balls, like little revelers invited to another kid's house for a party. One time, I pretended to be a slave, my chest bared, dressed only in a loincloth, a big fake chain around my neck. We can make fun out of anything. Never miss an opportunity to laugh and mess around. No, Man doesn't like serious things. If he had it his way, the word "serious" would be banished from the dictionary, never uttered by a single person.

His great friend, Marcel Duchamp, came up with a definition for him: "Man Ray: masculine noun, synonymous with joyfulness, playfulness, pleasure."

I must say, these three words sum up my life with him nicely ...

Joyfulness, playfulness, pleasure – this is also what people come looking for at the Bal Blomet. One evening, the very serious Paulette Nardal was pointed out to me. She's from Martinique and lives near Clamart with her sister Jeanne – they have both just finished studying at the Sorbonne and they host Black intellectuals and artists who are passing through Paris at their place. Africans, Americans, and, of course, Haitians and other people from the French Caribbean. Rumor has it that they sink into the Nardal sisters' velvet armchairs, looking smug while drinking tea with milk and chatting endlessly about colonization, slavery, apartheid, Négritude, segregation, decolonization, independence, the Harlem Renaissance, *Y'a bon Banania*, Creole *doudous*, identity, Black thought, the list goes on ... No topic is off the table! They come to talk among brothers, men cut from the same cloth, who inspire each other. They recite revolutionary poems, invent an imaginary future in which Black people are no longer white people's stooges, their porters, *Oui bwana*, cannon fodder, *Y'a bon Banania*.

I didn't spend much time with them, but I know about these things because we Caribbean folk talk among ourselves. To tell the truth, in the thirties, there aren't all that many of us living in Paris. It's a small world of hushed tones and high hopes. They know who's who and where you're from. They are as interested in trivial family stories as they are in History. Students, professors, and workmen read and reread the newspapers that write articles about them, those who have been colonized, exiled, the grandchildren of slaves: *Le Cri des nègres*, *La Race nègre*, *La Revue du monde noir*, *La Dépêche africaine*, and the fortnightly published by the Comité de défense des intérêts de la race noire. Narcisse, my older sister's husband, the one I lived with before moving in with Man, gets incensed when he reads them. They stir and spark things inside him: an old nameless pain, nauseating resentment, a nagging feeling of humiliation smoldering under his Black skin.

And then those arriving on ocean liners come with news from back home ...

Cousin Bertille's wedding sure was lovely, did you hear? Poor Théodore the neighbor died during Lent.

Do you know about the young aristocrat? The one who went to school with the nuns at Saint-Joseph-de-Cluny. She washed up in Le Havre, wanting to hide her big belly.

1934 ... It's already been six years since the hurricane. Six years. Lord ...

Alas! Back home, they haven't finished cleaning up the debris of the destroyed *cases*. But we mustn't lose hope ... God is great. Guadeloupe is being rebuilt stronger than ever. Never again will wood be used in the Caribbean. The French architect Ali Tur has assured us that cement is the sole miracle cure for hurricanes and earthquakes. They've just inaugurated a new courthouse. It's a remarkable piece of work! Construction on the new general hospital on Morne Jolivère is progressing rapidly.

Yes, they assure us, signs of the 1928 hurricane are gradually fading from the landscape and from memories. Pointe-à-Pitre is being reborn and preparing for the lavish festivities of 1935. Next year, there will be a grand celebration for the tricentennial of the French Caribbean departments' affiliation with France.

Those who return to Guadeloupe go home with a Parisian

accent and white mannerisms, dressed in the latest fashions from Paris. They stow newspapers written by communists and *nègre* revolutionaries in their luggage – the promise of a better world ... Along with souvenirs from Paname wrapped in tissue paper: a miniature Eiffel Tower, figurines of Great War soldiers in horizon-blue uniforms, a vial of Fleurs de Rocaille perfume by Caron for an elderly mother, Bêtises de Cambrai mints for the little *négrillons*. They're always peddling buckets of gossip, the *nègres* in the Métropole ... *So-and-so has managed to find success in France and nobody can figure out how – he can't even read. Whatshername is now leading a life of debauchery – she was caught rubbing up against old white men at the Bal Blomet ...*

It's all just chatter.

And I don't care.

Mind your own business!

In Paris, men whistle at me in the street, say I'm a looker, that I have a sweet Black doll face. I'm only nineteen years old and I like it. I'm no less attractive than Princess Aïcha. I could be a model, like her. Maybe even a showgirl at the Casino de Paris or Folies-Bergère. I dream about it, like all girls my age. I have my whole life before me. I could even be an actress in the movies. An island *doudou*, a *Fatou*, a Moroccan girl in a harem, a maid in a white apron ... Joséphine Baker played a Caribbean woman in *Siren of the Tropics*. Apparently she danced her Charleston to the beat of our drums.

What did I do in '34, besides dance?

Yes ... I saw *Zouzou* at the Moulin-Rouge. In the film, the orphaned Baker feeds Jean Gabin his lines. There are posters on most of the Morris columns in Paris. Joséphine is first and foremost a Black woman, then an American. A Black woman with café-au-lait skin, like me.

I looked after my older sisters' kids.

Spent a lot of time wandering through the streets of Paris, from Chaussée-d'Antin to Belleville, Faubourg-du-Temple to Montmartre, Rue de la Pompe to Opéra.

I know nothing of my destiny. Man Ray and I are yet to cross paths. I am walking toward something that is starting to take shape in an end-of-the-world fog. Will I live longer than my mother? Will the good Lord give me much time on this earth? No, tropical storms do not visit France ... Will there be another war in this world? Let's hope not. I want nothing but joy in my life. That's not asking for much.

Here we go! I step onto the dance floor, one foot in front of the other. My eyes are closed and I surrender to the Creole melodies. I float along to the bacchanalian music, allowing myself to be rocked and cradled. The bewitching notes flow to the depths of my insides. I'm surrounded by the ocean. By its roaring waves. The screams of night birds and the frightened laughter of the mermaids in the evening, the hazy conversations that hang in cigar smoke, the alcohol fumes, the sour smell of sweat mixed with cheap marine lotions, in chic, sweet, peppery perfumes, faraway scents.

My distant island.

It doesn't matter whose arms are wrapped around me. As Chevalier says, "In life, you shouldn't worry. I never worry. These little problems are only temporary. Everything will be fine ...."[2]

The sky softens. The sea quietens. The cyclone moves further and further away trailing its strong winds like a never-ending bridal veil. The bodies of Pointe-à-Pitre come back to life. The ghosts of Mathilde and Maxime smile sweetly at me. The sad broken faces of the Great War disappear from the landscape. May their ragged souls rest in peace. The unknown *poilus*, the bearded soldiers torn to pieces in the war, return whole in the trenches. Voilà! Normalcy has been restored. Death has found its way, without missing a beat. I cling to the man who has trapped me in his arms. Whoever he is, he is my savior.

That's why I'm here. To chase away dark thoughts, thumb my nose at misery, forget this mess and pain. *Joyfulness, playfulness, pleasure.* So, with a smile on my lips, I dance with anyone who asks me to. Go from one man to another, without looking for love.

First off, one of those familiar-looking Black men, light on his feet, like someone I might have known back home in my neighborhood in Pointe-à-Pitre. An Ivorian. A student with a bright future, or so he says. So Black that he is blue.

Next, a sweaty, lustful white man, escaped from his country town, clumsy, hanging around at 33 Blomet to see what's new in Parisian trends, ready to slum it and get down and dirty with a bonafide member of this subversive rabble of ethnic people. He

---

2 Words taken from Maurice Chevalier song, "Dans la vie faut pas s'en faire" (Paris: Pathé 2030/2031, 1921) (our translation).

whispers his name to me and I only just catch it through the hubbub. "Hippolyte." He wants to spend some time with me. I decline his invitation.

Then an overbearing fellow. A ladies' hairdresser with a thin, curled mustache and sideburns. Amazed by the scandalous reputation of the Bal Nègre.

And a shaggy painter who sees cubes and geometry in everything. This guy predicts that he will be famous any day now. I close my eyes and nestle my head in the hollow of his shoulder. Dreaming is not a luxury out of reach. We all have the power to add a few frills to our lives in our dreams. Paint the sky pink, see a triangle in a face, even smell the scent of café au lait just by looking at me. We can decide that life is a game of chess and happy coincidences.

Now I'm in the arms of a poet looking for inspiration. He sniffs the air and follows a smell in the alcohol fumes. He whispers, "Do you know Charles Baudelaire? *With strange wild odors all astir, and, from her lace and velvet busk, candid and girlish, over her, hovered a heavy scent of fur.*"[3]

Later, a man hungry for exoticism and debauchery. This fellow is a bit of a blockhead, frightens himself thinking he'll be bewitched in a Vodou ceremony. Wants to know if I have the temperament of these enchanting and feisty *doudous*, if I'm a depraved *diablesse*, a little trollop. He stepped on my toes twice.

And, here we go, a Martinican man, from Saint-Pierre. A nice, shy boy, peepers full of ash and desire.

Another comes up to me. "Would you like to dance, mademoiselle?" Large forehead, black hair and piercing eyes. He's already holding my hand. A smile forms on his lips. He is serious and joyful at the same time. I see it under his bushy eyebrows. He takes me in his arms. He's had too much to drink. The words tumble around his mouth, because of the rum and his accent. He whispers something in my ear. I make him repeat it because of the hustle and bustle. "I could take your picture!" he yells. "Why not!" I yell back. He compliments me, "You sure do dance well ...." I tell him he does too. Very proud of himself, he says, "A woman named Bérénice taught me, a very long time ago. But I was a natural, I have a good sense of rhythm." I continue, "I'm actually

---

3 Charles Baudelaire, "Un fantôme. Le parfum," in *Flowers of Evil*, trans. by Lewis Piaget Shanks (New York: Ives Washburn, 1931).

a professional dancer." He repeats the word, amused, "Professional! You sure are young ... And you're here all alone ...."

He likes to take photos of dancers from Caribbean folkloric troupes. Of the American actresses in the musical *Blackbirds*. All sorts of women, white and Black, have posed for him, their chests bared, needing no persuading. And everything is always above board – that goes without saying. Then he declares that he's a painter. His works are on display in galleries and museums all over Europe, all the way over in America. For the time being, he earns a living by doing portraits for well-known people. Artists, doctors, celebrities, and aristocrats who pay a lot of money. His photographic style means that he is also sought after by publicists. He tells me to open my eyes, to look at him. "Don't be shy, dear ... You run absolutely no risk in coming to my studio. You are a professional dancer and I am a renowned photographer. Would you agree to pose nude for me? Do you know about Dada, the surrealists?" I think about it. He continues, "I also photograph models, for fashion magazines, for big fashion house collections."

Is he trying to dazzle me? Is he being coy? His accent ... I observe him from the corner of my eye. His eyes sparkle. I ask him, "Are you English?" He shakes his head. "I'm American, from New York ... You have an accent, too – where are you from? The French colonies in the Caribbean?" I avoid the question. "No, I'm not shy. I'm not afraid to take my clothes off in front of a painter ...." I tell him I've already posed for a photographer, Roger Parry. It was not long after I arrived in France. Back then, I didn't really understand why Roger had a wooden indigenous African mask hung on his wall. A Panu mask from Gabon that reminded me of one I had seen at the Colonial Exhibition in 1931. Africa seemed so far away to me. I had worn my Creole *doudou* dress and hairstyle. I was docile and smiled at the camera on command. I was barely seventeen years old. Africa and its supposedly primitive art forms were in the savannah winds blowing over Paris. I took off my camisole. Roger took my photo, my chest bared ...

My dance partner doesn't let me go. He introduces himself while Léardée starts playing a new song. "My name is Man Ray. R.A.Y. Will you come and have a drink with us?" He's already taken my arm and he points out his group of friends. I say no, I want to stay on the dance floor. "I've been watching you," he says. "I noticed that you dance with your eyes closed ... Why do you do that?" I answer, "Because I go traveling …." He smiles, looks intrigued. We stand still and silent for a moment among the hypnotized dancers on the floor. "My studio is in Montparnasse, on Rue Campagne-Première," he blurts out. "Will you stop by?" I answer, "Yes, I think so …." He nods, "Right then, well … I suppose we'll see each other again someday, or night … Do you come here often? What's your name?" He has a mischievous look on his face. "Adrienne. People call me Ady …." He pauses for a moment, then murmurs, "Ady … That's sweet. A soft black cloud, with sun stripes running through it. No, I think I prefer *Ady, Little Black Sun*." He walks away and joins his clique. All of them cheerful, chattering, huddled together on a bench as if it were a raft, forming one single drunk body, vibrating with life, sailing toward a promised land. I don't know them, but I already desire and love them all.

Are black clouds soft?

Is that proper French, *les raies du soleil* … sun *stripes*? He surely meant to say *les rayons du soleil*, sun *rays* … Black sun … What does that mean?

Another bachelor tries to chat me up, followed by a foul-smelling eager beaver. Sometimes I open my eyes. I catch Monsieur Ray's mischievous glance. Ray of sun. Ray of light. He's not very talkative. He mostly drinks rum, laconic, as he listens to conversations with a mixture of politeness, indulgence, and nonchalance. Even though he laughs a lot, he still holds back, maintains a certain distance between himself and the world. He enjoys himself simply observing what's going on around him. Yet he gives the impression of not needing anyone else. He takes pleasure in the *human comedy*: the spineless, drunken, misguided men, the reluctant, lascivious women, the overbearing desire of some and the prudishness of others, white and Black people gathered in a pagan celebration where the only thing that matters is living in the moment.

Who is this Man Ray from America, then? I admit that I'm already a little attracted to him. But his group of friends get up in a flash, as if on shared impulse. They've had enough of the Bal Blomet and will continue the festivities elsewhere. Man Ray rounds out the pack. The renowned photographer looks like a rascal who lets life lead him wherever it wants, lets his steps guide him to a place where his memories disappear. Guided perhaps by the miraculous chance and sacred destiny that has already marked the road the two of us will travel together.

In the arms of a handsome young man, I forget Man Ray and his dreamy words. I stay on the dance floor. I sway, eyes closed. Taking a trip home. I welcome the images of my childhood overseas, one by one. They're already a little blurred, stained and sepia. They come to me as if in a storm, flash through my mind. I ask for more. Suddenly, I find myself really there, back in my beloved Guadeloupe.

Before everything was swept away, smashed to pieces.

Long before the country was turned upside down. Before the night of September 12, 1928.

Before I rose motherless from the remains of our *case*, the structure reduced to rubble, the beams toppled, the metal sheets blown away. Before 1930, when, as if under a curse, I became fatherless.

I wound up an orphan, having lost my father and mother, at the age of fifteen.

Like the bluebottle flies of yesteryear, the images of the evil hurricane swarm around me at 33 Rue Blomet. They whir, riled up by the laughter and the wildly cheerful music, still intoxicated by the stench of rotting corpses that littered Pointe-à-Pitre and surrounding areas after the great devastation.

How can I drive away these apocalyptic visions? I arch my back and grip my partner tighter. A weakling, this one ... I pull him closer, pull him in, take him along for the ride.

A frantic tempo has the couples on the dance floor in a frenzy and I no longer have control over my body. It sways to the rhythm of the *biguine*. My body, drunk and bewitched, seeks consolation. It tramples hardship, does the splits, straddles the sea. And the guy held tightly in my arms thinks I'm sending him an invitation. His thing stiffens wildly in his pants.

I don't care.

I've left my body.

I'm far from Rue Blomet now.

I have turned back into the little girl who tried on her older sisters' clothes in secret. Parma silk and pure organdy dresses, wobbly heels. I conjure up images of my former world. Upstairs, under the attic, the long dim hallway, the floorboards laid out in front of me, the solid doors leading to the three bedrooms: one for the girls, one for the boys, and one for our parents. Now, I make my way down the wooden staircase. The third step creaks under my feet, as usual. The dining room on the first floor, furnished with pearwood furniture, polished with beeswax and decorated with *Dames Port-Louis* lace doilies. The handsome living room hoping for guests, glimmering in the evening candlelight. The Oriental carpets, the varnished courbaril-wood console with its curved feet. The mahogany buffet filled with crystal, porcelain, silverware, embroidered tablecloths and napkins. The cane meridian covered in satin cushions stuffed with carded cotton. Children are not allowed to sit in this exotic sanctuary; only to clean the furniture with a faded feather duster. It's where manman's rocking chair sits: a repository of prayers, poems from the Caribbean, and important family secrets. And papa's armchair, carved in mahogany: a throne made to measure, covered with blue velvet.

My uncle Adrien Fidelin has been mayor of Pointe-à-Pitre since 1926. He is a public figure and a friend of Monsieur Gilbert de Chambertrand. He used to teach at the Lycée Carnot, and sat on the board of the General Council of Guadeloupe. When he visits my parents, he talks politics with papa. I remember a few names: Boisneuf, Mortenol, Légitimus, Gerville-Réache, Isaac, Lara, Candace, Sidambarom, Poincaré … The two brothers sip alcohol from the *M*étropole – Guignolet from Dijon, Armagnac from Château de Larressingle – and sometimes sit silently under the black-and-white portraits of the ancestors for long stretches, deep in thought. They are all dead, hanging on the walls, their eyes watching us like stern judges. Their faces, doctored in Indian ink, remain unperturbed within the crudely gilded plaster frames. They come from the Îles des Saintes, from a bygone era we rarely speak of.

Behind the shuttered double door lies the paved interior courtyard, strewn with potted plants with large leaves and stately tall stems that my mother cherishes as much as her Caribbean poetry. This small courtyard is the lungs of the house, overlooking the pond and two terracotta pots that are always leaking and dripping a little. The kitchen lies at the back, with its potsherds, orange-tiled benches, the collection of dented black pots and pans, the smell of fat, the scents of local spices.

I dance, carried away, back there. Back home.

So many images swirl in my memory.

They never leave me.

At five in the afternoon, my father, Maxime, leaves the Bank of Guadeloupe, where he works. With our mother's permission, my sisters and I sometimes go to meet him.

My mother Mathilde's fragile voice says, "Be sure to walk at the side of the road, my daughters! Be careful of the chaotic cars and the tilburies and carts! It will soon be dark!"

We stroll hand-in-hand under the sandbox trees, like good little girls. Day and night, never tiring, these giants spread their leafy branches colonized by flocks of fledglings. I raise my head and greet them. Using the tips of their palms, they repaint the blue sky with gray-black clouds. I can picture the town's brass band rehearsing in the blazing sunset, swinging under the bandstand of the Place de la Victoire. The brassy notes project extravagant sprays that soar into the air and fall in multicolored confetti. When I shift my gaze toward the sea, I see the Darboussier factory and its proud chimneys – implanted there, it seems, for eternity. From morning to night, it crushes and grinds sugar cane in its large jaw. "The Black man's burden," my father says.

I'm flooded by memories ...

The Vatable Canal and men fishing for guppy. Pointe-à-Pitre Harbor, immense before the naked horizon, frozen in the moist air, unaware of the imminent disaster. The harbor basin. The fishermen's boats lined up neatly in a row. People swarming, mingling, calling out to one another, chasing one another, coming and going all day long. The wharf and its adventurous sailboats. Not even a hint of a breeze. The evening scenery looks like a postcard of the tropics bending under the heat.

I can picture it all.

Everyone is in their place. Seated on small benches, the merchants with their large butt cheeks wrapped in madras cloths hail customers. "Get your coconut sorbet, freshly made today! Roasted pistachios! Potato cakes, nice and hot!" Lovers idling with adventurous hands, their mouths whispering sweet nothings. In the alleyways, nonchalant nannies watch over their mistresses' children with a melancholic eye. A worried chaperone follows a young couple's footsteps. There are these long benches besieged by little ten-year-old gentlemen dressed in white, wearing straw hats and waxed boots. I come across older politicians still wearing straw boater hats and pith helmets. Wearing starched suits, ascots, they chat as if life had no end. They always leave in their wake a scent of old age barely masked with hints of jasmine. Some block the sun's last few rays with a fragile black parasol meant for women, others parade around with precious knobbed canes. We wave to the poet and photographer Monsieur Gilbert de Chambertrand, now an art teacher at the Lycée Carnot. Manman knows his plays and poems by heart. She asks him for book recommendations at the Schœlcher library that they both visit often. She says, "Monsieur de Chambertrand is an important Caribbean artist, children. He writes, paints, draws, and takes photos. Everything he touches turns to gold."

My sisters and I never have time to get all the way to the iron gate at the Bank of Guadeloupe – we always run into papa on the way. He walks down the main street like a senator. He feels sort of like he's in charge of the place, since his brother Adrien is the mayor of Pointe-à-Pitre. Papa calms us with a wave of his hand. He can pull us back into line with a single look, reminding us that we are girls from a good family.

I remember. Yes, my childhood was only yesterday …

Not a cloud in sight.

When we arrive home on Rue Condé, papa takes a seat in the living room. Manman greets him with a "Good evening, my dear," which he answers with his timeless, "Oh, it sure is good to be home!" He lets out a sigh followed by a brief nod, then slumps back in his armchair. Manman presents him with a porcelain bowl filled with soapy water. He dips his hands in for a moment before waving them over the suds. I know they're not, but in my mind his hands are bird wings. My father's big beautiful hands. I see them flying out the window.

It's already so dark outside. Everything that is familiar to me in the daytime is suddenly enveloped in a big black sheet. In the cut-throat alleys and walkways, at the back of courtyards, along the wooden facades, under the worked balconies, these shadows wandering on the sidewalk are the scum of the earth. The night belongs to them. Evil creatures race toward their sacrileges. Seductive *diablesses* lust after lonely men. Prowling spirits lie in wait for innocent victims. Every night, the damned souls and other vengeful *soucougnans* that inhabit the legends and tales told by the elderly members of my family take to the streets …

Manman's voice sounds at nightfall, "Children! Close the

shutters and lock the doors!" Her every fear is contained within the order. And even the faintest sound outdoors sends a shiver of dread through me.

Grabbing a pitcher, manman drives away these diabolical visions. She carefully pours fresh water from a pot onto papa's wing-like hands. The water plays an improvised little waterfall melody, the gentle lapping of a river in Basse-Terre. She wipes her husband's long hands with a well-ironed white towel. Finally, bending down deferentially, Mathilde places a glass of a honey-colored drink on the stool next to the armchair. Maxime then bestows upon her a measured smile that conveys his appreciation for what a wonderful wife she is.

In my recollections, this daily ritual represents a fragile perfection that could be shattered by even the slightest utterance.

I am twelve years old.

I'm captivated, taking it all in as though I were at the theater. Mathilde and Maxime are actors. Each excels in their role, mastering their gestures and occasional soliloquies. The smell of eternity wafts through the small living room. I'm confident that the same scenes will be played out again and again, until the end of time. It's silly to say it, but I believe my parents are immortal. I can't imagine them suddenly disappearing from my life. Being snuffed out, one after the other, like the flame of a candle blown out in a brief draught. Now, the moment has come. Maxime picks a record from the stack. He dusts it with a chamois cloth then gently places it on the platter of the horn phonograph we've had since 1925. It's "Sensation Rag" by Scott Joplin and Joseph Lamb, straight from the Americas. The records come and go, a *biguine* by Léona Gabriel in vogue in Martinique, Johannes Brahms's *Hungarian Dance No. 5*, then Bessie Smith's voice, dark and on fire, performing "St. Louis Blues" …

"Hush now, children!" shouts Mathilde. She loves music as much as she loves poetry and her ornamental plants. The house fills with melodies and Maxime gently drums his fingers on the edge of a *guéridon* table. His feet tap to the beat. His eyes roll back under his lowered eyelids. I climb the stairs, go up to my room, put on my ballroom clothes and oversized high-heeled shoes.

Mathilde laughs and says I have fire in my belly. I already dance to all sorts of music. I kick my legs up. Do the splits. Strut and shake. Sometimes, I even conjure up an imaginary lover, a poor broomstick made from latanier leaves that I take in my arms and hold against my chest, imagining that I'll have my own prince one day, when I'm all grown up.

I leave the Bal Blomet dance floor in the early hours of the morning, a hellish racket in my head. The black sky is already cracking with a few whitish rays. But the crowd remains huddled together at 33 Blomet, still hungry for more, seething at the sight of musicians preparing to pack up their instruments. "One last tune, Léardée! Come on! Give us more. Hey! Please, conductor, one more little *biguine*! *Madiana*! Sêpent maigre!"

In Paris, I dance for my own pleasure, and also so I can buy trinkets and sit in brasseries ordering cafés like a chic lady. In '34, I dance in a troupe that performs in cabarets and *guinguettes* along the Seine. I dance in my *doudou* dress. I dance the *biguine*, the *quadrille*, the *mazurka*. No need for me to drink rum to get drunk. All I need to do is dance to ward off the darkness.

In no time at all, I learned to move my body to foreign dances that are all the rage in Paris: the Charleston, shimmy, foxtrot, one-step, Cuban rumba, tango ...

Man and I got together in 1936. There were all kinds of music at our home on Rue Denfert-Rochereau. We listened to jazz and blues: Duke Ellington, Cole Porter, Big Bill Broonzy, and many others. He also liked Bach, my little Manichou. And we would dance the rumba or the *biguine*, completely naked, holding each other close. What mattered was being together. Loving one another, having fun ...

"Dancing is not a profession! You do realize that, Ady, don't you? You're not from a family of dancers, as far as I am aware! What would your manman have said? How do you think your papa would have felt about this?"

In '34, I was living outside of Paris, in the Grande Couronne, with Raymonde, my elder sister. She wanted me to learn typewriting. Apparently, it's a job with a promising future. She said, "People need secretaries everywhere, Ady!"

"Manman isn't around anymore. If she were still alive, she would have said that I always had fire in my belly. I was dancing in her womb long before I was born. Plus, papa always loved music and ...."

A friend of my late mother is visiting us that day. She scolds me.

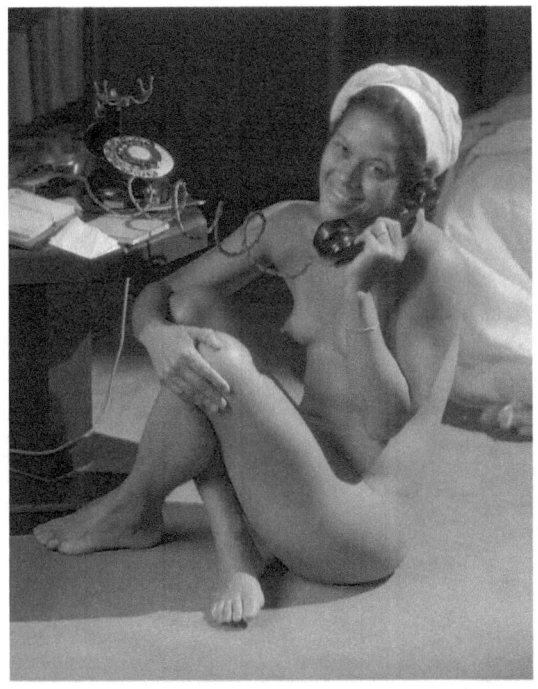

Ady, 1937. Banque d'Images, ADAGP / Art Resource, NY © Man Ray
2015 Trust / Artists
Rights Society (ARS), NY / ADAGP, Paris 2023.

"Show some respect! For yourself, for the memory of your parents ... May their souls rest in peace." She makes the sign of the cross and raises her eyes to the ceiling.

"May their souls rest in peace," I repeat. And bow my head.

The old friend softens her tone to coax me. She knows that at the very mention of my parents, my heart suddenly goes weak.

"Ady, be reasonable. Everyone in Guadeloupe is going to find out eventually ...."

"Find out what?"

"Well! Raymonde told me that you've been traipsing around in Paris alone, that you go to balls and cabarets ...."

"I don't care what they say!"

"What! Do you smoke?" The old woman smells the air in disgust. She grabs a lock of my hair and sniffs it.

"It's not me. People smoke everywhere in Paris."

"You reek of tobacco!" Raymonde bellows.

"And what does it matter if I smoke …."

"You're just a girl, Ady …."

"Women smoke in Paris …."

"And I bet you drink alcohol, too … Your manman spoiled you. You're a wild child, Ady! You're headed for trouble. You're your big sisters' responsibility. Forget about dancing … You're a girl from a good family, for heaven's sake! Lots of dancers wind up prostitutes, if they don't get their throats cut … I'm begging you, stop loafing around and go out and learn secretarial skills, Ady! Then you can get a job somewhere, like Raymonde said! In an office …."

"I don't drink, and I already have a job. I'm a dancer. And soon I might be a model for a renowned American photographer … He's an artist, you know. A surrealist."

"Sir what? Sir Realist? What on earth are you on about now?" says Raymonde.

"A surrealist!"

I suddenly remember that in July 1931, while France is raving about the Great Colonial Exhibition in Bois de Vincennes, I held a flier from the surrealists in my hands. "Don't visit the Colonial Exhibition!" Raymonde crumpled up the piece of paper without reading it and paid for the entrance tickets to see what we were all supposed to admire: the greatness of France, the vastness of its territory, the power of its empire, the expanse of its colonies, the benefits of its civilizing missions all over the world.

"There's plenty of women who pose for surrealist painters in Paris. Some of them even make films …."

"Black girls! Girls from the Caribbean!" The friend laughs. "And you think they can pay their way like that? You're dreaming … You want to play surreal African girls in the movies! Don't make me laugh … You're not American, you know … The Roaring Twenties are over. Don't go thinking you're Joséphine Baker, now! And don't you dare bare your chest! Don't even think about it, Ady …."

"Dancing is not a crime …."

"Dancing is not a serious job, Ady! You can't possibly believe it is. Don't bring shame to your family, you hear me! If you keep on like this, men will play with you like a Black doll … Then they'll throw you away …."

In mid-October that year, 1934, the newspapers announced that Violette Nozière was sentenced to death. At the age of eighteen, the girl had murdered her father and tried to kill her mother. "A monster in petticoats!" people spat. Along every sidewalk, her face was exposed in ink and paper to shoppers' eyes. Hundreds of Violette Nozières on the front page of papers pegged to newsstands. Violettes dressed in black, her face of white marble behind a black veil. From morning to night, men wearing sandwich boards and newspaper vendors riding bicycles hollered her first and last name. Violette Nozière! Like bunches of wilted flowers thrown to the wind. Violette Nozière! Alas, in every conversation this pale woman embodied the horror of patricide, of nausea, of the sordid silence of incest. I remember seeing musicians on street corners making a killing from the sad story. With their barrel organs and accordions blaring sinister notes ...

She poisoned her parents
The cowardly Violette Nozière
Laughed at their suffering
To squeeze money out of them
[...]
Vagabond wench
She committed this monstrous crime
So she could hit the town,
Dance, drink, make new friends.
Already getting around, precocious girl
In hotels and nightclubs ...[4]

The booklets containing these popular ballads were decorated with a photo of Violette Nozière and sold like hotcakes.

At the time, I vaguely remember hearing that artists and intellectuals, "surrealists," had sent her a sheaf of red roses. The little revolutionary gang condemned bourgeois morality, the hypocrisy of the establishment's defenders, the dirtiness of colonial France, plunged into recession, gangrened by its own failings, its bankruptcy, corruption, and scandals.

Years later, in old boxes abandoned in 1940 by Man when he

---

4 Author unknown, "Complainte de Violette Nozière" (1933) (our translation).

fled the madness of Paris amidst the Nazi invasion, I discovered – dating from 1933 and published by *Le Terrain Vague* – a collection of poems, drawings, letters, documents, signed by Breton, Éluard, Char, Ernst, Magritte, Giacometti, among others. There was one of Man's photographs on the cover, one of his works. A capital N with broken downstrokes, set on violets with crushed petals that looked like they'd been trampled. VIOLETTE NOZIÈRE written above it, in large characters and purple ink.

I have just run into Man Ray at the Bal Blomet. So, I've danced with one of the surrealists. I liked feeling his breath on my neck and hearing his voice whispering in my ear, his exotic accent lending a strange and cheerful ring to his words. I felt my heart beating against my chest. I felt warm against him, like I was being held by a big brother.

On December 24, 1934, Violette is pardoned by President Albert Lebrun, commuting her sentence to a life of forced labor. I think of Man Ray again that day, without really knowing why. And I rejoice at the news of the pardon, thinking that the red roses the surrealist artists sent undoubtedly helped to soften the terrible sentence.
Do flowers have powers?
Where is Man Ray?
Which friends is he celebrating with?
It's Christmas time, the beautiful month of tinsel and golden ornaments. The season of gifts and snowmen. We spend the day in the kitchen at my sister's house, preparing dinner, browning pig meat, making *boudin* with blood and offal bought at Les Halles. Without chilis or bay rum leaves, the *boudin* tastes like France. A bitter flavor of nostalgia. In the evening, we set a beautiful table and pray for the souls of our dead parents.
I miss Guadeloupe. I'm tired of winter. I think sorrowfully of my distant land ravaged by a hurricane.
I feel like a foreigner in France. A foreigner in the eyes of the French. A foreigner because of the color of my skin ...
And yet ...
In Paris, if I say I'm from Guadeloupe, people declare, "Ah, Guadeloupe! One of the oldest colonies in the French Caribbean!" Guadeloupe belongs to them, like a piece of land inherited from

an adventuring ancestor, an illustrious stranger. Even the farthest-flung Frenchman in his country town feels this deep-seated sense of ownership. These remote islands populated by Black people are part of his heritage. Even if he doesn't know how, he rejoices and boasts about it.

As I see it, my little country is bound to France by obscure ties of love and hate, memories of slavery, chains, and lashes, maimed *nègre marron* ancestors hounded by dogs and branded with a hot iron … In these tropics, we speak French and Creole. We were taught to cherish France and its *république*, Jean de La Fontaine and his fables, Schœlcher who freed us from the worst. Over there, *nègres* still walk barefoot in the streets. Over there, people live in *cases* that collapse like a house of cards at the faintest gust of wind.

The year is drawing to a close.

On the other side of Europe, in Germany, Adolf Hitler has become Chancellor of the Reich.

While preparing the invasion of Ethiopia, Mussolini's Italy celebrates its victory in the soccer World Cup.

The Japanese Empire begins to rearm.

The Congo-Ocean railway line, inaugurated with great pomp in July, has already stopped keeping track of the number of *nègres* lost in the name of civilization.

War is brewing in all four corners of the world.

The worst is yet to come.

II

She flew, she flew. Over the houses.
Through the half-open shutters, she saw her little companions.
Her little companions slept, their guardian angel
at their side. She saw the animals. They were asleep,
except for the cabritt-bois, *the roosters, the dogs,*
the mosquitoes, the fire beasts and the bats.

Thérèse Georgel[1]

---

1 Thérèse Georgel, "L'oiseau de nuit," in *Contes et légendes des Antilles* (Paris: Éditions Nathan, 1957 [1994]), p. 82 (our translation).

1928, Hurricane Year

My father Maxime didn't die in the war.
He's fifty-four years old when the 1928 hurricane strips him of
everything that gives his life meaning.
His dear, loving wife,
his life so sweet and all mapped out,
his *haut-et-bas* home on Rue Condé,
the prestigious Bank of Guadeloupe.

His Mathilde, no longer of this world.
His wealth reduced to a pile of rubble,
deadwood and crumpled metal.
His workplace in ruins.

It sounds like a poem, doesn't it? Or the lyrics of a sad *biguine*.
We can dance to the desolation and laugh at ourselves in derision
– it's common in the Caribbean, it makes life easier. You simply
need to let yourself be cradled.
After all these years, and after everything I've been through,
I can still see the child I was after September 12, 1928, still feel
every shiver of my body, recall the wildest apocalyptic thoughts
that went through my head.
In one short night, my father's entire life is turned upside down,
thrown into a muddy mire filled with traps and filth: broken
bottles, rusty nails, sharp blades, shattered glass, and tiles ... In
a few hours, under a black sky, the path beautifully paved for my
papa is transformed into a nightmare, spiked with wildly broken
branches, an inextricable tangle of dirty fabric, telephone wires,
vines ... Obscene clusters of anger, planks, and beams.

His world shattered, Maxime gives up on life. Just like that.

The morning after September 12, 1928, he ceases to exist in the Realm of the Living. His body is there, visible and whole, but his eyes are empty and his thoughts dwell in an embittered elsewhere, far away from this earth.

I'm only thirteen years old. But I feel it deep inside me. Because of a splinter sinking soundlessly into my heart.

I feel it as if I'd received a premonition from an angel.

I see black death in my father's eyes.

I hear something turn off inside him, blown out by the huge gusts of wind.

And then I watch a shapeless shadow emerge from his body. Rising up like the smoke from a *boucan*. And sink into stagnant waters where rats, chickens, and humans float among dead flowers, a monocle with cracked glass, folding fans missing half their leaves, soiled doilies, a funnel, a broken record player, the sad muddy pages of manman's favorite poetry: John-Antoine Nau, Saint-John Perse, François Villon and his Ladies of Yesteryear, Monsieur de Chambertrand ....

Maxime doesn't resist death's devious call for long. For two years, he lets himself be smothered and consumed by sorrow. Then he gives up, in too much of a hurry to join his Mathilde in the Kingdom of the Dead.

Official records state that he passed away two years later, on November 9, 1930. On that day, I learn the lesson that people die. That nothing lasts on this earth.

I am so old and worn out today.

Time could have shown me mercy.

I should have already forgotten Mathilde and Maxime, their faces and his wing-like hands, the fanfare on Place de la Victoire, the ragtime and poetry, and all the other things the wind blew away ...

I celebrated my seventy-fifth birthday the other day. It's funny, I didn't notice the time go by. My God, seventy-five years old already ...

Alas, distant images are like roses that never wilt. They stay planted in my mind, unaltered, their stems straight and their petals proud, like plastic flowers, their leaves always fresh, their thorns erect.

I remember the day before the hurricane perfectly.

In the afternoon of September 11, 1928, the wind picks up suddenly.

I am at Maison Caillé, with Lucette, our servant. Manman has sent us there to buy thread, needles, and six small pearl buttons, and we are making our way back when the clouds suddenly start to roll a little too fast across the sky. Lucette makes the sign of the cross and whispers a prayer to God almighty, asking for mercy and protection. Above our heads a gray and foggy web unfolds, with rough purplish brushstrokes in places, scarred with coppery lines that might have seemed threatening to me, harbingers of misfortune. But at the tender age of thirteen, I look at the sky in awe, like an ever-changing painting, similar to those I will see Man paint years later.

The sea is already churning and rumbling uncharacteristically in the harbor. Waves crash wildly onto the frail boats and moored ships. Masts sway, sails flap. Along the docks, a dozen fishermen hurriedly haul their canoes onto land. Looking toward the horizon, others babble and wave their arms around. One minute, they are tracing circles in the air. Next, they are drawing arabesque curves.

On Place de la Victoire, people are scarce, the benches are deserted. The giant leaves of the sandbox trees buckle under the repeated blows of invisible enemies. The birds have flown far away, abandoning their nests to the wind. A pack of stray dogs near the municipal bandstand sniff the air, tails tucked between their legs. They whimper anxiously, skittering around, spinning in place, darting from side to side, and then doubling back.

Lucette is sixteen years old. She's rather shy and comes from the countryside of Marie-Galante where silence is golden and words are an accessory she uses sparingly. When I stop near a *grabiot* and *tablettes-coco* vendor, she comes out of her usual shell and scolds me. Her face, usually so emotionless, displays a sudden panic. "We must go back home straight away," she shouts firmly. "There's a hurricane coming, Ady! Look around! Those dogs would warn you if they could. Look at the malice in the colors in the sky! Look at the fear in the trees! Can't you see the anger in the sea!"

I don't dare say anything back. I gather up my two holed coins and walk toward the house in a sullen silence, tinged – perhaps – with a hint of trepidation.

On Rue Condé, the serenity of the daily ritual is not in the least disrupted. Is Lucette crazy? Is she trying to scare me, just for a laugh? I couldn't see the malice in the sky. The fear in the trees … The anger in the sea … The poor girl is telling tales.

As usual, Maxime is sitting peacefully in the living room, tapping his fingers on the arms of his chair. Mathilde has, of course, already presented him with a bowl of soapy water. Papa's hands are washed and dried, nice and clean, rid of the filth amassed from handling and counting dirty bills and coins at the Bank of Guadeloupe.

Manman is about to place a glass of alcohol on the little stand beside him. A record turns and spins on the phonograph. I remember papa being very proud. He has only just acquired this record player from a music-loving docker, a certain Bibi Toche, who does business with the Black sailors from American ships that pass through the Pointe-à-Pitre port. The song is Ma Rainey's "See See Rider Blues," accompanied by the mighty Louis Armstrong on the trumpet …

I'm so unhappy
I feel so blue.
I always feel so sad.
I made a mistake
Right from the start.
Oh, it seems so hard to part.
Oh, but this letter
That I will write,
I hope he will remember,
When he receive' it.

See see, rider.
See what you done done.
Lawd, lawd, lawd …

Blissful, eyelids closed, savoring the music, Maxime remains seated in his chair until dinner. I think I get that from him: closing my eyes to see better, to drift backwards in time. Experiencing something that is both dark and bright, that escapes reality.

What did he see?

Today, I still wonder if my father went traveling far away from our little island of Guadeloupe. If his closed eyes took him there, to America, all the way to the banks of the Mississippi, to the segregated fields filled with Black bodies picking white balls, in Alabama, in Saint Louis, Missouri, in Columbus, Georgia ... Maybe he found himself in Chicago, in one of those famous jazz clubs where the same blues that sustained Black people captivated white people's ears. In New York, Harlem, at the Cotton Club and the Savoy Ballroom ...

I'm so unhappy,
I feel so blue.
I always feel so sad.
I made a mistake
Right from the start

The anger in the sea, fear in the trees, malice in the sky ... Lucette must have thought that Nature is, like people, capable of feeling emotion.
Does Nature have a soul?
I still haven't stopped wondering if it does ...

Later on, during my years with Man, I often hear him say that he aspires to function in the manner of Nature, with its infinite, ever-unpredictable, manifestations. Indeed, in his life and in his art, he leans into contradictions, the whims of his imagination. He is convinced that any problem that comes his way will resolve itself, just as Nature finds a solution for everything. Human beings have this deep need to live and to create, so Man says. They must express themselves in one way or another to overcome hardship, failures, foolishness. To get through misfortune and calamity, fed by their own resources, chance encounters, desire, inspiration. To survive the worst, with nerve and kindheartedness, driven by dreams, words, numbers, and colors. And to savor the simple things ...
On September 11, 1928, Nature is not pondering her palette of colors. The anger in the sea, fear in the trees, malice in the sky. I don't want to admit it, but I can see it all as I fasten the doors shaken by the gusts in the street. Ma Rainey sings the blues, and even though I don't understand the words, her deep, sad voice seems to foretell the doom on its way. I resist these bad omens. Outside, raging winds and devils may well decide to tear each other apart. I believe my family is safe under our roof; it has seen

it all before. Even if hell freezes over, nothing can reach us here, nothing can unsettle the peace and quiet of our lives.

I'm go'n away, baby,
Won't be back till fall.
Lawd, lawd, lawd …

In the evening, we enjoy a peaceful dinner before going to bed. Lucette washes the dishes and pots. She unrolls her banana-leaf mattress on the kitchen floor. I hear her pray and picture her kneeling, pleading with the Lord to spare us. With a poetry book under her arm, manman goes upstairs to her room. Papa is already in bed, waiting for her.

The wind picks up speed in the middle of the night. The black sky unleashes flashes of lightning and deafening claps of thunder. A steady downpour of heavy rain pelts the tin roof, unleashing sheets of water. Beneath the racket, the city is cracking on all sides.

I don't sleep. Far away, dogs struggle in their chains and bark wildly. It's a gloomy dirge. I remember a neighborhood infant bawling its eyes out. And a quarrel between spurned lovers with raised voices. One threatens to kill the other with a knife, with a single stab. In the wind that escapes from the darkness, a woman screams for help.

On the morning of Wednesday, September 12, Mathilde says, "My God, the sky is so dark. There's going to be a lot of rain today, my children. And all this wind! Make sure you keep the doors shut! You won't be going to school …."

Maxime adds, "It looks like hurricane weather. You never know, maybe I won't be going out either."

Alas.

Disaster is on its way.

At around 8 in the morning, the first round of nasty gusts is already blowing down doors and tearing off sheet metal. The rain cascades down on our roof worse than a deluge. Hammering and pounding without faltering for a moment. Growing stronger and stronger, in its stubborn resolve to break through at any moment, its patience unyielding. The wind is its faithful and furious ally. You would swear it was the devil himself paying Earth a visit. With all its screaming and snarling beyond the doors. It has claws and fangs out there. Stomps its hooves. Has one hundred big, mighty paws, and maybe even satanic tools and contraptions to uproot trees and bring down poles in an instant, smash and lift up houses, overturn canoes and carts and tilburies ... Its massive mouth blows mercilessly on us, on our little country. With damned gigantic jaws swallowing everything in their path.

We struggle on and on. A long day followed by a harrowing night. In a daze, in the confines of our house on Rue Condé, falling to pieces before our eyes. Young and old alike, coming to our rescue, calling out to us, looking for us in the dark. At the end of our rope, soaked, discouraged. Helpless. Fighting against the raging elements with our bare hands. Then armed with zinc buckets and leaf brooms. Sad pieces of wood and paltry nails. A shovel and a hammer. Wet candles, tears, fear in our stomachs. Prayers and signs of the cross. Screams and swears. Our Fathers and I believe in Gods, the Virgin Mary and all the saints in heaven.

And then a brief lull, interspersed with desperate screams coming from everywhere and nowhere.

And then a tremendous cracking sound from above. Long and plaintive, like a living body resisting being dismembered.

And then something tearing away, falling. Heavy, massive, murderous.

And then manman's voice. A single sound. A whispered "Ah!"

And then nothing.

Nothing but the rancid silence of the corrupted waters all around.

There has already been so much screaming.

We are all so tired after the long hours of fighting. Good Lord, we faced the incarnation of Evil that night. Watched the world unravel before our stunned eyes.

Papa tells us that manman has fallen asleep. We want to believe it, for as long as possible. The idea of the Sleeper, of Sleeping Beauty, is comforting. In the darkness, we glimpse her motionless body in an unusual position. Like an unloved doll, thrown in the corner, mouth gaping open. One arm on backwards. Its legs out of shape. Eyes wide open. When the sun comes up, the first rays break through our lives. Death stands beside our manman. Stiff, with that ugly implacable smile that we know so well. Dressed in black veils ...

I can picture Maxime on the morning of September 13.

My poor little papa ...

He's spent, disoriented. He stares at me with haggard eyes but does not see me. His gaze goes straight through me. His stained and torn pants billow at his ankles. He's not wearing a belt or suspenders. His very dirty white shirt is stained with blood. Mathilde's blood. She was hit on the head by a beam.

He staggers. His feet bare in the filth. The hurricane has stripped him of his shoes. He who is always wearing tailored shoes, handmade by Pointe-à-Pitre's most reputable shoemaker. And impeccably polished by manman.

The house is on its last legs. Disfigured, gaping, it has lost most of the roof. Under the steady, miserable rain, the hapless bits of sheet metal still remaining squeak and flap in the wretched wind. Half-bent and hanging on by two or three nails, they're enough to make you weep. The staircase is broken in the middle; three jagged steps dangle in the void. The entire first floor is in ruins, echoing with ominous, macabre creaks. From the ground floor, you can see the sky. It can see us, too. It's the eye of a voyeur, a blue, formless, enemy ogling us through the gutted flooring. High above us, a cloud passes, taunting us shamelessly. Our beds have blown away with the sheets and blankets and quilts. The rugs have disappeared. The wardrobes are empty, their doors hanging loose like broken wings. The wind left nothing behind. It carted away all the patchouli-scented laundry, ironed and folded, and dumped it at the bottom of Rue Condé and who knows where else, in tattered tree limbs, on the few surviving roofs in the neighborhood, in the dirty water from the culverts that have become rivers.

In the living room, the hurricane has ripped the furniture to shreds. We wade through the molasses-like debris, tripping over tattered curtains, blues and ragtime vinyls, manman's nice books, portraits of our ancestors. And the water keeps rising. What remains despite the frenzy? Papa's armchair. His throne remains almost entirely intact among the rubble. With its sodden blue damask canvas and feet stuck in the mud, among the trash, the scraps of broken crockery. The brass horn of the battered phonograph bubbles and gently sinks – it's a fascinating scene that keeps me riveted, and makes time stand still.

I wonder if the hurricane took pity on my papa. I tell myself that God left him his armchair as a reminder of the good times. Like a consolatory relic, the chair was spared because my papa can no longer stand upright. His grief weighs on him and cuts into his legs. In his chair, he reflects on his past happiness and mourns the sweet woman who stood by his side. He taps the arms of the chair with the tips of his fingers. Does he hear music? Maybe Ma Rainey's voice will help him recover ... Maybe the sound of Louis Armstrong will restore some of his strength to face the end of the world.

On this fateful day, I look at my father, abandoned in his armchair, a broken puppet. I can picture my mother giving him the bowl of soapy water. I can picture his wing-like hands. I can picture the porcelain pitcher, the splashing water, the foam making clouds in the bowl. I can picture the well-ironed, starched white towel unfolding. It escapes my manman's hands and is now floating in the air like a white flag begging for mercy.

In a single night, my papa's beautiful crimped black hair turned white. Maxime, dashing, always worried about his appearance, now looks like one of those old men in the General Hospital garden. Sometimes we see them behind the wrought-iron fence. They sit there, perhaps reminiscing about a fragmented past. Stare at you without seeing you, mulling over nostalgia for days gone by, their past glory, and no doubt the bitterness of some departed love.

Is happiness a fleeting mirage?

Which perhaps promises some kind of a trip.

What kind of trip? A page torn from the big book of life.

Manman's lifeless body rests on the dining room table. We covered it with an embroidered tablecloth reserved for special occasions. A salvaged tablecloth that serves as her shroud.

Every time she turns her eyes toward the mortuary table, my sister Rose, or "Wòz," as we call her, lets out a loud scream followed by a long groan. Sheltered in a wet corner, she has been sobbing and moaning for hours. She sits cross-legged on the floor. Swaying back and forth, back and forth, muttering part of a poem dear to our mother, *"But where are snows of yester-year ... But where are the snows of yester-year ...."*[2]

My other sister, sweet, gentle Aimée, or "Dous," is praying to God. Kneeling in a small puddle, she's shivering and her lips are quivering.

---

2 François Villon, "Ballade des dames du temps jadis," in *Poems*, trans. by Dante Gabriel Rossetti, 6th ed. (London: Strangeways and Walden, 1872), pp. 178–79.

I am the youngest in my family, our manman's last baby. I pick up one of my rag dolls. She is very cold and wet. I wring her out, twisting her from head to toe. I hug her close to warm her up. She's not crying, but I rock and pretend to console her. Just to do something, to keep my hands busy, to feel like I'm doing something useful, to feel less helpless.

In the middle of the day, Lucette takes matters into her own hands. She pushes open a door blocked by a heap of trash and branches. The hurricane killed three people in front of our house. One of them lost a leg. Another is naked, battered by the wind, her thighs spread. The third is missing half an arm.

All around, there's nothing but rubble. Lifeless bodies have been strewn carelessly all down Rue Condé. Corpses soaked in filthy water, their faces are wounded, blinded, withered, their arms and legs lacerated. Kids who have miraculously survived the havoc roam the street like zombies crying for their manmans. The Vatable Canal is overflowing. A wild barricade has formed at the end of every street: piles of stones, bricks, boards, branches, leaves, sheets, slates, tiles, telephone wires, wood, beams. The Ferret, Chauvel, and Massabielle hills are charred and scorched. In the distance, toward Place de la Victoire, several roads have become impassible, blocked by leaning buildings ready to fall. With its broken walls, torn doors, and windows, Monsieur de Chambertrand's house stands exposed to the elements.

I remember people talking about an impending tidal wave and an earthquake. The End of the World, the Apocalypse ... I don't remember anymore ...

What I cannot erase from my memory are Lucette's haunting prayers mingled with Rose's screams. The desperate screams and muffled sobs outside. The desolation on every face. The smell of carrion and the rumors of an epidemic. Good God, the sad procession of foul-smelling carts filled with corpses. The masses of bodies buried under the rubble.

Always the same vivid images of my wounded city ...

And then, in the days that follow, the unnamed dead unceremoniously buried in mass graves. Bluebottle flies everywhere in the air. Worms swarming in sacks of rice. Weevils, rats, vermin. Rationed water, infested water. The victims in the throes of death on makeshift cots, the vagrant survivors fallen into insanity, the empty-bellied wanderers crippled by the storm. And the bleary-eyed orphans who never stop screaming and crying and begging for a piece of bread. Little ones hanging off the breasts of frightened mothers in endless lines. The patience of the destitute on the sidewalk outside the police station, waiting for food, a basket, a pound of flour, a pint of red peas, lard, a filet of salted cod. Help us, please ...

Hold on, all this reminds me of something ...

The first summer in Mougins, in 1936 ...

At first, Man's friends look at me quizzically. He's already had a lot of women pass through in his life and leave marks of varying depth. Kiki de Montparnasse, Lee Miller, and so many other beauties ... They stay for a while and then set off ... It's just a few steps from the studio to the bedroom. From the darkroom to the white sheets, where pleasure and desire become entangled. And after jumping each other's bones, after the tears and punches and insults, there's a craving for suicide and alcohol ...

Maybe I'm just a passing fancy in their eyes. A frisky islander in search of a Parisian pimp. A blossoming exotic bird who will belly dance and pose bare-chested at the drop of a hat. But if there was any prejudice, it didn't last long. Nusch and I are quickly inseparable. Even though I don't talk much, we become soul sisters that summer. One white, one Black. Naked under the men's gaze. Naked in their arms. Naked and available for their pleasure in the Mougins sunshine.

It's late afternoon at the Vaste Horizon pension hotel. We're sitting in the pergola, pouring glasses of wine, smoking, stretching, lusting after one another, laughing and chattering endlessly. The sun is disappearing in the distance. Big, copper-feathered clouds seem to crowd around us like vultures. Suddenly, lightning lights up the sky. Terrified, I let out a scream. The night of the hurricane comes back to me. Once again, I see my dead mother and I am ready to collapse amongst the laughter.

That afternoon, Nusch told me about her childhood in Mulhouse – the circus, the poverty, the trapeze, the acrobats ... The thunder and cracking in the sky loosen my tongue. I speak about my country, ravaged by the hurricane – a story that Man already knows. I use my arms to help me as I describe the strength of the hurricane that engulfed Guadeloupe in 1928. My chatty hands describe the night of helplessness, the celestial wrath, the wickedness of the wind,

Picnic, Île Sainte-Marguerite, Cannes, France 1937 by Lee Miller. © Lee Miller Archives,
England 2023. All rights reserved. leemiller.co.uk

all of the fear in the world crammed into a wooden shack, back there, in the Caribbean. That's where I'm from. That small slice of Heaven on Earth. That hell. Silence surrounds us. Then someone yells out, "Hey! It looks like Ady has clouds in her hands." I hear laughter and meet Man's kind eyes. No, they're not making fun of me. They're laughing at the imagery, because of the clouds in my hands. And then Nusch comes toward me. She kisses me on the forehead, runs her fingers through my hair. She lets out a sad sigh and says, "My poor sweet Ady, you come from so far away ...."

The next year, in the collection *Les Mains libres*, Paul Éluard illustrates Man's drawings with his words. "Des nuages dans les mains" is a short poem that echoes my story. I know it by heart. And even if I get some of the words wrong sometimes, it is still mine. Man told me that all of us are in *Les Mains libres* in any case – friends, lovers, painters, poets ... All hidden beneath the words and drawings ...

That confusing despair
Tenuous rainy night spring
Far from the nascent leaves
Far from the cleanly tears
That disdain for the East
That livid paradise
That walking backwards
Incredulous and drained
Toward a few memories

The miracle cure a pact token credence.[3]

And then my papa dies on Sunday, November 9, 1930.

After a beautiful mass at Saint-Pierre-et-Saint-Paul Church, a hundred Black silhouettes follow his casket to the Pointe-à-Pitre cemetery where our family is already resting. He is reunited with his Mathilde. Tall people with stern faces kiss me, hold me in their arms. Some shake my hands in reverence. I think I remember women sobbing under their black veils. But not a single one of them came up to us. An elderly aunt stops me from looking at them.

My father had a son out of wedlock. In 1930, the little boy is twelve years old and makes the trip over to the *Métropole* with us. I don't know his mother, but I promised my papa to always consider this boy my brother. He's three years younger than me.

One of these women is likely his manman … I never met her. Never saw her at our door. She stayed far away, a shadow at the end of the street. Let the little one go on alone. Waited until the door of our house closed behind him.

We leave the cemetery. That's it! It's all over. Like that moment at the end of a ball, when the musicians pack up their instruments.

I truly believe my father died from grief. That used to happen back then, in Guadeloupe. People overcome with melancholy would decide to die from heartache. Their pockets filled with pebbles, wounded women walked resolutely into the sea. Armed with a strong rope, inconsolable fools climbed onto stools in the middle of their huts to hang themselves. Others sat quietly waiting for

---

3 Paul Éluard and Man Ray, "Des nuages dans les mains," in *Les Mains libres* (Paris: Gallimard, 1947 and Man Ray 2015 Trust / ADAGP, 2020), p. 95 (translated by Mehdi Étienne Chalmers).

death to release them from their painful existence. You could see them wasting away in front of you, and then, one fine morning, they would disappear without a farewell.

Dying from love ...

In the last days of December 1930, it is this quaint picture of love that I place at the bottom of my sorry luggage, between a salvaged Brahms score, a few pages of *Poésies antillaises* by John-Antoine Nau, and one of Mathilde's dresses, rescued from the mud, a survivor of the hurricane.

Like all the bereaved or dispossessed, we are fleeing desolation, poverty, death, and our shattered country. We board a Compagnie Générale Transatlantique liner for the long trip to France. I wave a weak goodbye to the people singing and crying on the dock.

Adieu foulard, adieu madras
Adieu grain d'or, adieu collier-chou
Doudou an mwen i ka pati
Hélas, hélas, sé pou toujou.
Doudou an mwen i ka pati
Hélas, hélas, sé pou toujou.

I'm fifteen.

Raymonde and her husband Narcisse have lived in France since the 1920s. They came back for papa's funeral, primarily to take us back with them – my little brother, my two sisters, and me. After 1928, we lived with Uncle Adrien who had welcomed us into his two-story home that had survived the hurricane. My brother-in-law is an insurance agent. They have a beautiful apartment near Paris. We must relieve Uncle Adrien and look forward to a brighter future ...

Born in 1900, my older sister is fifteen years older than me. Raymonde is like a fine lady to me, familiar and foreign all at once. The morning after papa's funeral, she declares that she's going to replace my manman. What a joke!

She's taking us to France; it's not up for discussion. Dous agrees. I'm not asked for my opinion on the matter. Neither is my little brother. Wòz, my other sister, the one who was reciting *the snows of yester-year* the morning after the hurricane, is pregnant by God knows who. She's twenty years old and is hiding her big belly under loose dresses. Thank God papa died without knowing that his Wòz was pregnant.

"No father, no mother, what use is there in staying in Guadeloupe when it's been crushed by suffering, gossip, and witchcraft ... We need to get you out of this hell, fast!" Raymonde says. "France will be glad to have you. You will be happy there with us. The damage is done. The child will be born in Paris, in a beautiful modern hospital. No one will have anything to complain about, believe me! The *Métropole* is the land of Maurice Chevalier, strawberries, apples, pears, and cheese. The land of snow and the French language. There aren't any nasty hurricanes in France ... No tidal waves or earthquakes. They don't even have any volcanoes. Just the four seasons ...."

My history and geography books had long prepared me for my exile. I learned to read at the desks of the private school run by the Sisters of Saint-Joseph-de-Cluny, on Rue François-Arago in Pointe-à-Pitre, close to home. Under the watchful eye of Mother Elizabeth, I dipped my Sergeant-Major quill in purple ink. I wrote rare words not seen in our tropics.

So, there you have it, I'm off to France, home of my ancestors the Gauls, the Holy Land of Joan of Arc, Charlemagne, François Villon, Napoléon. We're headed to the land of the French Revolution and the Declaration of the Rights of Man and of the Citizen, of Robespierre, Jean de La Fontaine, Voltaire, Diderot. And this immense and appealing motherland is home to a thousand streams and rivers, golden fields of wheat, vineyards as far as the eye can see ... France, the country of roses and poppies and daisies. And trees that do not bear fruit, planted for the sole purpose of filling out the landscape, drawing people in. I think of the poplars, the snow-covered fir trees of December and the plane trees of my dictations ... A thousand marvels, a thousand age-old beauties ... I think about the Palace of Versailles and the châteaux of the Loire Valley, the Eiffel Tower, the Louvre ... I have a heavy heart, but I already see myself on the Champs-Élysées, at Les Invalides, at the foot of the Arc de Triomphe ...

Leaning against the railing, I watch Pointe-à-Pitre and the *mornes* of Basse-Terre shrink until they join the haze of the horizon and then disappear altogether, like the outlines of a land that might have never existed. Beside me, my sisters are silent. My little brother wipes his eyes. He cried a great deal leaving his mother in Guadeloupe. I console him as best I can, setting some of my own sadness aside.

The handful of politicians on board try to comfort their compatriots, reassure them that the country will rise from the rubble. "Fear not, rebuilding is already underway in the devastated countryside. Ali Tur, a leading architect sent from Paris, is busy redesigning and building new administrative buildings, schools, churches, and marketplaces …." In their speeches, reinforced concrete is declared to be the great savior with the promise of resisting Nature, even the most monstrous calamities descending from the sky or rising from the belly of the earth. "Concrete, ladies and gentlemen, is the future of Guadeloupe. It will replace wood everywhere. No more flimsy structures or deadly sheet metal and beams."

In my head, a small voice keeps crooning, "People die … If nothing lasts, Ady … go, if nothing lasts … go and live your life …."

Among the passengers, young scholarship students in waxed boots and black redingote coats are headed to Paris to continue their studies. They always walk with a book under their arm. They can already picture themselves as doctors, lawyers, magistrates, government officials … I tell my little brother, "See how happy they are to be going to France! You too will become an important person one day, because you've studied in the *Métropole* …."

On deck, we come across a bunch of *nègres* in their Sunday best. They're wearing starched white shirts, cotton jackets, twill-cuff pants, shiny ascot ties. These poor souls have dragged themselves from the insalubrious outskirts of the city or perhaps the depths of the countryside bristling with sugar cane, where dogs bark with their tails, where witchcraft roams naked in the savannas. Eager to tread French soil, their feet cramped in hard leather shoes that blister their toes, they dance from one foot to the other, dreaming of being reborn in France. Raymonde says that they are hoping to land a job at the prosperous Renault factory, recently built on Île-Seguin in Boulogne-Billancourt, a stone's throw from Paname. Others are eyeing a job as a coachbuilder, or maybe a welder, at Citroën, on Quai de Javel in the fifteenth *arrondissement*. If they have a brother or a cousin who already works there as a laborer, that helps their prospects. As for housing, they're counting on resourcefulness and family solidarity. And probably on prayers to God.

Others, survivors of the Great War, hint at hypothetical reunions with wartime lovers in their conversations, the dressing nurse in a field hospital, the beautiful visitor who would read at the bedside of the wounded, a fearless washerwoman ... In sum, a real Frenchwoman from the *Métropole*, white from head to toe, hair with a satin sheen, rosy, silky cheeks, green or blue eyes. They dream of engagements and nuptials with all the bells and whistles. They dream of conquests and furious expeditions, their Black hands probing the diaphanous skin, the delicate porcelain flesh. Good heavens! They imagine their ravenous lips unlocking the great mystery of those pubis with such fair, fine hair, their avid mouths drinking from miraculous springs. And in the dark of the night, on their third-class beds, these Black men allow themselves to become masters in these oceans of whiteness. They know that those white dolls, once more inaccessible than Miquelon, now offer themselves up to *nègres*. Times have changed. War has come and gone.

Manman used to say, "Never sneer at a setback ... Sometimes, you may want to curse misfortune. But you mustn't. After night comes day. We don't know anything. We are on this earth to learn from challenges and grow, with faith in Our Almighty God ...."

It's true, if this hurricane had saved my family I probably never would have set sail for France. I never would have met my sweet little Man.

Ten days of travel across the seas.

Of incessant churning.

It's a real ordeal for pregnant Wòz. Her complexion is a shade of gray. Her enormous belly bulges and weighs her down. Aimée and I take turns watching her while Raymonde looks after her husband and three children. We count the days, hoping that the poor thing won't give birth in the middle of the ocean. To pass the time, I read her manman's poems. And when Dous whispers, "Soon, we will see the snows of yester-year, we will eat apples and strawberries in the *Métropole* ...." Wòz smiles, sometimes.

On board, many people in bad shape heave their guts out. Stay locked in their cabins writhing in pain and praying to make it to shore alive.

At lunches and dinners, those who aren't seasick slowly become accustomed to the French dishes that Raymonde and her husband know by heart. Potatoes in every sauce. Bitter chicory. Bloody beets,

Brussel sprouts, sausages with beans, veal blanquette, roast meats, beef tongue, peas and carrots, andouillette, navarin, béarnaise and ravigote sauce, cheese soufflé, *île flottante* ... Aimée makes a face and spits out the chicory. Raymonde isn't particularly pleased – that's not how people eat in France! Those are bad manners. You swallow even if you don't like it ...

Whenever Wòz sleeps a little, I wander the halls alone without ever getting lost. I can also spend hours with my little brother, watching the liner's hull smash through the thick, foamy waves. One morning, Dous and I are walking on deck when we overhear a conversation between two first-class passengers. They recount how in 1912 there was a shortage of lifeboats on a big liner that sank in the North Atlantic – the Titanic. Hundreds of bodies were fished out of the icy waters. Few survived ... I'm already aware of the fact that I could die before arriving in France. Die at fifteen, having seen nothing of the world. Dous promises me that won't happen. She predicts that I'll live a long life full of mystery and joy. To distract us from these dark thoughts, we follow the steps of happier people. We casually eavesdrop on their conversations. Here and there, we stare at travelers, imagining what their lives could be.

I'm curious to know what goes on in the cabins, behind all these closed doors. I think about the Black men and women making babies on the Compagnie Générale Transatlantique's white sheets. The ladies fascinate me. Even those from humble backgrounds take great care with their appearance. Not one of them goes anywhere without makeup. Not a single one walks barefoot or shabbily dressed on this boat. This is not the Place du Marché in Pointe-à-Pitre. At mealtimes, it's a parade of extraordinary outfits pulled from trunks. Falbala dresses and fabulous jewelry, even if it's just glass. Buns with hairpieces and layers. But these hairstyles are already outdated in 1930. Their finger on the pulse of the latest Parisian trends, Black and white avant-gardists sport short bob cuts, or sculpted, wavy and notched locks, plastered to their forehead like a work of art with spit curls on their temples. Thanks, Joséphine! Black women use Bakerfix Brillantine on their relaxed hair. All these women wear calf-length dresses. They've thrown away their corsets and switched to bras. Some even dare to prance around in pants. They size each other up with murderous glances. And then pay each other compliments, interspersed with big fake smiles. *Masques de poix* on their powdered faces.

Forgive me if I mix up the order of events. I'm doing my best. My head is filled with wobbly drawers that insist on staying wide open, filled with fresh old memories that are almost intact, nicely folded and smelling sweetly of hope and love ... Others spew out sad and crumpled things, a mishmash of painful names and dates. And then, as soon as I start rummaging around, I stumble across a hodgepodge of films floundering under the light of day, contact sheets, plates, and scratched photos where I see myself in my twenties, with Man. So, even though I can't believe I've been through all these things, the joy returns to my heart. That's what life is: happiness and unhappiness mixed together.

We arrive in Le Havre in the first days of January 1931.

You have to imagine the Caribbean people disembarking from the enormous liners in those terrible winter months, wearing cotton shirts and dresses, drill suits, and light shoes. While a lot of the passengers on these transatlantic voyages are regulars, many of them are unprepared for the harsh climate of the *Métropole*.

First, a bitter cold hits them right in the face, stiffening their jaws. Then they are enveloped in a treacherous cold that sinks into them, freezing their blood, before emerging as icy white vapor in their breath and their every word.

Then, there's the desolate picture of paradise. A low, heavy, colorless sky, ready to collapse, like a false ceiling colonized by termites. Black skeletal trees, stripped of their leaves as if burned to the core, looking like they might topple at any moment. These tall, steaming buildings with gray facades, where people rush in and out with worried faces, glancing left and right.

At once bewildered and filled with pity, disoriented and shivering, I board the train for Paris, wondering where we've ended up. I'm perplexed. So this is France! Where is the Glory? Where is the legendary Grandeur of our Motherland? Raymonde lends us black wool coats. Dous and I swim in them, but at least they shield us from the cold. Wòz is wrapped in a large checkered blanket. My little brother disappears in one of Narcisse's jackets that hangs past his knees.

At the Gare Saint-Lazare, the kid opens his stunned eyes. A phenomenal rush and my Wòz is screaming, holding her stomach in both hands. Dous opens her mouth in a wide O. My older sister and her husband stride through the crowd. White people like you've never seen bump into you constantly, without a single apology. A waltz of trunks and suitcases. A stream of porters in livery uniforms. Screams everywhere. Lovers, alone in this world, embracing. Cold on the wide-open quay exposed to the four winds.

That winter, snow melts as soon as it hits the ground. The Parisian sidewalks become filthy, muddy molasses. Everywhere disgusting puddles sully shoes and ruin pants. Paying no mind to this annoyance, bundled-up Parisians go about their business in the streets. About half the people thrown outside are attempting to sell something, either by auction or under the table; the other half are there to buy anything at a good price. Paname resembles a big makeshift fair teeming with rag-and-bone merchants, delivery boys, peddlers, knife-grinders, paperboys, sandwich men, glaziers, baker boys, hot chestnut sellers ….

I remember … There were horses in those days in Paris, even donkeys and goats. You have to be careful where you walk … Chickens and rabbits running around courtyards ….

Under this gloomy sky, men walk quickly – not at all like back home. That's what strikes me first. With their noses in the air, they walk confidently, seemingly indifferent to one another. I watch them disregard common sense and risk their life crossing the road, under the stern gazes of the police in *képis* and black capes. While some of them take the time to give cars a hearty scolding or to whistle at women on the street, they all have an urgency about them, except for the homeless and penniless hoping for some spare change from a charitable soul at street corners, the unemployed in front of the soup kitchen, veterans dragging their legs out of shady bars, children begging here and there. Alas, yes. There are miserable people in France, too.

Behind the windows of the bistros, restaurants, and brasseries lining boulevards and avenues, more affluent clientele eat and drink, from time to time hailing a server with slicked-back hair, a black vest, black bow tie, and large white apron. Men and women smoke and chat, paying no mind to the incessant stream of vehicles clogging the road. Streetcars, carriages, green Renault buses with out-of-breath travelers chasing after them, whirring sidecars, honking cabs, and backfiring cars weaving between cyclists, zigzagging like dragonflies.

The banks of the Seine are still crowded with lines of horse-drawn carts laden with crates, barrels, large baskets, and goods packed in heavy burlap sacks. All around, laborers, sailors and bargemen, wiry-framed porters. Chatty little commanders in caps, giving curt orders. Sunday fishermen and taciturn onlookers who every day rewrite the century to their own tune, as they watch the barges glide along the water ...

In those years, maybe until my twenties, I feel that Paris is a giant pigsty. Much to the dismay of my older sisters, I quickly take to strolling the streets alone. Sometimes I walk all the way to the Faubourg Saint-Martin, letting myself be led by the whims of the streets. I get lost in the Faubourg Saint-Denis. Some afternoons, I climb up Montmartre to get a closer look at the Sacré-Cœur. Afterward, I hurdle down the stairs toward the Marché Saint-Pierre, Boulevard Rochechouart, and the Dreyfus store where they sell the world's most beautiful fabrics. Sometimes, I wander around the Les Halles neighborhood like I did at the Pointe-à-Pitre marketplace. In Les Halles, you can find anything to eat and drink among a cacophony of screams. Other times, on Sundays, I take the *métro* and get off at Bienvenüe Station in the heart of Montparnasse. I blend in with the crowd of *flâneurs*. I take the pulse of Paris. Some people whistle popular tunes. Couples lock lips, eye to eye, walking in sync. On the edges of sidewalks, I eye plotting brats that look like miniature adults. There is spectacle everywhere in Paname. This city is also filled with flashy neon signs, huge advertisements painted onto walls, DUBONNET, BLÉDINE, GALERIES BARBÈS ... Colorful posters glued everywhere, announcing revues, expositions, boxing matches, new albums ... I confess, I'm not sure where to look. Always something new to see somewhere, concerts in neighborhood bars, a movie theater where you can sink into an armchair, a comedy to laugh at and distract yourself, no doubt from the grayness outside, a low and heavy sky, icy sidewalks, black trees.

My little niece is born on April 18, 1931. An adorable, chubby little girl, the same shade as the sapodilla fruit. I help Wòz. She's hanging in there despite her depression. I give the baby her bottle and I look after her while her manman goes out looking for work.

It's less chilly in April. The sky is brighter. And then, on May 1st, the cold suddenly disappears, as if by magic. New leaves appear on tree branches. Kids selling Lily of the Valley and ice-cream vendors flood the streets. On the sidewalks, in front of the department stores, you'll find everything from seamstresses with their sewing machines for alterations, to crêpe-sellers, shoemakers, sausage- or shirt collar-sellers, and edgy hawkers peddling their goods from behind their stalls. The sun puts a smile back on Parisians' faces. So they start to dress lighter and swarm café terraces. Spreading out like a human tide under the joyful trees, in parks, squares, and gardens where clans of kids and toddlers run around.

I'm sixteen.

It's my first spring in France. I eagerly join the crowds on the Grands Boulevards. With my nose to the wind, joyful, I push my little niece's stroller down the streets. We sit in the Jardin du Luxembourg at feeding time. While waiting for the baby to burp, I watch the Parisian women come and go. They are so beautiful. Even in their cheap dresses, they carry their heads high and display a natural easiness, an innate elegance. The men look dashing under their straw hats, shirts unbuttoned to show their chest hair.

When I come across a Black face, once in a while, I sometimes feel guilty about my joy and I think of my island. You can read so much in the eyes of these Black people. A hypothetical kinship, a reproach, a question and a command … "What are you doing here? Go back where you came from!"

At the Casino de Paris, Joséphine Baker sings "J'ai deux amours" to Vincent Scotto's music:

J'ai deux amours
Mon pays et Paris
Par eux toujours
Mon cœur est ravi
Ma savane est belle
Mais à quoi bon le nier
Ce qui m'ensorcelle
C'est Paris, Paris tout entier.

Quand sur la rive parfois
Au lointain j'aperçois
Un paquebot qui s'en va
Vers lui je tends les bras
Et le cœur battant d'émoi
À mi-voix
Doucement je dis "Emporte-moi!"

1928, Hurricane Year

Does my life seem beautiful then?
I don't really know anymore ...
I believe so, yes ...

I remember loving the idea of living in Paris, even if my heart
never stops reminding me to not forget Guadeloupe, even if my
café-au-lait skin raises a few white people's eyebrows in the street.

That's what it's like, everywhere on earth; there are good things
and bad.

When you travel, you always leave something behind.

Sometimes pain and tears. Sometimes laughter and love.

When you arrive in a new place, whatever your skin color, you
arrive with joy and sorrow.

At first, everything can seem strange and foreign.

But your heart beats. You live. You learn every day. You fall,
you get up again.

If you're homesick, you smile and you cry without tears.

Years pass. You forget things about your homeland. Your
memories are like old photos. You collect them. You caress them.

One day, you go back home and you realize that you yourself
have become strange and foreign in the eyes of your own people.

III

She
thinks she exists
and her life exists as a suspended bridge under a sky of clouds
I say exist
with Her
exist
while Heaven wonders where shared loneliness leads.

Léon-Gontran Damas, "Élydé"[1]

---

1 Léon-Gontran Damas, "Élydé," in *Black-Label et autres poèmes* (Paris: Gallimard, 1956 [2011]), pp. 44–45 (our translation).

31 bis Rue Campagne-Première

Man often spoke of his arrival in le Havre in 1921.

He chose the right season to come to France.

In summer, around the 14th of July, in the middle of the roaring twenties. I see oompahs, bal-musettes, confetti, and fireworks in his eyes when he talks about this period of his life ...

His train crosses the Normandy countryside to the Gare Saint-Lazare in Paris, villages popping up here and there with their quaint bells and rugged locals, a rustic stable, a meadow where cows munch on old loneliness while watching trains go by.

Man is so excited at the idea of living his dream. He arrives with all his valuables in tow: crates of canvases, photographs, objects, and drawings. Some friends offer to host him but the whimsical Marcel Duchamp has booked the Dadaist Tristan Tzara's hotel room, vacant for the summer.

He wanders the boulevards that same evening. Duchamp takes him to the Passage de l'Opéra, to Le Certa, the Basque bistro where young writers and poets from the Dada movement meet and debate. Éluard and his wife Gala are there, along with Aragon, Duchamp's friend. They give him a warm welcome, trying their hardest to exchange a few words with him in English. No prohibition in Paris! The concept of the "noble experience" holds no sway in Europe. Alcohol flows freely in broad daylight. No wicked bootleggers in sight. No need to shut yourself away in a speakeasy and guzzle whisky from a coffee cup.

Finally, Man is free to live his life as he wishes, no strings attached, free to earn a living from his passion: painting. He is in Paris and will learn French. Through sheer determination, he will likely become a famous painter, in the manner of Picasso or Foujita. After the Spanish man and the Japanese man, he, the American Man, is set to conquer Paris.

Anything is possible. He need only lean over a blank canvas and allow his imagination to lead the way. Man is the master of his own destiny. Young and enthusiastic. Life in Paris appears to him as a clean slate on which he will write his own story.

A beautiful story brimming with pleasure and laughter, amorous women, one-night stands, wine, friends, Exquisite Corpses. With lots of color, of course. Bold pencil strokes, muses, languid lovers, princesses, and grateful models of flesh and cardboard. Clay pipes, coat hangers, and funnels piled around a chess set, a dust farm. A dark bedroom, wrinkled sheets. Soap bubbles, glass tears. A clothing iron, nails, needles, and twisting wire, birds of passage. Dreams and revolvers put down on paper, hands cut out, free ... An eye on the pendulum of a metronome, a tree-rose, red lips, the Violin of Ingres, an ebony mask ...

Strokes of luck and chance.

Pleasure and freedom laid bare.

Frivolity, joy, poems galore, and endless words of love.

In Paris, in July 1921, the weather really is fair; it's the blessed season where women reveal a little more of their pink legs. They laugh from morning to night, simply because of a sliver of blue and the bright sun, up in the sky, hanging in the tree branches until 10 at night. It's a dazzling summer, with strawberries, cherries, plump apricots, and mountains of *mirabelle* plums on the market stalls. It's a time of love and parties in the street. It's all of Paris served up on a platter to a young artist from New York.

That night, Man feels immediately accepted among the Dadaists. After Le Certa, they whisk him off to an Indian restaurant for dinner, where bottles of wine flow amid laughter, curry, and white rice. Then they take to the lively streets that bustle as if in broad daylight. Near Montmartre, Man discovers a gigantic traveling carnival. Under the multicolored paper lanterns and the blue-white-red flags, entwined couples dance to a catchy accordion tune. There's joy and love in Paname. So, the band of Dadaists storm the wooden carousels, roller coasters, and pendulum rides, more enthusiastic than children. There are so many different attractions, they barely know where to begin. They jump into the bumper cars, screaming their lungs out. Next, they run from one stand to the next, shooting a gun to win a stuffed animal, fishing for a bottle of cheap wine.

Barely three years have passed since the end of The Great War.

"Never again!" the French keep saying, after the signing of the Armistice, as if to convince themselves that all events on earth are not destined to keep happening time and time again.

While the gunfire ceased on November 11, 1918, the erosion of peace continues surreptitiously within government offices and embassies. All over grief-stricken France, people are savoring victory, laying lavish wreaths at the foot of brand-new war memorials. The nation is infinitely grateful to the brave soldiers who gave their lives in the trenches, their blood in the snow and mud of the battlefields in the Dardanelles, in Picardy, on the Somme front, in the Battle of Ypres, in Artois, on the terrible Chemin des Dames, in the hell that was Verdun ...

Men often give women flowers, trying to steal their hearts.

Flowers express love as well as forgiveness, regret, sorrow.

There were always flowers at our place on Rue Denfert-Rochereau.

Flowers, music, poems.

And color on the paint palette.

The color of the joy in Man's eyes ...

When the Second World War was on Europe's doorstep, Man painted *L'Arbre est une rose*, "The Tree Is a Rose," for me, Ady ...

I was so afraid, especially after the annexation of Austria, what the politicians called the Anschluss, and then the Munich Agreement, when regions of the Sudetenland and Czechoslovakia were eventually ceded to the triumphant Führer's Third Reich.

Sometimes I would ask him, "Do you think Hitler will come to Paris? Do you think there'll be another war in France?" Man would shrug his shoulders. I understood this to mean that he knew nothing of the future, but that the worst could not be ruled out ...

Nobody really wanted to answer these questions. I myself had no interest in hearing a real answer. The war was like a hurricane forecast well in advance. But until we felt its breath on our necks, we doubted we'd ever actually see it blow over our heads.

In '37, Man had drawn *L'Arbre-rose* for *Les Mains libres* in Cornwall. One year later, in place of the nice sailboats, he painted this enemy warship that threatened our life in Paris. He painted us, both of us, naked, in the shadow of a swirl of pink, green, and blue petals. "L'arbre est une rose," he said. "*The Tree Is a Rose*, that's what I'm calling the painting, Ady." He painted us like Adam and Eve in the Garden of Eden … I'm the woman with café-au-lait skin, standing, my back turned, painted from behind, watching the sea. He's sitting, helpless, unfazed, waiting to see what happens next.

Now, whenever I see roses anywhere, I think of Man. I reflect on all the things we could have done if the war had not happened. Sometimes, if I have some change, I buy a bouquet of red roses at the market in Albi. I place them in a beautiful vase on the coffee table in my living room. And then I start to dance to a *biguine*. I close my eyes. I think of Man, young and full of hope, walking the streets of Paris in 1921.

He told me …

On the avenues and the Grands Boulevards, we still stumble upon widows dressed in black, and miserable orphans, wards of the nation that the Great War sowed in its madness. We give the maimed and crippled veterans a smile or a friendly tap on the back. We offer a handshake of thanks to the valiant Senegalese Tirailleurs, sporting their eternal red cap. They, the kind "*Y'a bon*", cut off Bosch heads by the thousands for France. Barely civilized, but well-trained in military discipline and handling weapons, machetes, and bayonets, they liberated the motherland alongside the white French army and the other tan-skinned conscripts from the Caribbean and faraway colonies who were given names like *bamboulas*, *bougnoules*, métèques, *bridés* …

During the twenties, capital flows and industry prospers. Factories in France are running at full capacity. Say goodbye to the years of tightened belts! Gone are the days of bare cupboards! The modern age has swept in at breakneck speed, promising growth and opulence free from suffering. Euphoria is all around.

Alas. On the other side of the Rhine, anger grows. Years pass. Worn out and starving, the Germans feel swindled by the Treaty of Versailles. The victors, not satisfied just occupying and ruining the country, brutally divide it, amputating its colonial empire in Africa. To add insult to injury, the enemies are aided in their infamous task by a battalion of *nègre* soldiers with shoddy morals. Barbaric subhumans claiming the right to dominate and govern a people from a long-standing civilization that birthed Beethoven, Brahms and Bach, Mozart, Wagner, and many others. These wannabe-whites lust after beautiful German women and make bastard babies! Day after day, conquered crowds seduced by Adolf Hitler lend an ear to the hateful propaganda of the German Workers' Party. They flock in droves to listen to the Führer, the charismatic Nazi orator. Beneath the party emblem, the swastika, he presents himself as their savior. He is the providential man giving faith and hope to his people. On his orders, the first Nazi militias, the sinister assault sections clad in brown shirts known as the Sturmabteilung, promise to restore Germany's glorious reputation.

In Italy, Benito Mussolini has already been elected by the National Fascist Party and is preparing to set his Blackshirts onto Rome.

In France, strange and venomous words, akin to flowers of evil, plague the pages of newspapers. Dictatorship, totalitarianism, fascism, nationalism, antisemitism, racism, the list goes on ...

Man told me ...

When he arrived as a young man of thirty-one, he had been furiously in love with France for quite some time. Because of the stories people told him, the French poems that his first wife Adon Lacroix read and translated for him.

More than anything, he longs for Paris.

"For the love of art!" he tells me.

He is convinced that Paris is where it all happens. That in Paris, art is undergoing a revolution. In Paris, especially in Montmartre and Montparnasse, painters create, innovate, seek to break away from the constraints of academic and figurative painting that photography has rendered obsolete. Paris is the incubator, the source, the nest. It's the launching pad for all new directions ...

In New York, Man was well acquainted with museums. He appreciated and was already inspired by the works of renowned European painters: Ingres, Delacroix, Corot, Rodin, Cézanne, Matisse ... He confessed, however, to having been somewhat disappointed by the paintings of American artists on display at the Macbeth Gallery on Fifth Avenue. Their so-called avant-gardist style offered a crude display of modern times, in all its misery and trash, drunks and prostitutes. Their paintings seemed gaudy and comical to him, devoid of the mystery that floated above European works.

The young Man often also frequented Stieglitz and Steichen, photographers and founders of Gallery 291, another Fifth Avenue establishment. He was a regular visitor and listener, often Stieglitz's guest at Mouquin's, one of the most famous French restaurants in New York at the time. Steichen, a friend of Rodin's and a great lover of art, divided his time between France and the United States. The latter further increased his desire for Paris.

As early as 1913, if I'm not mistaken, Man discovered modern European art at the "Armory Show" on Lexington Avenue. Pioneering artists seemed to be reinventing painting. Derain, Léger, Braque, Picasso, Archipenko, Brâncuși, Picabia, Duchamp, and many others ... Most of them lived in Paris. Post-impressionists, nabis, fauvists, Cubists, futurists, Marcel Duchamps' *Nu descendant un escalier, Nude Descending a Staircase*, had caused a scandal. He became Man's close friend. His lifelong friend and chess partner. When the Great War broke out in Europe, Man had to postpone his trip to France and painted *War* (*A.D. MCMXIV*), a monumental canvas, his vision of the world war that was bringing bloodshed to old Europe. Faceless men, horses, death, barbarism. His contribution. "Unconcerned but not indifferent," Man always said.

I think back to a different night in Mougins, during our vacation in Provence.

In '37, I think ...

Our sweet and tumultuous vacations at the Vaste Horizon, in the sun, just off the Mediterranean, with our friends: the Éluards of course, my dear Nusch, and Paul, her poet husband ... Picasso and the brooding Dora Maar. Lee Miller and Roland Penrose, who embark on a surrealist romance.

Yes, in '37 ...

Our lovely happy summer vacation, overshadowed by the tragic images of the war in Spain, the rise of fascism, Nazism, and antisemitism. As always, we enjoy the cool evening air under the arbor. Dora Maar shows us the prints of the photos she took of Picasso while he was painting his Guernica and when he completed it. A large horse bucks in the middle of the canvas. Around it there is barbarism, death, hope and despair, sobs, moans and agony beneath the bombs. Picasso speaks very little, apart from in his paintings.

At our place on Rue Denfert-Rochereau, I often see Man taking pictures of his own work. He files and dates everything he does: objects, drawings, sketches, photos, paintings. He keeps track, indexes everything – you never know ... I admired *WAR*,

Paul et Marie Cuttoli, Dora Maar, Pablo Picasso, Ady Fidelin et Man Ray.
Banque d'Images, ADAGP / Art Resource, NY © Man Ray 2015 Trust /
Artists Rights Society (ARS), NY /
ADAGP, Paris 2023.

his painting from 1914. Looking at it, I said to myself that while some men make war, others paint it, maybe as a confession of powerlessness or as a silent protest. They let out a stifled scream in the solitude of their studio. They flaunt their rage with large brushstrokes. Horses and men emerge from the nothingness of the white canvas. I thought about all of the horses that were led to the slaughterhouses in their strange wars.

I whisper to Man, "A big horse, just like in your painting!"

He doesn't react.

We stay pensive for a moment.

Someone offers wine.

And then Paul whispers, *"Lonely horse, lost horse, Sick from rainfall … And, loyal to the stones, Lonely horse waits for nightfall So he does not have to See clearly and flee …."*[2]

His poem recited in a soft voice mingles with the chirping of the crickets. Man straightens his beret and lowers his head while

---

2 Paul Éluard, "Cheval," in *Les animaux et leurs hommes, les hommes et leurs animaux* (Paris: Au Sens Pareil, 1920), p. 18 (our translation).

taking a drag on his pipe. Nusch closes her eyes under the stars. Pablo peacefully doodles a new work of art on a corner of the table. Sitting by his side, Dora devours him with her eyes.

Time flies by.
I'm twenty years old. It's 1935.
I've taken my independence. I live in the heart of Paris, not far from the Eiffel Tower. I went all the way to the top once, but only once. There was gray as far as the eye could see. A sea of slate and zinc and overlapping clouds. And spots of green, here and there – just like untouched islands. People looked like ants and cars like black beetles, moving in single file.

I'm renting a room with one of my dancer friends on the top floor of a temporary housing building in the fifteenth *arrondissement*. If you look out the skylight, you can see the Champ-de-Mars. I visit my sisters as often as I can. I look after my little niece from time to time. She's four now. She's growing up fast. She tells stories and rolls her r's like a true Parisian. I love her.

I've started dancing with a new company. We're sought after even in the countryside. One time, we landed a contract in Belgium. We also do private shows for individuals. One evening, we performed at Hôtel Lutetia. The French aristocracy love masked balls in the '30s. They call on our services to add an exotic flavor to their nights. Our impresario says that success is within our reach. In our shows, I imitate Joséphine Baker. I sing "J'ai deux amours," "La petite Tonkinoise" …

In between tours, I sometimes take my younger brother on walks in the Jardin du Luxembourg. When spring comes, we sit on a bench like turtledoves. We observe passers-by as we eat ice cream. I speak with him in Creole and tell him about the past, about Guadeloupe, stories about witches, *diablesses*, and *soucougnans*. He likes these stories and, trembling, asks me to tell them again. He gives me fresh news about Dous, who just got engaged to a guy from the Gard.

Nobody checks what time I come home anymore. I feel free and light. I'm living my life.

I also audition for film roles. Sometimes, I work as an extra, hoping for a little glory. I'm a silhouette in the background of films. You can make me out from behind in some of them. In front of the camera, the main actors walk by me in the streets without seeing me. I sit behind them on a café terrace and drink a soda or chat with another girl. I make a dreamy face so the director might notice me. One evening, a producer asks me to go home with him. He talks about a role that he thinks is perfect for me, a starring role maybe … I don't like the way he looks at me. I can't accept anyway. I'm supposed to be filling in for a dancer in a dance hall near Montparnasse.

In 1935, *VU* magazine dedicates a special issue "Exotic Flavors" to Caribbean women. I missed the opportunity to be on the cover, but I still bought a copy. A couple of weeks later, some of my cousin's friends, students at the Sorbonne who, like me, often go to the Bal Blomet, unearthed an old journal from an attic somewhere – *La Dépêche africaine*, from October 1928. We sit on a café terrace, and they make me read this article written by Jeanne Nardal. "Exotic Puppets." That's how they see Caribbean women like me who dance in island dresses.

"You've got to stop playing the Black doll, Ady! We're fed up with seeing you shake your ass for white people!" one of them yells at me. "You're embarrassing us!!"

I start to laugh, because the majority of these boys court white dolls and nobody bats an eyelid.

I say that no one will stop me from dancing. And if white people like it, well that's good for them.

"What world do you live in, Ady? Do you really believe you're French? We're foreigners to them. Nothing but Black people …."

"Nothing but *Y'a bon Banania*!" another one chimes in, readjusting his collar.

"Savages arrived from Africa! Subhumans, if you prefer … We're undesirables. Remember, they enslaved us. We fought for them. Black men died in the trenches and on the battlefield for them. Our fathers! Our brothers! All those Senegalese Tirailleurs, all those poor men from the colonies sacrificed for the glory of France … We are only good for being put on display in their zoos, for playing circus animals and puppets, acting out the good savage … Blowing a trumpet and making them dance …."

"I have nothing to prove to white people. I am not a colonized man … Call me negro, if you want! Yes, I am a negro. A negro from the Negro Renaissance," declares the bony little one. "And I'm going to fight for my race, for the defense of the Black cause.

As W.E.B. Du Bois says so well in *Souls of Black Folk*, 'I am a negro and I glory in the name; I am proud of the black blood that flows in my veins.'"

"*Souls of Black Folk*, what does that mean?" I ask.

"Ady, in French, it's *Les âmes des peuples noirs* ...."

The three of them teach me this lesson over the same black coffees we've been sipping for more than an hour.

"You have to read Césaire's journal, *L'Étudiant noir*, Ady."

"But I'm not an étudiante, I don't go to university ...."

"It's for everyone! For all Black people!"

"We have to be united! If someone offends or curses a Black person, it concerns all Black people ... Humiliation seeps through the skin of all Black people when a white person calls one of us '*Chocolat*' or '*Y'a bon*' or even '*Café au lait*' ... It's all racist. All of it."

"We must be vigilant. History is always repeating itself, Ady. Have you heard of those American tourists who think they're back in their segregationist country and don't want to find themselves surrounded by Black people on the dance floor? These people come to visit Paris by the busload and they're upset to see as many negros in the city as in their cotton plantations ...."

I pout doubtfully. I think of my papa, who would tease mama every time she recited François Villon's *Ballad*. Whenever she got to the refrain, "But where are the snows of yester-year?" papa would cut in, hollering, "But by God! Where are the *nègres* of yester-year? Ti Pocame, Hildevert, Télisfort, Comrade Fèfène, Mista Vanousse." And we would all start laughing, even Lucette. I smile at this happy memory.

"We're not joking around, Ady! It's a serious issue and we've got to tackle it head-on, do you understand?"

I go, "*Han han!*" And swallow my smile and nod my head.

"Yes!" says my cousin. "Yes, it's true! They're trying to please white Americans by kicking Black people out of Parisian clubs and restaurants! In Montmartre and Montparnasse. Can you believe it! These guys fought for France! It's all hush-hush, but it's still happening. Some people are even enforcing segregation on buses and ...."

They all fall silent for a moment, contemplating their pain. Tense, pensive, and bitter. And then they continue.

"In *L'Étudiant noir*, Césaire writes that 'we must plant our

Négritude as if it is a beautiful tree until it bears the most authentic fruit.' Do you understand, Ady?"

"The time has come for us to find our values again, to go back to our roots, to free ourselves from the chains of the colonizers ...."

"They have never stopped subjugating us with their laws ...."

"It all goes back to the Black Code,[3] which stated how Masters should whip their slaves. Everything was regulated. It was all legal. Slavery was legal, Ady! And no one had a word to say against it ... Personally, I spit all over French laws ...."

"Make a profit at any cost! That's what's important to them ... They don't care about the rest. Only the money they can make from it! Human trafficking doesn't bother them ... Who's really the barbarian? That's the question, and ...."

"One day, Africa will be liberated, you'll see."

"First of all, they need to stop seeing us as inferior to them. We've also had to get over our own inferiority complexes. Because of what they've been putting in our heads for centuries – to this day, too many of our Black brothers still believe they are inferior to white people."

The students are speaking loudly. Some patrons seem bothered and keep shooting us dirty looks, as Parisians do so well, rather than daring to actually say anything ... The server starts to stare at us insistently. He comes over twice to ask if we wanted to order another coffee.

We part ways on the sidewalk, promising to see each other again soon. Maybe even at the Bal Blomet. One of the boys walks away with his head down, hunched over, as if he's carrying the weight of the entire Black world on his back. One hell of a burden! And again, my papa's comical words run through my head, "but where then are the *nègres* of yester-year?"

Do all of these battles concern me? What does "the souls of Black folk" mean?

I walk for a while, over to Sèvres-Lecourbe *métro* station. I have to attend a rehearsal near Barbès. I run down the stairs and

---

3 The Black Code, or Le Code noir, was originally made law in 1685 by Louis XIV. It defined what enslaved populations and free people of color were forbidden to do, outlined appropriate punishments, mandated conversion to Catholicism, as well as regulating sexual and romantic relationships.

present my ticket to the attendant. I put on the serious voice of one of my old teachers and take the time to ask myself, if, deep down, I sometimes feel inferior to white women. "Do you, Ady?" The truth is, I'm me. I don't feel inferior to anyone.

In 1935, a lot of French people feel grateful to and are still moved by the Senegalese Tirailleurs who served in the colonial forces. Everyone remembers the Africans from the Black force who survived the Great War as legends, but also as blood-thirsty, ferocious cutters of Teutonic heads. After a while, one word leads to another, the French people "through and through" end up truly speaking their mind. The truth is they're forever fluctuating between feelings of repulsion, derision, and fascination. I can see it in their eyes. Most of them immediately feel as though they belong to a superior race that's destined to bring true civilization to the Black world. Others see the "*Y'a bon*" image everywhere. Some remember the savages presented at Bois de Vincennes during the 1931 Colonial Exhibit. They recall with fear their tour of the human zoo at Bois de Boulogne – the sensational attraction at the Jardin d'Acclimatation which showed "real cannibals", the Kanak people, brought in from New Caledonia. What a show!

Cannibals, savages, subhumans, *bamboulas*, shoe polish ...

Over the course of my existence, I have often had the misfortune of hearing these words from the mouths of certain white people.

There are also nice white people who describe themselves as antiracists. Unfortunately, while they are often filled with good intentions, these are tinged with condescendence and paternalism. When talking to a Black person, they become obnoxious little teachers whose sole mission is to explain how the world works. It's true, they haven't quite finished colonizing, exposing, and exploring Black people in any way they can. Subconsciously, they still want to civilize them to suit their own tastes.

Is there less racism?

I don't know.

Do Black people truly give the impression of harboring some great mystery? Something that white people can't quite grasp? Something that scares them yet attracts them at the same time, like a scarecrow? Something that disturbs and annoys them tremendously? Something that makes us terrifying, funny, stupid, or inferior in the eyes of white people ...

I know that after twenty years, my face has hardened.

No, I'm no longer as blind as I used to be when I was younger.

In the thirties, "*Y'a bon Banania*" poster ads featuring the faces of the brave and loyal servants of the motherland are pasted all over the walls of Paris and they make people laugh. "Banania, the most nourishing of all French foods." Just awkwardly mannered overgrown children, a little naïve, simple, easy to fool: that's what any given white person thinks about Black people. They love Joséphine Baker, her animal imitations, and her clumsy French. Even today, the most ignorant French people still believe that most Black people can only speak broken creolized French. They look so much like Chocolat, the famous Black clown from the Nouveau Cirque who took slaps and kicks for laughs. "Beaten and content," the chocolate Félix Potin makes his claim without shocking the average French person. Whether I want to or not, I can't help but notice the satirical drawings in newspapers where they caricaturize Africans. Their favorite, the hilarious Senegalese Tirailleur, wearing his red cap. Big eyes, big mouth. In ads, he can sell anything: mint candy, aptly labeled Cachous Négros, liquor, wine, shoe polish, rum, cigarette paper, musical scores, hand soap, laundry soap, toothpaste, even cheese ...

The Banania Tirailleur reminded me of an old uncle from manman's family. When we would go to see him in the Basse-Terre countryside, near Les Trois-Rivières, he would tell us stories about the adventures of Compè Lapin and Roi Lion. While shelling pigeon peas, he would talk about the past, which he called "long-ago-olden-days of great misfortune." He would speak softly of Black people from Africa enslaved on the land of Guadeloupe. The poor creatures had to fend for themselves and survive all this misery. And then he would talk about the *nègres marrons*, who had escaped from slavery, who had fought for their freedom. The adults did not like to listen to him tell these stories as old as Methuselah. When they approached, uncle would quickly gesture a cross on his mouth. This meant that we should not betray him, not repeat his words. Aimée, Rose, and I always wondered if all of this actually happened, if our old uncle wasn't just mixing up stories and nightmares to make himself more interesting in our eyes, we who came from the big city of Pointe-à-Pitre. He never went to school. Never learned to read or write. But he was family, we owed him these short visits.

In 1930, before leaving Guadeloupe, we made the rounds to say goodbye to friends and family.

I can picture the scene.

Tonton is sitting on a small bench in front of his ramshackle *case*, spared in the hurricane. He greets us shirtless and barefoot on the dirt floor, wearing only an old pair of underpants tied with an old rope around his waist. Raymonde tells him that we are leaving for France, "There's no longer anything keeping us here in Guadeloupe," she says, "life is too hard here, people are mean, nature is fierce ...." He shakes his head and puffs on his pipe. He gives me a kiss and whispers in my ear, "*Bon voyage*, my little Ady! Above all, remember the *marrons* who fought for our freedom. Do you hear me, don't let anyone take your freedom away from you!"

It pains me when I come across the "*Y'a bon*" smile on the walls in Paris. My uncle was a proud man.

Am I nothing more than a Black doll without a soul?

Am I a disgrace to intellectuals, to the Nardal sisters, to this Monsieur Césaire, the founder of *L'Étudiant noir*?

Should being Black stop me from living my life and trying my luck in Paris?

No, my Black skin is not a prison.

How can I earn my freedom in this world where men are still waging war worse than barbarians?

Since the 1920s, the Roaring Twenties, Black American music has been setting the cabarets in Paname alight. Crowds really get into swing and jazzmen are all the rage. Man photographed the white Nancy Cunard with her big Black man, the pianist Henri Crowder. These two are everywhere and don't give a damn about other people's opinions. At Casino de Paris and Les Folies-Bergère, Féral Benga and Joséphine are stars in the sky. The Martinican René Maran won the Prix Goncourt for his novel *Batouala*. Then there's McKay, the Jamaican writer. whose books are read in their French translation by Black student communities. *Quartier noir*, *Banjo*, *Banana Bottom* ... And promising young Black intellectuals who publish poetry and political manifestos in their journals, like Césaire, Damas, Sédar Senghor, Tirolien, and the Nardal sisters, to name a few.

The Black sports stars make the front page of the weekly feature magazine *Voilà*. Raymonde buys it every Saturday. World champion boxer Panama Al Brown is Cocteau's Black dragonfly. Raoul Diagne, footballer for RC Paris – called the Black Spider of the stadiums – wins with the national team … And we mustn't forget that in 1924, in Paris, the American William DeHart Hubbard becomes the first Black man in the history of the Olympic games to win a gold medal, with a long jump of 7.44 meters.

How can you be successful despite your Black skin? What does it take to break free from prejudice? Sound integrity? Talent, courage, perseverance, immense self-belief, a touch of madness and selflessness …?

Two days later, I hear people talking about Man backstage in a small cabaret on Rive Gauche. A Guadeloupean dancer from a troupe I know shows everyone a photo. She's posing with an African statue: the Bangwa Queen.

I've forgotten this girl's name.

She is very proud.

I remember feeling a pinch of sadness.

I would have liked to be sitting where she was, beside the Bangwa Queen.

I should have been sitting where she was.

I swallow my jealousy and ask the girl how it went, what the photographer is like. She blurts out that the American is a little outlandish and a bit of a rogue, definitely a ladies' man – no one will argue with that. His name is Man Ray. Yes, he is well-known in the business. His studio on Rue Campagne-Première is swarming with models. Artists, models for fashion houses, actresses … She met him in 1929. He spends quite a bit of time at Caribbean cabarets in the evenings. He works meticulously. Always has a stern and diligent look on his face while he prepares his material and takes photos. Afterward, he likes to fool around. He'll flash you a charming smile, offer you a glass of wine, and sweep you off to his bed. Of course, you have the right to refuse. He's not the pushy type. But he's not one to decline a roll in the hay, to pass the time, find entertainment in love, penetrate and appreciate women's bodies, talk nonsense …

I take a closer look at the photo. At the time, the sculpture seems crude. The queen is standing up, with her big butt. Her large breasts hang low. One arm is shorter than the other. She's holding a bell in her right hand. Bare-chested, her crotch covered with a printed silk stole, the girl seated next to her has placed her arm between the statue's legs, in a pose that is somewhat conquering, familiar, casual – almost disrespectful. To me, the Bangwa Queen seems reduced to a decorative object. Worse still, a war trophy stolen from Africa at the same time as enslaved people. I think of my cousin and his revolutionary friends ...

Later on, some people believed that I was the girl sitting next to the queen. It's true, we do look a little alike, but my chin is more prominent. This dancer could perhaps have become my little Man's muse. Like me, she follows the fashion of the time, reshaping her eyebrows with a small pencil line. Her forehead is bare. Her hair is notched and parted down the middle. She is very beautiful, but I'm the one Man fell for ...

All my life, I've seen this photo, here and there, in magazines with articles about Man Ray, about his work, his genius. I recognize Man's style in the way the model stands, the way she looks at the camera. As always, he plays with shadow and light, with history and people's stories, subjects, black and white, women's curves and flesh.

Underneath the photo, the journalists wrote: Ady Fidelin. That always made me smile ...

The dancer whispers to me that the Bangwa Queen has been on display at the Galerie Ratton. Maybe it is still there. Queen, woman of God, or priestess of the earth ... Brought out of the Kingdom of Cameroon Grassfields by treasure hunters, what mysterious roads did the Bangwa Queen travel before arriving in Paris?

In the thirties, Africa is increasingly put on display outside of ethnographic museums. Statues, talismans, and masks become primitive art in the eyes of the West. Collectors the world over clamor for more. Exoticism is in fashion in all shapes and colors: the Bal Colonial, the Revue Nègre, and Joséphine Baker, the *biguine*, the rumba, Black American music ... And this infatuation may well stem from the time of the explorers of the African continent; people like Livingston, Brazza, Stanley ... From fever of conquests, fury of colonization, dreams of predation ... From European colonial exhibitions ... And from the Great War, when victorious Black soldiers – "Banania" – marched in Paris.

I visit the gallery at 14 Rue Marignan in the eighth *arrondissement* several times. I would have liked to find Man Ray there, to pretend

I was interested in *art nègre*, in African objects, and sculptures, imposing statues, and other masks carved out of wood.

The gallery owner, Charles Ratton, is a loyal friend of the surrealists. Collectors and connoisseurs, they are his favorite clients. Art is undergoing a revolution, and these troublemakers are determined to undo the academic straitjackets of the painters of the olden days by any means possible. In Ratton's gallery, they gawk in amazement at the way Black people depict bodies and faces. They eat it up ...

In around 1906, Vlaminck and Derain are – supposedly – among the first to identify the artistry in the masks and statuettes of African empires displayed in ethnographic exhibitions in European capitals. At this time, secondhand dealers also sell off these picturesque pieces to collectors of curious objects and enthusiasts of *nègre* primitivism.

Picasso doesn't deny being inspired by them from as early as 1907, when he and Matisse discovered a large white mask in Derain's workshop. After a trip to the Clignancourt flea markets, then a captivating visit to the Musée d'Ethnographie at Trocadéro that reeked of mold and neglect, he paints *Les Demoiselles d'Avignon* the same year. His friend Braque paints *Le Nu debout*, "the standing nude."

I meet Pablo in 1936, in Mougins, then again at his place in Paris on Rue des Grands-Augustins. Everything inspires him. He doesn't speak much, but his eyes dissect the world. His sharp look strips you to the bone in no time at all. Picasso's hands are the formidable instruments of his mind, his eyes.

Man admires him greatly.

The two friends do not worry about the influences they may be subject to – there are too many. For them, everything in the world is a source of inspiration and emulation. The smallest bit of wood, string, funnel, the wind in the sheets, a face, dust bunnies, a posture, a cigar box, a comb, an electric whisk, a garter belt, a bodice ... Photography has helped modern painters to free themselves from the duty of faithfully depicting their models. There are other things they can do with a canvas, colors, and paintbrushes. According to Man, artists will always be sacred beings, whatever they produce, whatever paths they take to express their art. What counts is freedom and imagination, the unexpected, and the pleasure of creation.

Man is not at the Galerie Ratton. I wander around inside, planting myself randomly in front of a window. There, there are masks and ivory objects made by the Alaskan and British Colombian natives. The rare visitors nod their head, bewildered while consulting the catalog. Some scratch their head, others bite their lips.

That evening, in my sleep, I'm haunted by Alaskan Eskimos. The masks spin around me to macabre music. Gigantic and frightening, they get closer with each turn. Suffocating me. I wake up in a cold sweat and get out of bed. I walk over to the skylight in my small bedroom. An enormous white ball hangs from the sky, the moon seems to look at me in astonishment.

Later, I will learn that the Bangwa Queen was shipped to America. Exhibited at the Museum of Modern Art in New York. Poor Queen in exile …

The next morning, my brother and I take a walk on the Boulevard du Montparnasse. It's springtime. We walk through the nearby side streets, asking passers-by, until we find Rue Campagne-Première. I pictured it green, maybe with a meadow, a quiet donkey, a cow, goats, large trees, like a little piece of countryside within Paris. Man Ray did not tell me what street number. I ask a lady. No, she's not from this neighborhood. Then another walking out of a *porte-cochère*. The old lady tells me that this is indeed a street often frequented by artists. She has lived here for fifty years and knows a thing or two about it. She chews my ear off. Doesn't know the painter-photographer Man Ray. Tells me about Modigliani, who had his workshop at Number 3. Louis Aragon and Elsa Triolet live at Number 5. She remembers Foujita and Youki at Number 9, who left in 1917, the painter for Japan, his wife in the arms of a poet named Desnos. "Go to Number 29," she says, pointing at the Hôtel Istria with the tip of her cane. They will definitely be able to help me. "A lot of artists have stayed there – painters, poets, musicians, writers. People from all over who love to party in Paris, and make a lot of noise, especially at night …."

"Monsieur Man Ray is traveling. You will have to come back, Mademoiselle."

"He gave me an appointment. He would like me to pose for him."

The receptionist smiles before quipping, mockingly, "Of course, of course … Monsieur Man Ray certainly is in demand, especially by beautiful young women such as yourself."

"He forgot to give me his exact address. Could you please tell me where his workshop is?" I want to look professional. I take out a notebook to write down the number.

"Well it's right next door. Number 31. The enameled sandstone façade covered with plants, big bay windows, and a large black wrought-iron door. You can't miss it, it's the craziest on the street. His workshop is on the bottom floor."

I put my notebook away and we leave, looking very dignified.

"What do you want to do at this man's place?" my little brother asks me.

"Well, it's for a job that will bring me money. You see, you need money to live in Paris. Nothing is free. You have to pay for everything. It's not like back home, where you can just walk around in the countryside and pick a piece of sugar cane or gather breadfruit, a few mangoes or apples, and drink coconut water … You've got to have money to live here!"

We stand in front of the building. I feel moved without really knowing why. Feel like I'm betting my life on a coin toss. The blue sky looks like it's been cut into squares and rectangles in the large windows of the façade. I close my eyes. I see myself in this fortress, behind the walls. I imagine Man and his camera. He is a good painter. The dancer told me that there is an easel in one corner of his workshop, an incomplete painting, a color palette, and paintbrushes of all sizes. And paintings hanging all over the walls, alongside enigmatic African masks.

Later on, Man will tell me that in that beautiful month of May he was in Tenerife, participating in the surrealist exhibition organized at the Ateneo de Santa Cruz.

He already travels a great deal. In 1935, his work – photographs, drawings, objects, rayographs, paintings – is exhibited in London, the United States (Connecticut and Los Angeles), Barcelona, and at the Galerie des Cahiers d'Art in Paris.

He traveled, my little Man. Free like a bird that needs only a few twigs to build its nest here and there.

He traveled in his head and his works of art, did Man. Far away from the calamities that humans inflicted on one another.

He traveled, carried by the wings of his art that brought him fame all over the world.

Did he worry about the dark news from the other side of the Rhine?

Yes, of course he did. But I believe that he was extremely careful not to be shaken by the powerful turmoil outside. Nothing could ever be stronger than his will to create. He put a lot of distance between himself and the tragic events of the century.

In September 1935, when the abominable Nuremberg Laws are passed in Nazi Germany, legalizing racial discrimination against Jewish people, perhaps he thinks about his grandfather Radnitzky, a peddler from Kiev, a wandering Jew who stopped in Babruysk to sell his trinkets. There, the old man met Manya, a beautiful young girl ready to marry who, he had no doubt, would make his son, Melach, very happy.

In his heart of hearts, Man surely remembers that his father, Melach, lived in Alexander III's terrible Russia. He knows that in 1886, following the adoption of a new edict to expel undesirables, Russian, Romanian, and Polish people fled antisemitic Russia en masse. Melach was one of them, aboard a liner headed for New York.

Without a doubt, Man pictures his mother, the young Manya, leaving Minsk alone for America in 1888. In New York, she meets up with the peddler Radnitzky's son. They kept up a short correspondence through her grandfather and exchanged a few photos. They don't know each other well, but the future awaits in America. A promising tomorrow, far from pogroms and persecutions. And that's how, without any declaration of love, without sharing a single caress, they come to stand before a rabbi who promptly marries them.

Man was born in Philadelphia on August 27, 1890. That's right, he's American. He moved to New York in 1897, to Brooklyn, then to Broadway. Like most Jewish immigrant families, the members of the Radnitzky family don't talk much about the past. The Old Europe that so brutally drove them out is relegated to the attic of their memories. They keep moving forward.

This is where Man Americanized his first and last names. Or rather, he fabricated them, in the same way that he fabricates mysteriously beautiful and useless objects, never before seen, then names them at his inspiration's whim. In a way, he reinvented himself. He is Man Ray, the first person to bear his name, an original creation, a work of modern, surrealist art. Similar to his work on certain canvases, he has covered his Jewish name on old paintings with new colors. He is Man, the man. He is Ray, the light that breaks through the darkness. He is the Man of Light.

In Paris, wherever we go, he always asserts his Americanness. If he meets Jewish people, he doesn't suddenly feel familiarity, or pain, or brotherhood. He enjoys solitude, the company of a few intimate and select friends. He loathes captive crowds, bleating herds of easily manipulated sheep, forever prone to lurching into hate and violence.

I know that he did his bar mitzvah back in New York. But he is not a practicing Jew.

Is art a religion?

Is painting a prayer?

On this earth, a few billion believers get down on their knees or prostrate themselves every day and pray to God up above, begging for mercy. They raise their eyes to the sky and look for the light, a patch of blue, a rainbow, a constellation in the depths of the universe.

At our place on Rue Denfert-Rochereau, I see Man standing in front of his canvas for hours on end, eyebrows furrowed, eyes steady, silent. Shirtless, barefoot, dressed only in a loincloth. I stay seated in a corner of our apartment in the fourteenth *arrondissement*. I watch him with love and admiration. I watch him trace the contours of his dreams. I watch the paintbrush graze the color palette delicately and meticulously. I watch the birth of an impassioned work of art. I watch Man bring beauty to our days. I watch him expand the world. I watch his beautiful hands that know just how to caress me.

No, he does not pray to any god, but he believes in his talent.

It's a gift. He paints out of gratitude. He is thankful to have this in his life.

His gift brings him all his joy.

His gift helps him to live in this world.

No, Man does not hurt anyone.

He is kind and attentive to everyone.

He is against war and all its atrocities.

He stands for love, joy, pleasure, freedom.

His art is his faith.

One day, in Mougins, Paul Éluard shouted that Man draws to feel loved. He also wrote that in *Les Mains libres*. It's the truth.

What else is there to do on this earth, if not enjoy life, take pleasure in it, love each other, use our talents to create different kinds of beauty ...

In the fifties, people were surprised to hear me speak about painting with such authority. But it's because I lived so close to Man Ray, a great artist, for nearly five years. That's no mean feat! I wasn't trying to show off how smart I was or trying to make myself more interesting or what have you ... I savored every minute with him, you see. Like a big delicious cake, licking my fingers so as to not waste a crumb.

Yes, whenever I evoked modern art, the words came to me naturally ...

On Rue Denfert-Rochereau, there were paintings on the walls, sculptures, works of art in every corner. Alongside Man, I often met with many of his painter friends. He would take me everywhere with him, Man ... To artists' workshops, museums, exhibitions, dinners, conferences, private shows ... We also socialized with art merchants, collectors, gallery owners, and critics. In Paris, Antibes, and Mougins, painting came up in every conversation. I have my little Man to thank for my ability to appreciate and recognize painters. To love them ... The living and the dead, for the love and beauty that they breathed into the world.

Later, at the end of the sixties, when life separated us for good, I stopped broaching the subject. I would keep my mouth closed when people around me spoke of the latest work by Man, Dalí, Picasso, Miró ... No, not out of spite ... More so out of gratitude. Yes, I am grateful to him for giving me these moments of joy with him. Perhaps I stopped talking because I no longer had the strength to face the wide-eyed stares of people who would look down on me or question my words, as soon as I mentioned Man Ray's name. Without a doubt, also, to keep the treasures that he had left me for myself. To nourish myself with them when the good times had come and gone ...

What's the point of flaunting your knowledge! It's useless ...

Shut up, Ady! I would tell myself.

Stop babbling on about Man and Pablo and Paul! No one will ever believe you knew them that well.

Wrap it up, girl! No one can take what you shared with him away from you.

Once, I watched a documentary about Man on television. They spoke at length about his work and his muses: Kiki de Montparnasse, Lee Miller, Juliet Browner ...

One day, a great nephew of my neighbor in Albi recited *Liberté* de Paul Éluard in front of me. I didn't say a word. Just closed my eyes, went along for the ride, just like I used to ...

On my notebooks
On my desk and the trees
On the sand on the snow
I write your name.

In my head, suddenly, there was Île Sainte-Marguerite and my friends, free love. La Garoupe Beach, the midday sun, the reeds, and crickets. I could hear my little Nusch's bird-like laughter again. I felt her kisses gliding soundlessly over my skin, then flying away one after the other.

On all the read pages
On all the blank pages ...

Lord, they were all there, Lee and Roland Penrose, Paul and Man, Pablo and Dora ... Above all, my darling Man, my sweet ghost.

On the wonders of nights
On the white bread of days
On the engaged seasons
I write your name ...[4]

I was over sixty years old. But all of a sudden, I was transported back to my twenties. Suddenly, when the kid finished reciting his poem, the charm disappeared.

No, I'm not bitter ... just erased from history, like a silhouette in a movie, a piece of furniture in the background.

---

4 Paul Eluard, "Liberté," in *Poésie et vérité* (Paris: Éditions de la main à plume, 1942), pp. 5–8 (our translation).

Ady Fidelin, Roland Penrose and Nusch Éluard, Mougins, France 1937 by
Lee Miller. © Lee
Miller Archives, England 2023. All rights reserved. leemiller.co.uk

I continued to go to museums all my life. To discover what was
new. And to rediscover the paintings I had seen come to life in
Man's friends' workshops.

IV

It is She! – None other than She,
The tender, slightly mystical, Serious soul,
Had such a soul, blue, winged;
None other would have said, so warmly compassionate,
Those gentle words that make one weep ...

John-Antoine Nau
"Lied dément"[1]

---

1 John-Antoine Nau, "Lied dément," in *Hiers bleus* (Paris: Librairie Léon Vanier, 1904), pp. 42–43 (our translation).

Twenty-one / Forty-Six

It's March 1936 when I see Man again.

We come face to face on Rue Blomet. It's past eleven, I'm coming out of the ball, he's running in.

Alone, just the two of us.

Coincidence has a way of toying with our souls.

"Once is a coincidence, twice is a sign. When something singular happens more than once, it's coincidence crying out for attention." I can't remember where I heard this fine saying.

Is our second meeting a second chance?

Was it imperative that we meet again? For what reason?

What can we call this force pushing us toward one another?

I like to believe that destiny wanted to unite us, Man and I, in this sweet month of March. I like to think that some obscure, unknown force came together that evening and decided to draw us together, definitively.

Our eyes meet under a streetlamp.

He pauses. Exclaims joyfully, "We know each other, don't we?"

"We danced together once, here actually, at the Bal Blomet." I say. "You've forgotten …."

"No! No, but it's hazy …," he says. "Your face really does look familiar … Please don't hold it against me!"

"I forgive you," I answer. He's already won me over, I'm delighted to see him again.

"So, we can dance again tonight … We have the whole night ahead of us, don't we! Come with me, I'm going to join some good friends. They'll be happy to meet you. I'll introduce you as an old friend. We'll make them jealous, you'll see …."

I hear his accent again, see his smile, his sparkling eyes shining through his sullen gaze.

"No, I'm going home. I have to get up early tomorrow morning. I need to get some sleep."

He looks back at me suddenly, as if his memory were coming back.

"Yes, yes, I remember you ... You were dancing with your eyes closed, so you could travel in your mind, weren't you ... What's your name again?"

"Ady, my name is Ady ...."

I avoid his gaze. I don't want him to see the desire that is suddenly jumping out of me, that is written on my face. I don't know why, I want to seek refuge in his arms. Want to touch his skin. To feel his heart beating next to mine. Our lips to meet and bring silence between us.

I know very little about Man at this time. Still, there is something familiar and alluring about him. This is without a doubt how moths burn off their own wings when they are intensely attracted by the captivating lantern lights. Maybe I'm a moth tonight. A slight shiver. The bottom of my dress beats against my calves. A long rustling. I bat my wings in the fresh air this March.

He puts his arms around my shoulders. "It looks like you're cold. Look at me, Ady. You're not shy, are you ...."

He lifts up my chin. My heart skips a beat. I wonder if this is what romance is. I've seen these kinds of scenes in films and photo stories. Starlets falling under the spell of too-handsome gentlemen. Dark and mysterious princes who'll make them miserable as soon as they're unmasked.

No, he doesn't kiss me. He's making conversation.

"So, Ady! Will you come and pose for me?"

"Not long ago, I looked for your workshop on Rue Campagne-Première," I stutter. "In the hotel next door they told me that you were out of town."

"No, there's no more Campagne-Première. I've moved since then. I'm at 40 Rue Denfert-Rochereau now."

We stay and talk for an hour on the sidewalk. No, I don't want to go back inside and dance.

"No, Man! I'll come next week, Monday, I swear!"

He looks me right in my eyes. "It'll be April then, right ... This isn't an April fools' joke, is it? You will come, won't you?"

I feel like I'm a dead insect on an entomologist's board. Or maybe a dying fish at the bottom of a fishing boat …

"OK! It's a date. Next Monday! Meet me at my place. Don't forget! 40 Rue Denfert-Rochereau. Come at three in the afternoon. We'll take advantage of the light. I'll be there. Waiting for you."

He takes my hand, seamlessly. Kisses me on the cheek, so very close to my rose-tinted mouth. His lips smell like tobacco and musk.

He laughs.

Then I laugh.

We stare at each other for a long time, like two children about to play grown-up games.

He whispers, "Little Black Sun …" and strokes my cheek.

It's a gentle burn that could bring me to tears.

We say goodbye. Both of us go our own way. No, he doesn't follow me like in the movies. I turn around and see him disappear under the garlands of red lamps at 33 Blomet. It's as if he's been swallowed up by the infernal fire burning inside.

I guess there's a big age difference between us.

What else makes us different?

His skin color,

his social class,

his art,

his culture,

his country,

his language,

his ethnicity …

They say that opposites attract. They also say, "Birds of a feather flock together." People say all kinds of things …

I must admit that I believe in our relationship right away. It's a sort of intuition …

After this promising conversation on the sidewalk, Man doesn't leave my mind. I think of our date the whole week. In my small room under the roof, I sing "Mon homme" by Mistinguett at the top of my lungs, as if our fate were already sealed. As I dance to *biguines*, I imagine myself in bed with him, with Man. The bed floats like a small raft on water. Man grabs the sheets and declares them the sails of our boat. Around us, there are no islands, only a fragmented landscape of surrealist paintings and African sculptures.

When the fateful Monday comes around, I'm at the *métro* stop at least an hour before our appointment. I walk up and down Rue Denfert-Rochereau three or four times. Then, when I can't stand it any longer, I ring the bell at Number 40. At a quarter to three.

Man is there. Wearing a white shirt with no tie, the sleeves rolled up to the elbows. Well-ironed black pants. He gestures with his hand for me to sit in an armchair. Then starts fiddling with light boxes and lamps. Finally, he sets up his camera. From time to time, he glances in my direction. Suddenly, he darts over to a corner of his workshop and pushes a crate in front of me, into the middle of the room.

"Make yourself comfortable, Ady. Take off your jacket."

I squeeze my thighs together and place both hands on my little purse.

"Would you like a glass of wine, perhaps?"

No need to rush into anything – I'm familiar with the glass-of-wine move.

He comes closer. Strokes my hair, twirls it in his fingers.

I made curlpaper the night before. In those days, before going to bed, I do what most Caribbean women do and separate my curly hair into locks that I wrap and twist tightly around strips of newspaper. When I get up in the morning, I undo it all and my hair is curly and easy to style.

I remember that, in the beginning, when I first moved in with Man, I was too embarrassed to put in my curlpaper before going to bed. It wasn't very glamorous, as they say. But when I got up in the morning, I was irked and my hair all bushy. So, I started up again, every now and then. It made Man laugh. He thought it was a very original hairstyle. He even hoped I would go out in public with the curlpaper in my hair. Not a chance! It would have been like walking around in hair rollers. In 1938, for the International Surrealist Exhibition at the Galerie des Beaux-Arts, I helped him wrap his mannequin's synthetic hair in clay pipes studded with glass bubbles. We had quite a laugh. He christened his cloud mannequin coat rack *"Adieu foulard."* It sounded like an advertisement. In his own way, he was starting a new trend.

But we're not there yet.

Back to the first modeling session.

Twenty-one / forty-six.

"You're very beautiful, Ady. You know, I'm not the big bad wolf. Don't be scared. We're just going to take a few photos. Let's go! Let's go! Loosen up a little, darling ...."

I take off my coat.

"Do you want me to put on my *doudou* dress?"

"Wait a minute. I'll let you know when. We had planned to do a series of nudes, if I'm not mistaken ...."

I have a moment of panic.

I think of Queen Bangwa. She's not here to protect me. It's just the two of us, Man and me, cooped up in this apartment. He has lured me into his lair under the pretense of taking photographs. I have surrendered to him like a silly little girl. Oh Lord! He might decide to hold me captive. Who would worry that I'm gone? I don't answer to anyone. I've declared myself a free woman. Who would know where to find me? It'll be a long time before my sisters and little brother worry about my disappearance. Maybe a month ...

The back of my mind is a never-ending whirlpool of fear and desire, love and repulsion. And images reel past, too, obscene and erotic. Our bodies tenderly entwined or fighting to the death on a raft. Café au lait, island bird, Creole *doudou*, exotic puppet. Whitish skin, cakey skin, chalky skin. Me and him, lovers. Mouthfuls of promises. Me and him. Man and Ady, white and Black in love. Me and him, dominoes, arm in arm, in the streets of Paris. Me and him, forever.

I'm not hiding anything, you know ...

I've had a few friends since I arrived in Paris. Black boys, Caribbean boys, naturally. Boys my age, harmless and approachable. No, I'm no longer a bashful virgin. But these boys were from the same milieu as me, the same race, the same generation. I was on familiar territory with them, so to speak ...

I think of the students, friends of my cousins. What would they say, seeing me with this middle-aged white man? No doubt they'd be appalled. Would I be ashamed? Maybe I'd have to lie low to hide from their stares ...

I posed for Roger Parry with my chest bared, but I wasn't in love. Man Ray looks a bit like him, oddly enough ...

I can't help myself. The words just come out. I ask, "How old are you, Monsieur Man Ray?"

He laughs. "Does age really matter, Miss Ady?"

I pause for a moment. "Er! I just wanted to know how long you've been working as a photographer?"

Man, unphased, explains, "Oh, about a century ... If you like, you can put on your *doudou* dress. Your pearl necklace and your earrings are beautiful ... You're already perfectly dressed like this, believe me ...."

I look around for a place to change. He points to a screen.

I slip on my white petticoat, my big madras skirt and my immaculate starched lace camisole. I fasten my hair and style it with my handkerchief. Voilà! I'm all set.

"Sit on the crate," he says without looking at me.

I sit there, obediently, all smiles. While he calls out his instructions, I can stare at him contentedly. He is very focused. You can tell he's a professional by the way he handles his camera and his equipment.

"Okay, we're ready!" he says after a moment. "You can't move, you know. We have to stick to an exact exposure length."

My jaw clenched, I hold my smile as long as I can. All sorts of bizarre and comical thoughts plague me. No matter how hard I try to shake them off, they keep coming back. Then there's a flash. I burst out laughing and my body suddenly relaxes. He takes more pictures. I keep smiling and posing, playing along.

"OK, this is a trial run," he murmurs. "It looks like you're a little more relaxed now. Maybe you would take off your bodice ... And we can see what's hiding under there."

A popular saying swirls around in my head for a moment, like a long satin ribbon, "Till April's dead, change not a thread."

Yet by the time the afternoon rolls to an end, I've cast all my threads aside. As if I'd just come out of my mother's womb.

I stripped naked beneath his quiet gaze for the sake of art. How could I say no to him? I soon realized that I had an artist at work in front of me. Man is very meticulous. I'm a subject under his expert eye. He chose me and I don't want to disappoint him. I've had enough of all the airs and graces. We all need to play the game, give it our best, on both sides of the camera. Him behind it, me in front.

When you see him, both tense and calm at the same time, it looks as though he's trying to capture or extract some unimagined treasures from reality, to hunt down the hidden beauty of the banal, to reach far beyond this carnal shell that I so trustingly offer up to him.

The hours fly by.

I'm quite sure I've lost all sense of time. This first shooting session takes me far away from the pretenses of everyday life. Far from the "what will people say". Far from decorum and good manners. Far away, in a parallel dimension where nothing else exists around us. Man and I are alone in the world. We have no belongings, only a camera to show us the way …

After all these years, the image that comes to me of these intimate hours is that of a glass or soap bubble swept along by the winds of a dream. Man and I are nestled inside this sphere, big enough to hold us both. A little drunk, we let ourselves be lulled into a state of utter giddiness. As if we'd consumed some euphoric substance. Connected to each other only by the thread of our gazes, we speak to each other with our eyes. It's magical! We float, enclosed and vulnerable behind a translucent wall that could burst at any moment. We weigh each gesture, without a thought for yesterday or tomorrow.

In some parts of the world, people refuse to be photographed. They believe that a photographer can steal their soul, imprison them forever in a picture.

As I look at Man behind his paraphernalia, I am reminded of Monsieur Gilbert de Chambertrand, a poet-painter-photographer in Pointe-à-Pitre. Manman used to say he had gold in his hands.

I remember manman.

I remember Guadeloupe …

I remember the day when, in the big Pointe-à-Pitre market, an old woman selling vegetables chased a white man on vacation who had been hoping to take home typical images of his trip to the islands. It was 1925, and I was ten years old. The woman threw a big yellow yam at the amateur photographer's head and he tripped, taking his tripod and camera with him. She cursed him, his black cape and diabolical machine, calling him a devil and the like, forbidding him to ever set foot in her sight again, *ad infinitum*. She sounded like a harpy. Dumbfounded, manman pushed me ahead of her onto the sidewalk, muttering that these country folk were backward and a disgrace to Guadeloupe with their ignorance of the modern world.

I don't know if Man stole my soul that day. I only know that I'm not the same person once the session's over. I think to myself that this man has gold in his hands, like Monsieur de Chambertrand. Gold in his wing-like hands ... And so much love in his heart.

By the end, we're exhausted, but emotional. Both of us happy. The room is suddenly heavy with a strange silence. He hasn't done anything out of place, or put a word wrong, but I can no longer bear to look at him. This very chaste session, full of flashes and clicks, has given rise to a sudden intimacy that has left me alone with my thoughts, overwhelmed by uneasiness and questions. Granted, Man is used to seeing women naked. You could say it's his bread and butter, and he enjoys it ... For me, though, stripping naked in front of a man is a promise to offer myself to him, for better or worse. So, I stand there, naked, motionless, expecting him to take off his clothes and walk toward me without further ado. When he tells me to get dressed, I feel like a fool. I pick up my belongings and run behind the screen. In my head, a nasty voice whispers, "You exotic puppet! What an embarrassment!"

Then he starts chatting.

"You catch the light very well, Ady."

From behind the screen, I say *"Han han!"* Just like back home. A way of inviting him to keep talking.

"Would you like to have dinner with me? My treat ...."

"Han han!"

When I've finished putting my clothes back on, I find him sitting at his desk, numbering his plates.

"First, we can take a stroll around the neighborhood. We can even go over to the Observatory, if you like ...."

"Han han!"

He repeats, *"Han han!* Does that mean yes in your language?"

I move closer to him. He puts an arm around my waist. I plant a kiss on his forehead. On the wall, facing me, there's a painting: huge red lips floating in the sky above a dark landscape. Lips that strangely seem to be spying on us. A large mouth, silent, desirable, bearing witness. Is this art?

He follows my gaze, "You don't know a thing about painting, do you? So, tell me! What do you see? Take your time! Look carefully! How does this canvas make you feel?"

I begin, "It's, uh, sur ... surrealist, maybe."

"No! No, Ady! Don't use words you don't understand! Just be yourself! Trust your eyes ...."

"Well, I see painted lips with no face. Is this a memory of a woman you loved, a woman who left you? It's dark all around like a sad landscape ... Maybe you were unhappy and needed to paint this woman's red mouth to keep a part of her close to you, to remember the moments of love and joy you shared ... I don't know ...."

He smiles. He kisses me. We hold each other for a long moment, like castaways stranded on an island.

I ask in a tiny voice, "Man, do you paint what you can't photograph? Do you paint your dreams?"

This is how it all begins between Man and me.

That evening, our lovers' footsteps lead us to Parc Montsouris. We stroll along the alleys bordered by enormous cut stones. We watch the ducks in the pond. We race after a gaggle of youngsters, up and down the stairs. At one stage, we sit on the steps of a kiosk like the one on the Place de la Victoire in Pointe-à-Pitre. When he kisses me again, passionately, not far from the Flatters monument, I feel as if a new page of my life is turning before me. Resuming our walk, we try to catch a glimpse of the fragmented reflection of our bodies in the large mirror at our feet. "It's supposed to measure the height and speed of clouds," Man tells me. Finally, he plants his feet in front of the Observatory. We walk around it, as if on a pilgrimage.

I get the strongest feeling that we're suddenly bound to each other by strong, invisible threads. I feel it intensely inside me. There is nothing to say. All I can do is live inside this bubble of love. And I don't care if it only lasts an hour, three months, a year ...

On Rue Victor-Considérant, Man shows me a building. Laconically, he murmurs, "That's where she lived at the end ...." Then, we walk to the restaurant in stunned silence. For a moment, it seems to me that the woman with the red lips, or perhaps her shadow, has crept in between us. I imagine her to be slender and beautiful, draped in veils like a ghost.

I know my stuff when it comes to ghosts and how they move back and forth between this world and the next.

You shouldn't count the wrinkles and white hairs on old people like me. Our hands are ugly and stained. We carry all the pain of the century in our tired bodies. But even if death awaits us, we mustn't forget that we were once young and beautiful and full of life ...

And the past is there to haunt us, with its eternal ghosts, good and bad.

No need to set the cogs of memory in motion. People we've loved come back to us without warning. Long, long after everything has been torn apart, we are left with so many recollections of them, the shreds of a story, the scenery of a forgotten era, a faded photograph that turns back time, a house blown over by a hurricane, tears in the middle of the night, bursts of laughter, frissons of a body in love. We are left with joy, bitterness, regret ...

To this day, at the age of seventy-five, I can sometimes catch a glimpse of my mother's face. Feel her close to me. Hear my poor papa's voice slowly growing more and more faint.

I can picture Man, flamboyant and forty-six on Boulevard du Montparnasse ...

I return to my twenty-one-year-old self. Already so deeply in love.

An American in the flesh.

A little Guadeloupean girl.

What can ever become of the two of us?

We don't ask ourselves too many questions, I think. We just go with the flow. That evening, we are just happy to be walking side by side on the Boulevard du Montparnasse, like two travel companions, people from elsewhere whom Paris brings together.

We're here. It's a chic restaurant. Valet service. Attentive doorman. The interior is sumptuous. A real palace! Phenomenal chandeliers hang from the ceilings, unfurling their glittering tassels. The walls are covered in paintings of chubby cherubs and diaphanous nymphs, immense mirrors with elaborate gilded frames, gigantic bouquets of artistically arranged flowers. Man has done things properly: there's a table reserved for us. White tablecloth, immaculate napkins, silver cutlery, gleaming glasses. I take my seat in the crimson moleskin booth. Man settles into a chair and lights a cigarette. Wherever he goes in Montparnasse – I'll come to realize later – Man feels at home. He knows everyone, from the color merchant to the local bistro owner, the bookseller to the baker. Theaters, cinemas, nightclubs, jazz clubs; he's got his foot in every door. Montparnasse is his village.

A battalion of servers are at the ready, offering obliging bows as they whirl around the guests, elegantly and deferentially. I feel truly intimidated and flattered to have been invited to this palace. I must confess that I've never been afforded this much consideration in the neighborhood cabarets and brasseries I usually frequent. But I know how to behave. My parents gave me a good French education. They taught me how to handle silverware. I know how to swallow soup in silence. I know how to cut my meat and chew it with my mouth closed. Even if my skin is somewhat black, I'm not some wild girl who fell out of a tree with a pink feather in her backside.

As soon as we're seated, Man orders a bottle off the wine list. He consults the menu with an expert eye and asks me if I like seafood. "Seafruit," in French, *fruits de mer*. I nod without asking any questions. The truth is, I don't know that the families of crustaceans, shellfish, crabs, and other lobsters are considered *fruits*. I imagine that they are French species unknown in our tropics. Juicy fruits perhaps collected on the shores of the Mediterranean, on the beaches of the Atlantic Ocean.

While we wait for the meal, we drink wine. Man is cheerful – so long, sorrow of the red lips! He wants to get to know me. He enjoys anecdotes and backstories. Who are you? What do you do? Where are you from? What are your interests?

At first, I describe Guadeloupe to him as if it's a kind of paradise. The sun, the coconut trees, the bathing in the river, the sugarcane fields ... I come from one of those beautiful, tiny French colonies, stranded in a turquoise sea. I'm from those laughing islands where life is good, where you can dance in the wind, laze around from morning till night ...

He cuts me off, looking skeptical.

"There's something I don't understand ... Why did you leave your island paradise, then? What are you doing in France?"

"I don't really want to talk about sad things with you, Man ...."

"Ady, believe me, you can tell me anything. Please don't tell me any tall tales, though."

He pours a drop of wine into my glass.

"Ady, the world is quite a bleak place overall, that's a secret to no one. But we can try to make a go of it by staying on the fringes of chaos, just a little out of the way, far from disaster. Needless to say, it's an exercise in balance and flexibility ... Whatever happens, we try our best not to sink into depression."

A little nod.

"Come on! Spit it out, Little Black Sun!"

I launch into it, not seeking to move him. I don't want his pity. But I have to tell it like it happened, in a furious, messy way. And my words, I remember, tumble out in every direction and gather in a mess, like the planks and metal sheets in the streets of Pointe-à-Pitre in 1928.

The hurricane, that great destroyer. It struck my family.

I lost my parents, Man. I witnessed the end of a world. Everything crumbled around me. I saw death firsthand ... my poor manman! My whole country destroyed.

In a single night. The Apocalypse ...

And the next day, the streets lined with bodies. The hole in the roof.

My God!

And my papa. Dead as well. Two years later.

No, there was nothing else to do, besides look ... wait ... hope for who knows what ...

For the world to be magically brought back to life?

For everything to go back to how it was?

"Guadeloupe is the lost paradise of my childhood, Man ... That's why I left my country when I was fifteen ... That's why I set sail for France ... I still remember so many images from the day I left: the docks, people crying and singing, cradling their sorrow ... *Adieu foulard, adieu madras, adieu grain d'or, adieu collier-chou ... Doudou an mwen i ka pati, hélas hélas sé pou toujou ....*"

And suddenly I catch myself singing! *Adieu foulard, adieu madras ...*

Strangely, my memories of the past no longer seem so haunting when I tell them to Man. He listens to me in silence, with curiosity and interest. His eyes say, "What can you change? The past is dead. Live your life, Ady. Live in the present!"

In all the time we lived together, I loved him for his eyes, his kindness, his joyfulness ... And his taste for freedom, his determination to live an unconstrained life ... And his sense of humor and the detachment that concealed his helplessness against the world's greatest evils. Barbarity, war, natural and human disasters, tyranny ...

He hums the chorus with me.

Adieu foulard, adieu madras, Adieu grain d'or, adieu collier-chou.

He asks me to translate the verses for him, insisting that he likes the melody of my Creole language. Perhaps, one day, he'll be able to learn it the way he learned to conquer the French language ...

It's my turn to ask him questions. It's a game with no pre-established rules, where we attempt to get to know each other. Two worlds collide, and we welcome the collision.

No, he has nothing to hide.

The lips floating on the large painting are those of Lee Miller. Man loved her to the point where he feared he would lose sleep and sanity ... A splendid American woman! She landed in Paris in the late 1920s to learn photography. Lee became his student, then his assistant. She soon became his lover and muse. When she tried to make it on her own, Man's pride took a beating. She was a beautiful woman who would not compromise her independence. While the surrealists theorized about freedom, this was a woman who followed their principles to the letter. Nothing was to stand in the way of the unyielding Lee Miller! She posed as a model for fashion magazines, tried her hand at acting for Cocteau, and became infatuated with a new man from one day to the next. He had taught her everything ... and she had left him for insignificant rivals, to be independent and open her own photo studio on Rue Victor-Considérant. Alas, Lee was born under a lucky star: she was both talented and lucky. Success awaited her on both sides of the Atlantic.

Abandoned, he wanted to put an end to his life, by any means necessary: a rope, a one-way poison with no remedy, hard liquor, making a murderous metronome ... a gunshot, bang! At the time, he had immortalized his grief in a series of grim photographs, staging himself in his suicidal state.

What remained of these defunct loves were many wonderful portraits of Lee, a few good nude photos, some collaborative photographic creations, an *Indestructible Objet*. And this painting ... À l'heure de l'Observatoire – les Amoureux, Observatory Time – The Lovers.

An eye, a metronome, and lips ... It just goes to show that everything leads to art, doesn't it? Like old rags, the whole fabric of life can be recycled into a work of art ...

At the end of his story, I ask, "Do you still love her? What if she comes back to you ... would you take her back?"

"Who knows," he murmurs.

I nod.

"Things are a little frosty between us," he went on, pouring himself another glass of wine. "After we separated, she went back to the United States. She opened a photo studio in New York. Now she's living in Egypt, in the triangular shadow of one of the pyramids. Over one hundred degrees in the desert sands. It's her choice. She's been married since 1934, apparently very happily, to a purebred Egyptian prince."

The matter is closed. He runs his fingers between the glasses and takes my hand.

"You know, I promised myself I'd never get attached to a woman again ...."

"I'm not asking anything of you, Man ... We'll just see what happens ...."

"You're right, let's see what happens before we start getting carried away ..." he says. Just then, a very exclusive server places a platter and its metal stand in the middle of the table. It's filled with big shiny red crabs, gray and green oysters, beautiful langoustine tails, and a variety of small shellfish. There is an art to the way all these critters are arranged. There's beauty in the wine glasses.

When I confess my misunderstanding about *seafruit*, Man starts laughing about the traps of the French language. This kind of mishap has happened to him many times. Then he declares that I have the imagination of a surrealist. Perhaps one day he'll be inspired to paint mollusks and seashells in the trees of a Mediterranean landscape. That would be unheard of.

By the end of the meal, I know a little more about Man. In his words, sketching the contours and broad strokes of his life, he has laid himself bare, so to speak.

American. New York.

Officially married to Adon Lacroix. "No rush, it's just paperwork." Nobody waiting for him anywhere. End of story. No more to it. No children. And whose fault is that? No answer.

Transatlantic journey. Paris! July 14th, 1921.

Surrealist and Dadaist friends. Notorious quarrels and lofty declarations. Wine. Strong coffee and all-nighters. The exhilaration of Paname.

Women in all their curves and scents. Even in brothels. The Roaring Twenties, so much excess of all sorts ...

Extravagance, bombast, frenzy, and insomnia ...

Love. Kiki, darling of Montparnasse. Model sought after by

painters. Beautiful young woman. Grand promises. Disappointment. Rumor has it that she now sings at night at the Cabaret des Fleurs.

Love again and again, this time with the American woman ... These romances start out very well. After a while, they invariably turn sour. It's a chemical mystery or a curse. Who knows? No, no regrets. But he has made some sound resolutions. No more romantic relationships. He'll never do that again! Never again ...

He has lived in France for fifteen years. Painting, taking photos. His life is full, to the brim.

"How about you, Ady? Tell me, what do you like? Aside from dancing ...."

"Well, I like music and poetry." I don't want to sound uncultured.

"Do you write, or compose? I have a few poet friends I'll introduce you to sometime ...."

"No, I *read* poetry. I write down the ones I like best in a little notebook and learn them by heart. After, I recite them."

"Go on, recite a few lines for me!"

While Man shells his crab, not taking his eyes off me, I launch into a poem by Daniel Thaly.

> ... *O spells set from evoking under the skies of Paris*
> *of a peaceful childhood the devout recollection*
> *And in this Luxembourg with flowered terrace,*
> *To breathe in the smell of the Antilles farthest region!*[2]

He nods without saying a word. Then I think of Saint-John Perse ...

> ... *And I did not know all Their voices, and I did not know all the women, all the men who served in the high mansion made of wood; but for a long time to come, I remember the soundless faces, shade of papaya and boredom, who stopped behind our chairs like dead stars.*[3]

Man is silent for a while. He asks me if I know Mallarmé, Éluard, Apollinaire, Desnos ...

---

2   Daniel Thaly, "Le jardin des Tropiques," *La Nouvelle Revue Française*, n. 32, 1911, p. 246 (translated by Mehdi Étienne Chalmers).

3   Saint-John Perse, "Pour fêter une enfance," in *Éloges* (Paris: Gallimard, 1911 [1960]), p. 21 (our translation).

I say no. I try to apologize and add that I have written down poems in my notebook by Lamartine, Baudelaire, Verlaine, Villon, and ...

He cuts me off. "Come on, Ady, have some of this shellfish!"

The salt from the seafood makes us thirsty. We down two bottles of Bordeaux. The cherubs painted on the walls talk to us of love. Nymphs circle around our table. Flowers perfume the room as if in a tropical garden. The chandeliers on the ceiling dangle dangerously. We leave the restaurant, very dignified, stumbling.

On the Boulevard du Montparnasse, we're well aware of the fact that we're a little tipsy. Arm in arm, we croon softly,

Adieu foulard, adieu madras ...

It's after midnight. The fauna of Parisian nightlife is in full flight, intent on taking over the trendy dance halls and clubs. We're not going dancing tonight. We're walking toward Rue Denfert-Rochereau. Number 40.

Adieu foulard, adieu madras ...
Adieu grain d'or, adieu collier-chou ...

No, there will be no more living with women ...

Things always seem clearer after a good night's sleep.

Nighttime, lovemaking. Nighttime, kisses. Caresses. You and me, legs and arms intertwined. You and me, inseparable, one within the other.

What good is there in refusing the grace we've been given?

Nighttime, tenderness, comfort, and more kisses and caresses. Nighttime overflows into early morning like milk on a stovetop. The gentle, frantic nighttime. And the scent of plenitude and perfection laced with the threat of heartbreak.

At first light, he whispers, "Stay, Ady. Stay with me ... Stay, my Little Black Sun ...."

I'm already entirely his. Poised to worship and serve him as if he were my little god.

So, he reneges and makes room for me in his life. In his bed. In his heart. In his dreams. In his hands that yearn for me. I am present for his pleasure, which is also my own.

There are twenty-five years between us. But what does that matter? We love each other, and that's all there is to it …

The days stretch on in peaceful bliss. Outside, spring is blooming, but it's of no interest to us.

We've gone almost a week without leaving the apartment. We're bound by love. By the fear of chipping away at something fragile.

He takes photos of me at all hours. Is he stealing my soul? I walk around his apartment naked. I dance under his gaze. I laugh and sing for him. He likes having me around.

He's my darling little Man. I adore him, my little Manichou. I want to believe that he adores me too … He tells me to leave the little attic room under the Paris rooftops that I share with my friend. He says he'll take care of me. Not to worry. He'll earn money for both of us. He tells me to bring my things and make myself comfortable. He makes room in his closet for my dresses and frills. He frees up shelves in his wardrobe for me. He clears out a bathroom cupboard for my lotions, makeup, and cosmetics. He shows me a chest of drawers in the bedroom, "The second drawer is for you, my darling! You're my Little Black Sun …."

He tells me that his home is mine.

I brought three suitcases. When we start emerging from this soft den, our bodies long for each other, all day long.

We whisper wild things in each other's ears.

We caress each other endlessly.

We make love all over our apartment.

On the floor and on the furniture.

There is love everywhere …

I'm twenty-one years old. He's forty-six.

The age difference is irrelevant.

In the mornings, he paints with a serious look on his face. In the afternoons, he rushes off to appointments or receives clients who have come to have their portraits taken. I dash off to my rehearsals. I sometimes show up late. He goes out to dinner. If he gets home before I do, he waits for me. When I come home, we make love.

The apartment is big enough for his activities and our life together. On one side is the photo studio and on the other, behind a glass door, our home. He designed all the furniture. His rayographs and solarized photos hang on the walls, along with his paintings and those of his friends. Cubist kings and queens are set on chessboards. Here and there are statuettes of African empires.

A multitude of photographed faces, naked bodies, masks ... This world is mine now. It's a new world. A multicolored, motley universe in the image of this new man, my Man, my love ...

And behind the yellow curtains that open onto Rue Denfert-Rochereau, I'm in paradise. Everything is alright. I've found my Prince Charming. Man and I love each other like Adam and Eve. I keep telling myself: everything is right, Ady! Everything is alright! This will never end. Everything is alright! There are no hurricanes in France ... Everything is alright, nothing will destroy your happiness ...

Everything is alright ...

In April 1936, rumors begin to spread that the Popular Front will win the legislative elections. The speech given by the communist Maurice Thorez on Radio Paris has left its mark on people's minds. French citizens are heading for reconciliation to ward off the threat of fascism. If Hitler insults France, calling its people "bastardized and negroid", France won't stand for it. France is strong. France is great. France is civilized.

Everything is alright ...

The following month, on May 3, in response to a call from Maurice Thorez, the people of France will vote "for well-being, against misery, for freedom. Against slavery, for peace, against war." The French will choose a "strong, free and happy France."

Everything is alright ...

I also feel strong, free, and happy.

I also have chosen freedom and joy.

At the end of the month, Man takes me away in his little car.

"It's a surprise!" he declares, sounding mysterious.

We're heading west of Paris, to Saint-Germain-en-Laye. As we approach our destination, he says, "Close your eyes, Ady!"

The car slows down and comes to a stop.

"Open your eyes, now!"

We're parked in front of a modern, Art Deco-style house: pillars, large bay windows, concrete roof, small yard, and garage.

"You see, when you've had enough of Paris, you go to the countryside ... I can't pretend to be a rich American, but I'm comfortable enough in light of the hard times we've had of late."

He's proud of himself, my little Man. This country house is a testament to how far he's come since his early years. Now, Man lives off his art, governed only by the rules he sets for himself. His reputation has been built. He is thriving and enjoying himself at the same time. His works travel the world. He scatters them and finds them again, like the white pebbles in *Le Petit Poucet*. It's the artist's dream life.

I'm perfectly happy to share in his joy, but I'm still a little cautious. I'm not that naïve, this beautiful dream is going to come to an end sooner or later. "You can be sure of it, Ady! The devil will wake up soon to take away all this happiness," whispers the little voice inside my head. Sadly, I'm no fairy-tale princess. Ever since I was thirteen, I've known that the good life always ends. Suddenly. Overnight. In no time at all. So instead of admiring Man's house, I stare anxiously at the clouds. I look for wickedness in the sky. I try to spot fear in the branches of the trees. The sea is a long way from Saint-Germain-en-Laye, perhaps it's already raging on the Atlantic coast, battering the sea creatures and the friendly fish, beating at the rocks in all its rage. The few dogs on their leashes trot along at a leisurely pace. They all look like their masters. They move along, grinning and quiet, without looking up.

"You don't like the countryside, Ady?" inquires Man, reaching deep into his pockets for his key. He looks disappointed. I suppose he expected me to gush a little.

I smile again. Plant a kiss on his cheek.

"You're not happy!"

"Yes, yes, I *am*! If you're happy, I'm happy."

"You know, I have a cleaning lady. She comes every day. You won't have to lift a finger, Ady. I'm going to show you. I have design ideas. I've already drawn up the plans. I'm going to hire workers soon. We'll be happy here, Ady, you'll see …."

Life with Man.

Man is very orderly. Everything in its place. He has boxes upon boxes in his apartment, where he keeps his negatives, photos, correspondence, and so on. Everything is arranged in alphabetical order. The names of the clients contained in the boxes are written in large, clearly visible letters. If a magazine requests a portrait of a celebrity, Man knows exactly where to find his photos. Everything is dated, numbered, referenced, cataloged, and inventoried. He also has compartments with countless index cards. Notebooks filled with names and addresses near and far. And notebooks with pages full of sketches. He also photographs each of his works, methodically. You never know ...

Joyfulness, playfulness, pleasure ...

Joyfulness
Yes, I laugh a lot. I roar with laughter. He's funny and easygoing, my little Man. He tells stories and makes jokes. Nothing ever seems to rattle him. Nothing is ever really an issue. Something amazing and funny will come along and turn things around. At any given moment, you can see beauty in ugliness. In the same way that he can turn a broken, useless object into a work of art, he always manages to find happiness in the midst of misfortune. He has a keen sense of humor and is quick to make fun of himself. Sometimes he'll try to provoke and deride, just for a laugh, to see a client's face turn green. He's tender underneath his grumpy exterior. He's a good egg, as they say.

Sometimes, he sits silent and pensive in an armchair, smoking a pipe. I suspect he's thinking about building extravagant machines. He's delicate and generous, Man. He wouldn't hurt a fly. All he wants to do is dream, draw, and paint. Give him a little gouache and a few big white canvases, and he'll keep quiet and out of trouble. I see him as a child trapped in the body of a grown man. Yes, he carries the treasures of childhood that so many adults lose along the way.

A thousand projects are simmering in his mind at once. Everything interests and stimulates him. He's smart, Man. Really very smart.

Today, he's making a movie. Tomorrow, he imagines a library, a chess set, a box of tricks. He draws them and entrusts his sketches to a craftsman – everyone has their own part to play. He bends coat hangers. He fiddles with lamps. He brings together objects that have no business being together. He paints. He plays with clay pipes and glass bubbles. He cuts up paper. He takes photographs of everything in his path. After we make love, he sleeps. I watch him as he sleeps, so vulnerable, surrendered to his dreams. No, his nights are not peaceful. When he sleeps, everything is a mess. He wanders through it like he's in Wonderland. He collects ideas, images, and objects all night long. He wanders amidst technical words: distortion, solarization, superimposition ... He digests surrealist speeches, "poetizing reality, derealizing the photographic medium, sublimating technique …." So, when he wakes up, he draws his dreams in the little notebook on his bedside table. After that, he gets up cheerfully and starts rummaging through his photographs. Draws a picture from a picture. Gives new life to his solarizations. Reframes photos …

Years earlier, freshly arrived in Paris, he showed the Dadaists the paintings he had brought from New York and stored in his small hotel room. His friends immediately decided to organize an exhibition. The Dadaists shower him with praise. Man is flattered. He enjoys good fortune in his encounters because he is a good person, a beautiful soul. Soupault had just opened his gallery near Les Invalides. On the evening of the opening, Man is freezing cold; the gallery has no heating. He meets Erik Satie, who invites him for a hot toddy in a nearby café. On his way home, Man walks into a hardware store, buys an iron, upholsterer's nails, and glue. He uses these to make a work of art. He wants to give it to the gallery owner or one of his new friends, so he calls his object *Cadeau, The Gift.*

This is the kind of unbelievably far-fetched idea that pops into Man's head …

In the evenings, we often have friends over. He loves parties, costumes, derision, wacky wordplay, miscommunication, and anything unexpected. Every day brings something new, a chance to create something, a time to dream up your own life. The most fantastic part of the story is that we never know what will happen next. What will this new day bring? He looks forward to every moment. What will my little Man's imagination come up with next? What surprises will chance throw our way?

Man astounds me. He asks for so little. His freedom, and just love, I think. A lot of love, I can tell …

Playfulness

He takes his camera everywhere we go. In Guadeloupe, my younger brother would drive around in a little toy car my father had given him. Man's toy is his camera. When he is armed with all his paraphernalia, he transforms into a great sorcerer, a magician, a master of lights … Then he exults … When I hear him say that he has had enough of photography, I laugh quietly. He's put off by the technical, chemical, and tedious side of the profession. But he knows that you have to go through that to achieve marvelous, poetic things ...

Painting ... During our five years together, I watched him drift daily between photography and painting, depending on his mood, on the weather ... He says that what he pursues above all else is freedom and pleasure. The last thing he wants is to be identified with a specific style that he has to commit to. He approaches each new theme with a distinctive inspiration that he makes up as he goes along. He creates unusual objects to amuse or provoke thought.

Chess ... especially with Marcel. When his clients pose, Man likes to place a chess set in the frame. Chess mimics life. You move the pieces forward. You see what your opponent is scheming with their rook. You have a plan. You anticipate. You bluff. You think. What does the bishop do? Where do I put the queen? You accumulate experience. You process it all and grow smarter in the real world.

Pleasure

Yes, we make love.

Pleasure intoxicates us and sends us reeling into the void. It's a scream, an effort, a discovery, a victory. Every time. Pleasure makes us more alive. Pleasure consoles us from the horrors of the world. And we take pleasure in the life we've been given. In the present, in small miracles, bursts of laughter, light April rain, a glass of wine, a rainbow, a caress, a smile ...

We make love and go out a lot. For dinner, to exhibitions ... He introduces me to all his friends. We walk arm in arm through the streets of Paris. I accompany him to the big fashion houses, where he is responsible for photographing the new collections for French and American magazines. I go with him to masked balls, all the rage in Paris at the time. I smoke, I drink, I sing and dance. I recite poems. He takes my photo. Life is good. I smile. He tells me, "Even when you're asleep, you smile, Ady!"

At home, we're an uncomplicated couple.

We make love and I get up to make him breakfast. We make love to jazz, to Johann Sebastian Bach's *Toccata and Fugue in D Minor*.

We make love without thinking about the war or nasty hurricanes.

We make love and look each other in the eyes intensely, so that we never forget.

We make love under the big red mouth, watching us night and day.

We make love, as if to lose ourselves in one another.

V

The Gift

She is fig stone thought
She is the sunlight beneath my closed eyelids
And the bright warmth in my outstretched hands
She is the Black girl and her blood cartwheels
In the night of a ripe fire.

Paul Éluard and Man Ray
Les Mains libres[1]

---

1 Paul Éluard and Man Ray, "Le don," *Les Mains libres* (Paris: Éditions Gallimard, 1947 and Man Ray 2015 Trust / ADAGP, 2020), p. 26 (our translation).

1936

The war is goose-stepping its way closer and closer. There is fear in the trees.

Wickedness in the sky.

The sea is far away, and calm by the sounds of things.

Anger has taken root in the hearts of men ...

On Sunday, my brother-in-law Narcisse is having lunch with a couple of Guadeloupean dignitaries passing through Paris. He is a doctor, Black. She is *mulâtresse*, head of the house. We've heard that she leads a battalion of highly docile servants.

"Everything has to be impeccable!" Raymonde tells me. The guests epitomize the *petite bourgeoisie* of Creole society and live in Pointe-à-Pitre, not far from Rue Condé and our old place. Their cut-stone house survived the 1928 hurricane. They knew our parents well and watched us grow up. They attended the funerals ... My elder sister wanted me to be there. To share our memories, to smile, perhaps to show how wonderfully we have risen from the rubble left by the disaster ...

Things got off to a good start with pleasant conversation. The latest news from back home. Ali Tur's current construction projects. The celebrations marking the tercentenary of the Caribbean's annexation by France ...

Madame remarks, "In 1935, we didn't know where to turn. There were so many balls! We were invited to banquets, inaugurations ...." "And to dinner parties, too – they were never-ending and sumptuous," adds the doctor.

"The *Mé*tropole was not to be outdone, believe me," Raymonde comments. "Did you hear about the great Caribbean night at the Paris Opéra? President Lebrun was there in person. What a great turnout! And the stage showcased the very best of Creole tradition. There were dancers in full costume, beautiful *biguines*, a flamboyant quadrille demonstration ...."

Laughter, nostalgia, sighs.

Followed by, "Do you remember this? And what about that?"

Faces filled with emotion as we reminisce about lost relatives and the great devastation of 1928.

The shadow of an angel passing overhead, escorted by ghosts.

But, alas! All of a sudden, war is upon us. Clatter, drums and trumpets, tanks, sound of boots. No doubt these gentlemen have had enough of this hodgepodge of vapid blather, female sentimentality, general inanity. Yes, I think they've had enough of the forced smiles, politeness, and manners and what have you, exchanged over silverware, china, and crystal ... I swear that war is a topic of conversation more suited to men, really gets their blood pumping.

The doctor throws out a question, "Did you know that as early as 1925, in *Mein Kampf,* Hitler attacked the bastards of the Rhineland? Soldiers from the occupying forces' colonial troops consorted with German blondes and started sowing seeds. Now these half-bloods have become the undesirables of the Nazi regime."

Raymonde and Aimée furrow their brows as if the topic of conversation were pornography.

"On the other side of the Rhine, these poor souls are the embodiment of Black shame, an intolerable stain compounded by humiliation. According to Hitler, the Jews are plotting and pulling strings behind the scenes. They supposedly orchestrated the presence of *nègres* in the Rhineland – in order to bastardize the Aryan race, lowering its cultural and political level ... The Jews' ultimate dream, their dark project, is supposedly to dominate the white world."

"What nonsense! *Nègres* being seen as instruments of the Jews and the negrified French, negrophiles, degenerates, traitors of their race ...," adds my brother-in-law.

"This hatred of Black and Jewish people is alive and well everywhere," sighs our guest.

The conversation is getting heated.

"In 1933, *VU* magazine printed images of a Nazi concentration camp. Dachau, I think ...."

"And who in France cared about that back then?"

"The question is: who are they going to lock up in these camps? Nègres? Jews? Refugees, political prisoners, *métis,* bastards ...? I'm sorry to say, the world has gone haywire ...."

"And what are we to think of these laws on the forced

sterilization of people with psychiatric disorders or genetic illnesses? It's unacceptable! I wanted to send a letter of protest to the medical association. But I was talked out of it ... Hitler is insisting that this sterilization program be extended to include bastard children in the Rhineland. The horrific Nuremberg Laws have outlawed interracial relationships and marriage between Aryans and people of mixed descent – Black, Jewish, and *métis* people."

"I hear it's hell for Black and mixed-race people in Germany, especially those from their former African colonies ...."

"They're being hunted, of course ...."

"I heard about a young Black dancer in a theater company, a man named Gilges, who was assassinated by the Gestapo in Düsseldorf ...."

"What's the Gestapo?" asks the eldest of my nephews and nieces.

"It means that you have to prove your identity," answers Aimée. They smile.

"On a more serious note," continues the doctor, "German Wehrmacht battalions are in the process of remilitarizing the Rhineland."

Sighs all around.

"Where are we headed! All the treaties are being violated one after the other and we, the French, are just sitting back and letting it happen ...."

The tension rises. Wòz offers salad and cheese. The doctor's wife purses her lips, collecting a few crumbs beside her plate. My nephews look terrified. Dous is lost in thought.

Worked up now, the doctor, a veteran of the Great War, brandishes his knife like a bayonet.

"Europe is sick," is his diagnosis. "The noose is being tightened. People from the Caribbean, from Martinique and Guadeloupe, are being dragged into this turmoil. I personally know several of the families affected, former patients, who are urgently repatriating their German daughters to French soil. We need to get to the heart of the matter before the gangrene starts to spread ...."

I ask, "That Black dancer – do you really think he was murdered because of the color of his skin?"

Around the table, they ignore my question.

"Friends, you must taste this *baba au rhum* from Guadeloupe!" says Raymonde.

Narcisse muses, "And who cares about the empire of Ethiopia, hounded and threatened with invasion by Mussolini's fascist troops? Who will hear the cries for help from Negus Haile Selassie? Good God, it's unbelievable! What is the League of Nations doing?"

At these words, he strikes the table with a useless fist. The glasses rattle. The children flinch, stunned. My sisters wince.

The doctor's wife is accustomed to weighing in on men's conversations. "The minute it comes to Black people, no one gives a damn!" These forceful words uttered, she dabs the corners of her mouth with the tip of her napkin.

My polite brother-in-law nods, swallowing his dessert mechanically.

Carrying a pile of plates in her hands, Raymonde exclaims, "Go to your room, children! This is grown-up talk."

My nephew and nieces retreat in silence. The conversation continues between the two men.

"Now that the Popular Front is in power, maybe Europe will improve a little. We must give this new government a chance ...."

"We'll just have to wait and see," says our guest.

"At least they're pro-peace. They're going to order the dissolution of the fascist organizations that are plaguing France ... Croix-de-Feu, Action Française, Camelots du Roi, Front Franc, and the like."

"One can only hope ... If the Popular Front follows its reforms to the letter, France might just be able to get its head above water ...."

"Hitler and his clique will simply have to pack up their prerogatives and leave us in peace ...," Madame intervenes. "What does he care if German women marry Caribbean men? We're not lepers now are we! Let people live, for God's sake!"

"It's not that simple," says the doctor. "Hating otherness is a contagious disease. Our race's experience of slavery is proof of that ... Racism is a wound and it will never heal in this world. The *nègres* should watch their step ... For the time being, of course, the Jews are the ones in the firing line. But who knows what will happen next? It's not looking good ... What do you think is driving all these poor people to flee Poland and Nazi Germany? I'm telling you, Blum's going to have a tough time of it with his detractors ... Maurras – the one who called him "human garbage" – won't let go of him so easily. They nearly lynched him on the Boulevard Saint-Germain just last February ...."

"Lynched him!" exclaims Madame. "What for?"

"Simply because he's Jewish!" replies her husband.

"White people! Pfff! They've been lynching *nègres* for centuries with complete impunity in the United States – in Georgia, Alabama, Carolina, Indiana, Minnesota, Florida ... How awful! Good God, haven't you seen the photographs of those poor devils hanging from the branches of trees, their tongues hanging out, genitals cut off ... Women and children, too ... And all those white people laughing their heads off, like they're at a party ...." By the end of his tirade, my brother-in-law has broken a sweat, as if personally threatened. He blots his temples with his napkin.

"Not all white people are racist," says Aimée. She's just got engaged to a nice white fellow. His name is Édouard and he's promised to marry her soon. They're going to live in the south ...

Madame begins, "Barbarism is a ...."

"For heaven's sake, can we please talk about something else?" exclaims poor Raymonde. She's on edge. No one has complimented her on her delicious meal. And, to add insult to injury, people are filling her living room with sordid images. She was up at four in the morning, labored away all day in her kitchen to treat their taste buds. And what was the point of going to so much effort? Her pleasure has been spoiled by a stream of ugly words, images of *nègres* hanging from trees ...

The men fall silent. The friend lights a cigar. Narcisse picks his teeth. They are now sipping an aged Negrita rum. The doctor's legs are crossed. His striped suit is immaculate.

Every now and then, we get snippets of news from Germany in the cinema newsreels, right before the film. The French comment on all this at bistro counters. Rumors and stories abound. It's clear that the Jews have been a topic of conversation ever since the Dreyfus affair. I hear snatches of nauseating chatter on café terraces. Slogans and whispered words that crop up over and over again. "France is for French people, the Blum Jew, the Jewish plot, Jewish immigrants, Jewish traitors, the Dreyfusards, Jewish fortune, foreigners taking opportunities from good French people, all these *nègres* and barbarians landing on our shores ...."

On several occasions, Man and I have found ourselves sitting in a restaurant next to people rambling on about antisemitic and racist propaganda like *L'Action française* and *Je suis partout.* Man turns a deaf ear. I look away. A deaf man and a blind woman ...

He's Jewish, I'm Black. The two of us are certainly not a couple to everybody's liking … We pretend we're not affected by these matters. We live our lives in our own little bubble, without really letting ourselves be troubled by what's going on around us. We resist, as best we can, until it all blows up in our faces …

Aimée and I leave the guests to their political conversations and join our older sister in the kitchen. Since I left Raymonde's home, we've stopped talking about anything that might cause a stir, which is just as well. While she washes the dishes, I lean against the bench. I congratulate her on a fine meal. Pork ragout prepared just like back home, served with her very French gratin dauphinois.

"Wòz is doing better, isn't she?"

"Yes, Thank God! Where is she?"

"With her daughter, in the children's room. She's taking a nap," Aimée replies.

"So, are you getting married soon, Dous?" I ask.

"Yes! Very soon! How about you? Are things serious with your photographer?"

"We're not talking about marriage. We're in love, that's all there is to it …."

Aimée laughs. Armed with steel wool, Raymonde gets to work on her *canari* pot.

I change the subject. "Will you give me your *baba au rhum* recipe, Raymonde? I'm going to try my hand at baking."

She hands me a tea towel. "Here! Make yourself useful, Ady! Dry the glasses."

Aimée returns to the living room. Raymonde and I, each occupied by our own task, don't utter a word. It's always difficult to find the right words with her, and to put them together carefully so as not to stir up the dust of our family's past scattered throughout History. When I visit her, we comment on articles in *Voilà*. We talk about fashion in Paris, the weather, the warm seasons that go by too quickly or the winters that stretch on endlessly. Our conversations are guarded and colorless. Most importantly, we avoid making eye contact. She thinks I'm too cheerful. My smile bothers her. She always sees insolence and irony in my face. I see disapproval in her eyes. That afternoon, I really want to tell her how happy I am. To tell her that Man is the love of my life. His name is Man. Man, meaning *homme* in French. This Man is my man. My lover, my father, my brother, my friend, my great love.

She eventually asks me, "How are things with you?" She chewed over the question at least a hundred times before asking it. I can tell by the tone of her voice that she doesn't want to hear the answer. She looks at my ring, a mother-of-pearl bead in a small scallop shell. "You've got some nice jewelry there, haven't you ... You're looking well ...." She looks me up and down, lingering on my white linen pants. Saying nothing.

A little later, we say goodbye on the doorstep of her apartment. The guests have taken their leave. Wòz is sleeping, Dous is playing with the children. My brother-in-law has dozed off in his armchair. The glass of rum resting next to him reminds me of my papa, of Guadeloupe, of happy days and ragtime.

My nieces and nephew give me a kiss goodbye, begging me to come back soon and take them for a walk in the Jardin du Luxembourg. They want to see Guignol again, take a pony ride, jump into a cart pulled along by a little goat.

Raymonde stuffs a piece of paper into my hand and closes the door.

The *baba au rhum* recipe.

The stems of my Lily of the Valley have been soaking in a Cubist-inspired ceramic vase for four days. The French tradition of offering Lilies of the Valley on May 1st is alive and well in Paris. There are little sellers on every street corner, at every *métro* entrance. Man brought me home a pretty sprig. "You'll see, it brings good luck," the vendor whispered to him. The white bells, frilly and immaculate, have turned brown. They look like lace petticoats soaked in mud.

On May 1, 1936, all over France, workers took to the streets, arm in arm. In Paris, there was a tremendous rally at the Place de la Bastille. Workers sang revolutionary songs in one loud, desperate voice behind the unionists of the Confédération générale du travail leading the procession. I spotted a few familiar faces – Caribbean metalworkers from the car factories who are regulars at the Bal Blomet. They fancied themselves at a big carnival, singing and dancing just like back home. On the flags and posters: celebration, unity, peace, struggle, beautiful hands, men marching off into the distance, one brotherhood. On that day, there were no more *métèques*, no more *bougnoules*, foreigners, Jews, *bamboulas* ...

Artists gravitate around Man. Many of them are foreign – writers, painters, sculptors, poets ... All creators of objects, forms, words, and images. Although they deny it, most of them seem to be permanently plagued by torment. They look like scientists on the verge of discovering a miraculous potion. As if they were tingling with something: a superhuman quest, an insatiable hunger, a stubborn rage ... With the tips of their brushes, they try to touch the stars, pierce the canvas, and make it yield. Their heads are filled with storms and tempests. They hear a sound far, far away, a peculiar kind of music that they chase impatiently until they burn their wings. They are on a mission to find the unique, eternal masterpiece that will speak for Humanity and the Universe, the meaning of life, the color of passing time. Their mission is to wipe the slate clean of old practices. They want to reinvent art right down to its very foundations. They are in competition with themselves. An inner enemy consumes them. An authoritarian voice speaks within them. It insists, it scuttles.

No, the world as they see it is not enough. And yet, they come from every corner of the earth. They met in Paris at the turn of the century. Lured by the sparkling lights of Paname, they swooped in with their colorful tongues, their luggage filled with canvases and blackened pages. They traveled so far beyond their very selves to land in Paris, where others just like them were already waiting.

There are stonecutters and woodcarvers – I'm thinking of Brâncuşi in his workshop on Impasse Ronsin. At the end of a paved alley lined with plane trees, a cathedral of whiteness inhabited by a scowling, long-bearded hermit. A beautiful soul, Constantin Brâncuşi uses words sparingly and looks at you without ever smiling – or very little. At his request, Man taught him photographic techniques. His darkroom is submerged in whiteness. Brâncuşi lives in the museum on a daily basis, where he roams like a chimerical, solitary ogre. His studio blends into his living-dining room. A massive plaster table is fixed to the floor. We sit on tree trunks adorned with pads. The surrounding works of art bear surprising names that force the mind to travel beyond the visible. Fairy-like birds, never-ending columns, a sleeping muse, a *négresse blonde* ... When we leave Constantin, our clothes are covered in a thin film of plaster, angel dust. Man snorts with a smile.

Then there's Pablo, the kind of painter who mixes mature colors, standing in front of the canvas. He's always defying and confronting some sort of superhuman creature. He's constantly playing for his life, stretched to the limit. His brushes are *banderillas*. Each of his works is a massacre. The canvas is on borrowed time. Soon to be inhabited by characters with tortured faces, horses, and monstrous women – grieving, mutilated, yellow and green. Picasso is a man of few words. He lives everything intensely and enthralls women.

Duchamp has been a close friend of Man's since New York and the Armory Show. They met quite some time ago. Back then, Man was living in Ridgefield, in a commune of free-spirited young artists. Marcel had visited him there, forming a friendship that would last a lifetime. When he comes to Rue Denfert-Rochereau with his companion Mary Reynolds, he and Man play chess. The two friends exchange a few bittersweet words from time to time. They chuckle over memories of theater and cinema. Talk about their trips and a certain suitcase in the making. I make dinner with Mary.

There are poets ...

The first time he sees me with Man, Desnos tells me about his wild nights at the Bal Colonial on Rue Blomet. He loves Caribbean girls. He's already tried very spicy *boudin* and salty cod accras. He's survived all that. He used to live at 45 Rue Blomet and go down to the ball like he was going over to a neighbor's place, with his intellectual and artist friends. He smoked opium. Yes, he stopped. With his googly eyes, Desnos says he knows a thing or two about the Caribbean. He was a friend of Léon-Gontran Damas, a French Guianese poet who, alongside Césaire, founded the Négritude movement. Robert traveled to Cuba in 1928. He leads me in a rumba and whispers in my ear, "Ady, you know they dance the rumba in Cuba ...." Desnos was well known in the surrealist gang for falling asleep very quickly during "sleep sessions," when crude poems emerged from his mouth. He had a falling-out with André Breton. But he impresses Man. Breton finds him narcissistic and reproaches him for his journalism. Man made a film inspired by one of Robert's poems, "L'Étoile de mer," "The Starfish."

Éluard and Man sometimes work together. One writes, the other paints, draws, and takes photographs. Both of them dream in words and images. On the pages of *Facile*, a collection Man recommends to me a few days before the Exhibition of Surrealist Objects, poems and photos dance, caress and embrace the frail body of a brunette woman. "It's Nusch, Paul's wife," Man tells me. "You'll see her at Ratton's place."

There are women poets and sculptors and painters ... Leonora Carrington, Alice Rahon, Meret Oppenheim, Valentine Hugo, Leonor Fini, and many others I have never met ... I had the chance to leaf through the famous *Negro Anthology* by Nancy Cunard, a poet and activist editor who wore ivory bracelets. She was Aragon's lover, before she met the Black American pianist Henry Crowder. He introduced her to the harsh conditions faced by Black people living in 1930s America.

I remember Max Ernst, of course. He left Germany to come to live in Montparnasse, but, above all, so he could be with the Dadaists. He is a painter and sculptor who also creates collages and does grattage and frottage ... He paints diabolical creatures and lots of birds. Man says that Max himself resembles a bird of prey. His female conquests are legion, including Gala – Paul Éluard's first wife, and Leonora, whom he met in London.

Then there's Soupault and Ré, Sadoul, Tzara and Greta, Aragon ... Giacometti. Yes, I remember. In 1937 ... the albatrosses.

Man is commissioned by *Harper's Bazaar*, the American magazine he often works for. He asks Giacometti to sculpt birds to liven up the background for a fashion photoshoot for the new Chanel collection. The models are sumptuously dressed in evening gowns. Tall, slender-waisted girls sway in fluid, wispy fabrics. I stand in a corner to admire them. Man shows them the slightly affected way of holding themselves and displaying their hands. At the end of the session, he says to me, "I can see you with these birds, Ady." I can already picture myself in a Chanel dress. "Take off your clothes. Keep your jewelry and your bonnet, if you like." I don't know how to say no to him, to his eyes, his smile. So, I take off my clothes while the models get dressed behind a screen. I think of my dad's wing-like hands. Wearing my white bonnet that was fashionable back then, I pose in front of Giacometti's albatrosses, my chest bared.

Juan Miró is a Catalan painter and poet, like Pablo. Man and I meet him after the tragedy of Guernica, the ill-fated town bombed by the Nazi Condor Legion. Miró fled his country. In 1937, one of his paintings is shown in the Spanish pavilion at the Exposition Universelle in Paris. Pablo's great work, *Guernica*, is also there. In their own way and with their art, painters show their solidarity with the Spanish people. The following year, when we visit him in his studio, Juan is painting *A Star Caresses the Breast of a Negress*.

Picabia, painter and writer, was born in Cuba in the Greater Caribbean and has lived in Madrid, New York, Paris, Barcelona, Lausanne ... Man had run into him in 1913 at the Armory Show in New York. Francis loves cars, boats, and the casinos of Monte Carlo, where he gambles heavily. Man has never forgotten that Picabia was one of the first painters to commission photographs of his work. It was during the twenties. Man had just arrived in Paris. Money was tight ... Gratitude.

I remember when Frida Kahlo came to Paris. In March 1939, I think. Springtime was already in the trees ... Mexico was being showcased in Paris and Breton had invited Frida to exhibit her work. But nothing goes according to plan. He has no showroom. No money. Frida is very angry, remembering that she generously hosted Breton and Jacqueline Lamba at Casa Azul in 1938. Alas, we're a long way from Coyoacán and long conversations about independent revolutionary art, with Diego, and Trotsky, who had sought refuge at the Riveras' place in Mexico. Breton was now in his element, surrounded by his devotees and admirers. "Mexico is the surrealist place *par excellence* ... Frida's art is a ribbon around a bomb," he declares. But Frida leaves him to his grand tirades. She hates Paris and the surrealists, "damned sons of bitches, cursed intellectuals" who think they're the gods of the world and spend hours in cafés blabbering about art, culture, and revolution ... Marcel Duchamp and Mary Reynolds are the only ones to escape her wrath. After a month, the exhibition goes ahead at the Galerie Pierre Colle, thanks to Marcel.

Before leaving Paris, Frida comes to the studio to pose. She is in pain from multiple surgeries and kidney inflammation. The intellectuals call her Madame Rivera this, Madame Rivera that. At the end of the session, she tells Man, "Frida Kahlo is my name. And you should know that I'm not a surrealist, I don't paint my dreams. What I paint is my reality." I remember her thick eyebrows, like the wings of a black bird over her eyes. I remember her mustache and her hidden pain. I remember her big silver rings, her hair braided into a crown. I remember her psychological fortitude and physical fragility ...

There are the theoreticians of the surrealist movement. Breton, Soupault, Tzara, Aragon, Boiffard ... The pope, the dissidents, the repenters, and the revolutionaries. The free-spirited, the belligerent, and the perpetually dissatisfied. Fratricidal tensions and dissensions shake the group. We have reservations, feel communist bitterness. We play the game of truth. We undress. We gather for sleep sessions. We hold debates on sexuality. We travel into the darkness to reach the abyss of thought. We surrender ourselves to dreamlike experiences, hoping to reach the depths of the unconscious. One person is asked to leave for going too far. Another is absolved if they pledge loyalty. Self-appointed judges institute trials. Laws are dictated. We forbid. We circumscribe. We censor. We quarrel, then reconcile. We cherish freedom. We rebuild the world, in surrealist style ...

Man doesn't take sides. In truth, he bickers with no one. While the surrealists and the Dadaists battle it out, he sails from shore to shore, remaining aloof. Silently, he slips through the cracks, unaccountable to anyone. I get the feeling he's very lenient with artists. He understands their proliferating doubts. He is familiar with their quirks and wandering thoughts, their fragility, and the tensions that fuel them. He himself admits he's full of contradictions, and doesn't feel the least bit guilty about it ...

He never sets himself up as a judge, my little Man. Especially when it comes to art, he sees no ranking or hierarchy! As far as he's concerned, the way an idea is expressed is entirely up to the artist.

During our years together, I mostly saw him as attentive to and curious about others. No, I never really heard him criticize a creator's work. He's as interested in the anecdotes that punctuate artists' lives as he is in their works. He lives in the moment, passionately. Never imagining the future, he says that problems will eventually find a solution, in the same way that nature manages to escape from all situations. He's never bored. His imagination is always on the move, on the lookout, poised to invent something new and to color his days like a canvas. His art is his distraction, his food, his breath, his joy, his consolation, his whole life ...

In the course of our encounters with other people, I discovered that his friends all consider Man to be rather quiet. Picabia calls him the silent man, while Robert Desnos sees him as an unflappable crocodile. Perhaps he has kept the habit of staying silent from his first years in France.

Man told me.

As a young American arriving in Paris, he could barely grasp what was being said around him. When he tried to express himself, people couldn't make out what he was saying in his broken French. There was also the problem of misplaced accents, which turned words into their opposites, or made them obscure or comical. On the hunt for vocabulary, he often got entangled in Parisian slang, false cognates, anagrams, and puns. Duchamp advised him to find a girlfriend with whom he could learn the art of conversation. Which he did.

The two of us talk a lot, when we are alone together. We talk about anything and everything ... Using French, English, and Creole words. We always understand each other, even with just a look. The two of us have never argued.

For five years, he lived with me, Ady Fidelin, a girl from Guadeloupe. Man looked after me well and I took good care of him.

For five years, we loved each other ... And no one can ever take that away from me.

For five years, he heard me sing and speak Creole. He tasted my Caribbean cuisine and relished it. I read him the pages of the poets of my island – those my mother adored, of course, and those others whose collections I found in bookshops in Paris: Daniel Thaly, John-Antoine Nau, Saint-John Perse, Gilbert de Chambertrand ... I told him about Compè Lapin's tricks, the terrifying stories of the *soucougnans* and *diablesses* ... I told him about my visits to my old uncle in Basse-Terre who looked so much like the "*Y'a bon Banania*" Tirailleur. I made him laugh telling him about the yam merchant in Pointe-à-Pitre who was afraid a photographer would steal her soul ... By 1940, Man already knew a lot of Creole words. He would even answer me in Creole with his American accent. We had plans ... to go to Guadeloupe together, at least once ...

No, you can't erase five years of your life that easily.

Man can't stand still. The great exhibition of surrealist objects will soon open its doors at the Galerie Charles Ratton on Rue de Marignan. From May 22 to 29, 1936. Man is jubilant and bursting at the seams. He wears many hats. He flutters. Fidgets. Files, cuts, reflects. He makes late-night phone calls to his friends.

Long, impassioned conversations ensue, centered around one word, one name: Breton. He holds meetings at the local café. I get the impression that the little gang is plotting a coup d'état. They're all counting their ammunition in their studios. Some are curating collections of this and that. Others are putting the finishing touches to a painting, while their companions are unearthing foreign treasures: masks, dolls, pottery ...

We walk briskly toward Rue de Marignan.

Before we leave, I ask him, "You won't leave me all alone in a corner will you, my little Man?" He looks at me for a long time. "You'll be the most beautiful, Ady! You'll be the most attractive thing at the party ... Believe me, I know several people who'll be jealous of my Little Black Sun ... And if anyone at all disrespects you, I'll beat the living daylights out of them."

On the way, he tells me about his run-ins with the Cowboy of Montparnasse, lover of the beautiful Aïcha Goblet ... It happened a few years earlier, at the Jockey, a popular jazz club on the boulevard. The guy, a Russian painter, was completely drunk and wanted to force Kiki to dance with him. After a while, Man stepped in and grabbed the guy by the collar. There were limits to his patience. In no time at all, both of them were on the floor. They had to be separated. But Kiki was a no-nonsense fighter, as they say in Paris. She chased the Cowboy to the sidewalk, hurling insults at him as she went, and gave him a thrashing, armed only with a small camera. Kiki sure was unpredictable. She had terrible fits of jealousy and the like, but that's another story ...

A crowd has gathered in front of the Galerie Ratton. The surrealist *Tout-Paris* has assembled.

Man introduces me left, right, and center. Ady, Ady, Ady ... People gawk at me from top to bottom. They offer tight smiles. Excessive embraces. Oblique glances. Clenched hands, limp hands. Ady, Ady, Ady ... After a while, he joins a group of chattering men. He listens, nods. Looks over each of their shoulders. Smiles at women and greets them from afar with his mischievous little look. He's in his element.

I can't take my eyes off my little Man, thinking he's the most elegant of them all. Some of the men are disheveled and bedraggled. Their shirts hanging over their creased pants. Shoes muddy and unpolished.

One day, upon returning from the Saint-Germain-en-Laye market, I find Man sitting on his bed, sewing a button back onto his shirt. I open my eyes wide: it's the first time in my life I've seen a man sew anything. He laughs and says,

"Ady! You can't begin to imagine all the things I know how to do!"

His father was a tailor, his mother an embroiderer and seamstress.

Back home in America, a room in the apartment serves as a workshop. His papa makes tailored jackets. Everywhere, neatly arranged in boxes, there are pins and needles, threads of every color, scissors, buttons, and fabrics around a sewing machine that keeps food on the family's table. Tergal, linen, poplin, satin, silk, cotton, velvet ... And hands, big and small, bustling about, sewing, cutting, trimming, pulling the needle. All this beauty at the service of fashion.

So now that he can afford it, Man wears custom-made suits from Tailor Shirtmaker Knize, at 146 Avenue des Champs-Élysées. His sister regularly sends him American shirts. I love his polka-dotted and striped ties, his impeccable shoes. And his crimped hair, so well-styled whenever he goes out.

Things keep spinning round and round in the Galerie Ratton. I get the impression that there are more and more people. The crowd has spilled out onto the sidewalk. I can't see Man anymore. I don't really feel like I belong here among these white people when he's not in sight. Sullen-faced intellectuals. With pompous speeches. Standing in front of a canvas doll, lecturing and swooning.

I'm a fly writhing in a bowl of milk.

Suddenly, a woman grabs me by the elbow.

"Ady!"

"Yes!"

"You look a little lost among all these wild birds."

She bursts out laughing.

It's Nusch Éluard.

This is the first time we meet. On May 22, 1936, the day of the inauguration.

Her smile lights up her face. She embodies light. Her milky skin, her perfect face, with all its features and contours, reminds me of the painted picture of a little Virgin Mary that my mother used to keep preciously in the Bible on her bedside table.

"Man asked me to look after you. I'll chaperone you for a while ... My name is Nusch. Welcome to the troupe!"

While the artists discuss the works, she takes me under her wing. She has an accent. She tells me she's from the east of France. She grew up there, in Alsace, when Mulhouse was part of the German Empire.

Man's cosmopolitan world makes me dizzy. All these people are odd and seem foreign. Most of them speak French with an accent. When they don't have enough French words, they finish their sentences with words from their mother tongue. They mangle the French language and don't give a damn. Understand whatever you want! The native French speakers just have to deal with it. France has made it known to the world that it is the country of the Rights of Man and of the Citizen. Well, the whole world is here in Paris, flocking from all over the place. They've come to taste these words that speak volumes ... *Liberté. Égalité. Fraternité.*

But I, too, have an accent. I hear it rubbing up against other accents and it sounds funny. Like these people, I navigate between two languages. I come from a pocket of this elsewhere, a somewhere that disappears into the margins.

Full of hope, most have turned up here with their suitcases packed with pain and great expectations. Behind each of them, gigantic pantomime shadows bellow their nefarious names. Dictatorship. Persecution. Poverty. Expulsion. Antisemitism. Pogrom. Massacre. Nazism. Ethnic cleansing. Sterilization. Natural disaster. Colonization. War ...

The introduction by André Breton in the exhibition catalog cautions any visitor who may have lost their way. Nusch and I catch a few phrases on the fly: "The conglomeration known as *garçon* or *carafe* in the part corresponding to the dining car ..." and "Any wreck within arm's reach must be regarded as a precipitate of our desire ..." or " ...the contemplation of cyclones at a safe distance, the god-objects of certain regions ...."

We don't understand a thing.

We stop in front of the display cases. We look at the objects for a while and then continue our visit. I wonder what all the fuss is about, in this motley assortment of objects. We elbow our way to the front. Lean forward a little to get a better look at a black-and-white photograph. It reads *Portrait d'Ubu*, by Mademoiselle Dora Maar. Further on, a work by Meret Oppenheim, *Cup, Saucer and Spoon Covered in Fur.* Hopi dolls, Eskimo masks, Zapotec pottery. Dalí has delivered *Le veston aphrodisiaque*, the *Aphrodisiac Dinner Jacket.* According to the catalog, some of the objects are recovered, others are disturbed, interpreted, oceanic, mathematical, or American, like the mummified Jivaro heads ... Man offers *Lanterne sourde et muette*, "Deaf and Mute Lantern"; Duchamp two readymades, including *Porte-bouteilles*, "Bottle-Holder." I feel like I'm in a cabinet of curiosities. We pull up in front of a display case filled with twisted decanters, flasks and ciboriums, melted, tortured forks. It says that this collection belongs to Governor Merwart. These pieces, kindly lent to Breton, were collected from the ruins and remnants of the Mount Pelée volcanic eruption in Martinique in 1902. The objects are said to have been "disturbed," as in, modified by nature. The artist's choice of these objects makes them surreal. Nusch takes me to the natural objects. A carnivorous plant plans to eat us. Sulking stones remain silent. An Aepyornis egg listens to us. We stop in front of the *Galet gravé (*îles Loyauté*)*, the "Engraved Pebble", from the Paul Éluard collection.

Nusch is speechless. As if hypnotized, she gazes at the pebble. A soft look in her eyes. A flutter of the eyelashes.

"Voilà! We've come full circle!" she exclaims. "Now you know a little more. Come on, let's go! I'll introduce you to my husband."

There are other displays we haven't seen yet. But I've seen plenty. I've got enough to give me nightmares for an eternity.

We find Man and Paul in the company of Breton and his wife, Jacqueline Lamba. André is the only one talking. He looks satisfied. Nobody really seems to be paying attention. Man smokes his pipe pensively. Éluard, tall and thin, sways on the spot.

"Ah! Finally, here's the Ady everyone's been talking about!" he says, wrapping his arms around Nusch.

Breton stares at me for a long moment. This must be how he examines objects before declaring them to be surreal. Man watches him out of the corner of his eye, as if he'd thought about playing a practical joke on him. A slight smile flits across the corners of his eyes.

I fiddle with my catalog.

Man asks, "Did you see my deaf and mute lantern, Ady?"

I nod, hoping he won't ask me any complicated questions.

"She doesn't speak? She's mute, like the lantern ...," says someone behind me.

"Well she lights up my life, that's already something!" retorts Man tit for tat, quietly taking a puff from his pipe.

"We'll get to know each other better very soon," murmurs Nusch. "Man says you'll be joining us in the south. We'll have a great time together, in the southern sunshine, at the seaside."

The Éluards take their leave.

The exhibition room empties little by little. Behind the glass, the surrealist objects look like old toys abandoned by children: tea sets, dolls, masks, and carnival costumes. What remains is the smell of tobacco and, in the heavy silence, the memory of Nusch Éluard's sparkling smile.

It's three in the morning on Rue Denfert-Rochereau. The window is open. The month of May is already warm. Outside, revelers come and go under the streetlamps, singing verses of popular songs.

Man and I are in bed. When we returned from the exhibition, we made love. I know what he likes. I offer him my body. Draw him into my world. I have this power over him. He surrenders in my arms. Tastes my skin, inhales my underarms. Delves deep inside of me. I wait for him and he harvests me, night after night.

Then he lights the lamp and gets up. He pours himself a cognac. Completely naked, he strolls around the apartment with a cigarette in his mouth.

"What is it? What's the matter, my little Manichou?"

He comes back to the bedroom, sits on the edge of the bed. I rub his back.

He says, "You know, one day, when I was with Kiki, someone asked me if she was intelligent. I curtly replied that I was smart enough for two ... I saw how intimidated you were at the gallery. Ady, don't ever let the arrogant, know-it-all types and their pals impress you. You're you. You're young and beautiful and smart. You're sweetness itself, Ady. Anyone who sees you with me and judges you or questions our relationship is not my friend."

That same evening, he asks me, "How do you say 'to make love' in Guadeloupe?" I reply, "*Koké*!" He nods and thinks, looking disappointed. I add, "In Martinique, they say *Koupé*!" He's startled. A big smile appears on his face. He repeats, "*Koupé*! Like *couper*, to cut, like with a knife or scissors ...." I nod yes. The following year, for *Les Mains libres*, he'll draw a woman lying under a large, menacing pair of scissors.

The trips continue.

June. Man is in London. I stay in Paris to take care of my little niece. The New Burlington Gallery organizes the International Surrealist Exhibition. Among other artists and actors in the movement, Man and Paul are guests of Roland Penrose, a young English painter and heir to a wealthy family.

When Man returns to Paris, he's very excited. He tells me everything, in vivid detail. Paul gave a lecture on the sulfurous Marquis de Sade, a sensitive and provocative topic. Decrying Sade as a "martyr for freedom," he left the audience stunned. Numerous works were displayed. Most of his surrealist friends were in attendance, each trying to demonstrate more creativity than the next. Wearing a diving helmet rented for the occasion, Dalí spoke of the depths of the unconscious. A herring was found hanging from a Miró painting. Twenty-five thousand visitors came. Man seems delighted. According to him, the UK has just moved into the surrealist era.

When he's finished, I ask if he met any beautiful girls in London.

Man sits at his desk. He arranges his photographs, rattling off names like a list of errands, "Valentine, Meret, Sheila, Alice, Nusch ... One of them was very attractive. Sheila Legge ... She served as a perch for pigeons. Hid her face behind a hood of red roses. They called her the 'Phantom of Trafalgar Square' ... Can you imagine? A woman with a head entirely covered in flowers. Every man wanted to go and see what was hiding behind that charming bouquet ...."

Silence. I run into the bedroom and close the door behind me. I lie down on the bed and undress. I slip under the sheets with my stuffed animals and rag doll. I close my eyes.

After a while, I hear the door. He stands there naked, his camera ready to shoot.

"And you, Ady? Did you meet any nice people at the Bal Blomet?"

To which I reply with a few lines of John-Antoine Nau.

It is She! – None other than She, The tender, slightly mystical, Serious soul.

He takes a few photos. I smile and gather the stuffed animals around me. Then he puts down his camera and pulls back the sheet. He lies down beside me. He takes me in his arms and repeats, *"It is She! – None other than She ...."* He starts tickling me. I continue, *"None other would have said, so warmly compassionate ...."* We laugh. We can't keep a straight face. We're laughing about playing this game – it's a little conventional, perverse, childish. *"It is She! None other than She ...."*

We laugh in our love.
We laugh in the poetry of love.
We laugh in the desire of our touch.

On July 12 we leave Paris for Saint-Raphaël, Cannes, Antibes, and Mougins. The road is clear. Man and Paul are looking forward to seeing Picasso again. We all stay at the Vaste Horizon. Nusch assures me that we'll be roistering from dawn till dusk.

There's rumba in the air. Picasso is in love. Things weren't going well with his wife anyway ... Dora Maar will be in Saint-Tropez, but he'll invite her to Mougins. She's a photographer. Already renowned for her work with Brassaï and Man. She has her own studio on Rue d'Astorg. Advertising, fashion, reports from the inner city, from disadvantaged neighborhoods, poetic photomontages, she delves into every field of her art. I remember her as the creator of *Portrait d'Ubu*, widely acclaimed by the small surrealist community at the Galerie Ratton. They say she has talent and a strong character. Picasso wants her. Everything he wants, he gets, Nusch tells me.

Man claims that it was in his studio on Rue Denfert-Rochereau that Pablo first saw a photo of Dora. He was spellbound and fell instantly in love, begging Man to give him the photo and promising one of his works in exchange. Paul, meanwhile, recalls an arranged meeting in January 1936. Dora, herself desperate to be introduced to Picasso, was at the café Les Deux Magots, where the painter was a regular, along with Éluard and his secretary, Jaime Sabartés. Sitting alone with her glass at a nearby table, Dora tries to attract his attention. She stabs the table with the blade of a small penknife at regular intervals, between her splayed fingers. It makes a sharp, mind-numbing noise. Tap tap tap... She has taken off her black leather gloves embroidered with pink flowers. Knock, knock, knock ... Suddenly, a few beads of blood appear on her white fingers and crimson-polished nails. The table bleeds a little. They look like shapeless rose petals. Picasso pushes back his chair. Hooked, he walks over to her. Dora remains stoic. No, she's not in pain. Will not shed a tear. Dora is not the kind of woman who cries that easily. She offers to photograph him and summons him to her studio. Dora has a high opinion of her work in those days. They stare at each other. Pablo smiles as she slips her bloodied hands into her black gloves.

Mougins. The Vaste Horizon.

The beach, the sun, the sea.

Love, poetry, painting.

Pablo can't keep still and takes us on a mission to Saint-Tropez. Dora is already there, staying with her friend, the poet Lise Deharme. Whether she likes it or not, we have to get Dora back to Mougins. She had hoped we would, of course. She is intentionally making herself a little attractive, that's the tender game she has to play. She's not just anyone, Dora Maar. Not the kind of girl you just pick up off the street, like Nusch, fortune-teller, highway whore, mindless ninny promoted to model and muse. Or an exotic Ady, Creole dancer, island *doudou* who laughs at anything and everything. Lise offers us a drink on her terrace. Suddenly, Pablo asks Dora if she'd like to take a walk on the beach. We all watch them walk away, betting that he's going to woo her and she's going to cave. Dora is only a woman, after all, and her heart is already beating for the wrong boy. They take a long walk along the beach at Les Salins. They turn their loss into a win. Pablo puts all his cards on the table. You have to take him as he is. He wants her in his life. She'll have to deal with Marie-Thérèse and little Maya. There's nothing to discuss. Dora thinks she'll be able to mother him. She's convinced that, in her arms, he'll forget all about his wife and mistress, and all the others yet to come. Dora is jubilant. Her bags are packed and ready in a flash.

Back to Mougins.

Pablo wakes up at the crack of dawn and heads straight for the sea. He goes for a swim while Dora lies in bed. He does at least an hour of frenzied swimming. Man puts on his espadrilles and joins him on the beach. Kasbeck, Pablo's faithful dog, trots ahead of them. The two friends stroll along the shore, here and there picking up a piece of driftwood, a shell, a cuttlebone, a sea sponge, some horsehair weathered by salt water: all potential surrealist objects to become jewelry for the women or works of art. And then they climb the rocks and contemplate the horizon, the ships in the distance, the strange worlds they will later paint. They speak very little. They are silent artists. Gathering and feeding on images of the landscape. It's their breakfast. Éluard joins them a little later on.

Nusch and I get to know each other better while our men explore their surroundings. We drink coffee on the guesthouse terrace. Nusch is not at all snooty. She looks and moves like a queen, but she's a simple girl who doesn't put on airs and graces. Man has photographed her many times. Picasso, who adored her, painted several portraits of her. Naked, pensive, offered up, graceful. Her beautiful face also appears behind a spider's web. Dora took the photo, for a cosmetics advertisement. The caption says it all: "The years are waiting to catch up with you."

Dora photographed Nusch for her beauty, but they don't have much to talk about. Dora is an intellectual, an artist, a political activist. She reads. She writes in her notebooks, looking focused. Often, she sulks and mopes, watching us with dismay. We swim in the same waters ... We pedal together on a tandem bike, bringing back groceries from the neighboring village, but we're not really friends. We only spend time together because of our men. No, Dora doesn't really take part in our girl talk. She's more comfortable mingling with the men. She's trying to carve out a spot for herself among these gentlemen. She weighs her words hoping they pay her a little attention. It's not a battle Nusch and I want to fight ...

"He looks big to you, and to me he's tiny, no thicker than a twig. But he's fragile, my Paul," confides Nusch. "He had tuberculosis when he was young. Have you heard of the sanatorium? It's no picnic, believe me. His lungs still hurt and he has to go to the mountains from time to time to help him breathe properly. He goes to a place near Davos, in Switzerland ... That's where they treat him ... That's where he met Gala, his first wife. Now she's married to Dalí. Do you know who he is? Well, you'll get to know him if we go to their place in Portlligat. It's near Cadaqués. The Costa Brava is beautiful ... Dalí! You should have seen him in London!

He was wearing a diving helmet ... Anyway, my Paul comes back to me after the treatments he does in the mountains. He's a great poet, you know ...."

She urges me to tell her about when I met Man, if I want to. "I don't mean to be nosy, Ady. It's just that I love love stories."

I tell her about the Bal Blomet. Yes, she knows it. 33 Blomet! Desnos had taken them there once. She remembers the bodies touching, the noise, the sweat. Black and white figures tangled together, as if possessed by the music. An atmosphere of confinement, fury, and despair. A desire to flee ...

"And you, how did you meet Paul?"

"Ah, it's a long story ... I come from the circus. When I was a kid, I was an acrobat, and a clown, and a magician. I started theater in Berlin. I got small roles at the Grand-Guignol in Paris. Would you believe me if I told you that I was a hypnotist and a medium ... I even made dead people talk ... But I wasn't earning any money, as you can imagine ... The truth is that Paul picked me up off the streets, or rather on the Grands Boulevards, right in front of the Galeries Lafayette, where there are all kinds of women walking around. He was looking for women with René Char, another poet. They offered me coffee and croissants. I was starving. In those days, I was a fortune teller and a card reader ... I also did a bit of begging and worked the sidewalk, to eat, you see ...."

I open my eyes wide. And look at her. Her face always looks like the Blessed Virgin in my mother's pious picture. Smooth, bathed in light, full of innocence and goodness. We have the same hairstyle, tied back with a thin satin ribbon. We love each other very much. At my sister's, my mother's old friend had predicted that I'd end up a prostitute if I kept up my life of merriment. I picture Nusch, roaming the streets of Paris. I see myself, depraved, offering my body to the masses on the Grands Boulevards ...

"Don't judge!" She bursts out laughing. "It's nothing, it's no secret, you know. Paul doesn't hide it. We took a cab back to his place that night. We spent the night together. And he kept me after that. Now I'm Madame Éluard. Just goes to show, anything can happen. I take care of him, do the housework and the cooking. If he asks, I pose for him, for his friends ... We both love making love ... He sleeps with other women. No, I'm not jealous, it doesn't bother me. I know I'm the one he loves ...."

Man takes photos. Nusch and I pose nude, arm-in-arm. He

1936

Ady Fidelin et Nusch Éluard, 1937. Banque d'Images, ADAGP / Art Resource, NY © Man Ray
2015 Trust / Artists Rights Society (ARS), NY / ADAGP, Paris 2023.

says, "Bring your lips closer together. Kiss each other." He doesn't really give orders. He directs us like actresses. We play the game of desire. We laugh, we kiss. She's tender, Nusch. The two of us are there to serve art.

Avignon, L'Isle-sur-la-Sorgue, Marseille, Antibes, Golfe-Juan, Saint-Tropez … One day, we race to a village. The ruins of Château Lacoste tower, at the highest point. Man and Paul are very excited by the idea that the Marquis de Sade once lived there. Man takes photos, does sketches … He tells me to pose between the old stones.

Dora photographs her Pablo. She's desperately in love. She doesn't smile much. She goes with the flow, but it's clear that she would have preferred to be alone with Picasso. We sense that Dora is always a little unhappy, bitter, chewing on some dissatisfaction or old anger. We don't know what's going on in her head. Sometimes there's a strange gleam in her eyes. Her gaze is like a haunted house, populated by ghosts.

Otherwise, it's utter bliss. We're a happy family. We all get into our cars. We drive down roads at random. We laugh. We kiss and touch. We also visit friends who have homes in the region: the poet René Char and art dealers Yvonne and Christian Zervos.

The friends give each other wacky, mysterious nicknames that they use among themselves. Hammer, faucet, pipe, *soupe à l'oignon*, lioness … They laugh. Dora and I are a little out of the loop. Nusch says she'll explain it to me one of these days.

On July 18, we hear about the civil war in Spain. There's been a military coup d'état, announces the guesthouse radio, which unleashes thunderous words: Mussolini. Fascism. Francoism. Totalitarianism. Blackshirts …

On August 1, the Olympic Games begin in Berlin. The Reich puts on a show of greatness and power. The Nazis strut about in front of the League of Nations. The Black American, Jesse Owens, wins four gold medals in the athletics events.

Picasso paints Dora.

That same month, we travel back and forth between Saint-Tropez, Antibes, and Mougins.

The great factory strikes are behind us. The Front Populaire and paid time off set people in motion, on vacation. They feel the need for fresh air. Bicycles, birdcages, trunks are strapped to car luggage racks. They say that in Paname, the train stations are under siege. Some Parisians have pitched tents on the banks of the Marne, others have ventured as far as the sea or the mountains, into the remote French countryside.

In the Midi, it's seaside and sunshine every day.

Every day, it's lovemaking, poetry, painting, wine. My skin takes on a darker, coppery hue. Man and Dora take photos.

Pablo paints, Paul writes.

Nusch and I enjoy the beach. We lounge and pose. Nusch's body is always on display.

I loosen up. I imitate her.

Roland Penrose, Ady Fidelin, Picasso and Dora Maar, Cote d'Azur, France
1937 by Lee Miller.

We're twin sisters. Black and white. Every day is filled with joy, games, freedom, desire. The war is a long way from Mougins ...

Man unearthed a ukulele from a knick-knack stall in Antibes. We get dressed up. He strums the notes like an amateur Django Reinhardt. Clad in my costume, Nusch is a Creole *doudou*. One afternoon, she's a Japanese woman wearing a kimono. And I'm a Tahitian ... Our bodies are bare and veiled. All day long, our bodies graze and rub up against each other under the watchful eyes of the men who love us ...

We swim with the fish. We dive in the clear, perfect waters of the Mediterranean. We know secret coves and isolated beaches, friendly holes in the rocks. There's always a camera around somewhere.

The images of that time are frozen for eternity.

It may sound lewd ... but I have no regrets.

I remember that feeling of freedom vividly, it grows stronger with each passing day that summer ...

Even today, I can still feel it inside me, sharp and fresh.

How can I describe that freedom in words?

... A great wave in the distance that sweeps you into the depths of your being ... An intoxicating whirlpool ... An endless *biguine* ...

... Morning breaking brightly, chasing the night away like an old dog ...

... A seed in the ground that bursts its bodice, releasing a stem that grows and grows ...

... An ointment that soothes and numbs pain.

... A breath of euphoric air, perhaps. It was all there ... Yes ...

We were on vacation, joy and naked bodies under the Mougins sun. Wide awake, daydreaming. Far from all the horrors of the world ...

And I'm overcome with dizziness in the face of the possibilities that lie before me. For the first time in my life, I feel as though I've escaped the shackles and judgments of conventional society. Escaped all the stares ... I am free to be myself, not a character, a Black doll, a puppet made of canvas and cardboard.

I listen to the men.

They debate right and wrong. Lost innocence. Taboos ...

"What's not right?"

"What's wrong?"

"Why should friends who love each other refrain from making love?"

"When we love, friends or lovers, we touch, we kiss ... Who says that's wrong?"

"Who dictates the laws? Who forbids things? Constraints, corsets, diktats ... Enough is enough!"

"To hell with it! With this damned bourgeois morality!"

"Love is for everyone. Pleasure is for everyone. Freedom is here. It's up to us to seize it ...."

One evening Paul reads us a poem, a glass of wine in his hand, stars in his eyes.

A woman is more beautiful than the world I inhabit
And I close my eyes.
I step out on the arm of the shadows,

1936

I stand at the foot of the shadows
And shadows are waiting for me.[2]

While Paul reads, Nusch comes over to me. Puts her silk-soft hand on my neck. Her fingers in my hair. Then she reaches for my mouth and tongue. She caresses my breasts. She leads me into a bedroom. I can't resist. The men sit smoking and drinking. Man and Paul smile. Later, they join us.

In Mougins, nobody belongs to anybody. Nusch is made available to Man and Pablo. Paul caresses me and makes love to me in front of Man and Nusch. We love one another. We cherish one another. We caress one another. We choose love over war.

Paris.
Autumn. There is rust on the tree branches. Sticky, suppurating leaves rot and die a slow death on the sidewalks.
Rain, wind, cold …
I'm reminded of the 1928 hurricane.
I feel so sick to my stomach as winter approaches.

November '36. Man leaves for New York. He has a contract with an American fashion magazine and makes the most of his trip to take part in the "Fantastic Art, Dada, Surrealism" exhibition organized by his friend Alfred Baar at MoMA.

He pulls a suit out of the wardrobe, telling me he'll be back in the first half of January 1937. He assures me that he would have liked to take me with him, but that he will be very busy.

Suddenly, I remember that I'm a Black woman.

I know what they do to *niggers* in his country. Hang them from trees. Men, women, and children, without a second thought. I know some showgirls who were born there. They remember white people in the South going with their families to see Black Africans exhibited like animals in freak shows. In those years, you'll have heard Black Americans in Paris talk at least once about the "Jim Crow laws" that forbid different races from mixing. And you'll have heard a story about the white knights of the Ku Klux Klan getting away with burning down houses and killing *negroes* in the

---

2 Paul Éluard. "Absences. II," in *Capitale de la douleur* (Paris: Gallimard, 1926), p. 97 (our translation).

Southern states. White people on one side, Black on the other. The same as in Hitler's new Germany, where *die Neger* are murdered gratuitously ...

I'm in my robe, sitting on the bed. I watch Man fold his shirts and pants. I wonder if Americans from the North are less racist than those from the South. To keep my hands busy, I start shining his shoes.

He goes to the bathroom and comes back with his razor and toiletry bag. Two towels, his toothbrush.

Maybe Man would be embarrassed to walk alongside me on the streets of New York. Maybe living with a *négresse* isn't something people do there. New York isn't Paris ... I'm sure that even in the North, some people look sideways at a Black man.

Crates of paintings and surrealist works are already in Le Havre, ready to be shipped. He leaves most of his suits in the closet. But I'm worried. Will he come back to me? He tells me to wait for him, promises to write and check up on me. I watch him roll up the canvas with the big red mouth and slip it into a case. He gathers photos and rayographs left and right.

He buckles his suitcase.

"Don't worry, my Little Black Sun! Time flies. Go dance at the Bal Blomet! Let your hair down! Don't change anything, have fun with your little nephews. Visit your family. If you need anything, give Nusch and Paul a call ... Go to Saint-Germain-en-Laye and see what the workers have done. I've given them instructions ... I'll write to you ...."

He leaves me money. He pats my hair, caresses my cheek, kisses me.

The door slams. I hear his footsteps on the stairs.

I run to the window. He looks up and blows me a kiss.

I see him get into a black cab.

The cab disappears at the end of Rue Denfert-Rochereau.

I tell myself he'll fade from my life one day. It's a kind of clever intuition, and it hurts.

VI

I know, myself, now, that if I had it over again
I'd be even more free with my ideas, with my body
and my affection. Above all, I'd try to find
some way of breaking down, through the silence which imposes itself
on me in matters of sentiment.

Lee Miller[1]

---

1 Note from Lee Miller to Roland Penrose, September 9, 1947.

'37–'38–'39

Lee, Nusch, fashion in Congo, "Adieu foulard ..."

In January 1937, Léon-Gontran Damas's *Pigments* was published by Guy Lévis Mano. Robert Desnos wrote the preface. I remember that *Facile*, by Paul and Man, was also published by GLM. Damas is friends with Césaire, Goffin, Desnos, and many others, Black people and white.

I only met Damas once, in a café on the Boulevard du Montparnasse. What do I remember about him? His generosity and kindness, the torment etched in his ember eyes, the flayed passion of a poet. While he talks with Man, Robert, and another friend, I imagine Damas walking a tightrope between heaven and earth, between dreams and the absurdity of life, a great fighter for all humanity.

On the cover of *Pigments*, a Black man is freeing himself from a stiff shirt collar with a bow tie. Around him, the landscape opens up for him to burst out. To the left, a modern city is smoldering and teetering. To the right, there are coconut palms. Behind him, a crowd of *nègres* hungry for freedom. Robert is effusive when he speaks of Damas and offers me the collection. "I'm sure you'll like this poetry, Ady." I give him a kiss, to thank him.

I turn the pages. I read, at random.

S.O.S.

In that instant alone / won't you all understand / when that thought does come to them / soon this thought comes to them / of wanting to gobble up some nigger / in Hitler's way / gobble up some Jew / seven days a fascist week ...[2]

---

2 Léon Gontran Damas, "S.O.S.," in *Pigments* – Névralgies (Paris: Présence africaine, 1972 [2005]), p. 51 (translated by Mehdi Étienne Chalmers).

I get chills.

And then, on another page.

Lament of the Negro

Set forth once more / my daze / of olden days / of being hit with whirled rope / of charred bodies / charred from toe to backside / of dead flesh / of ember / of hot iron / of broken arms / under the raging whip / under the whip that makes the plantation run / and gives blood to drink my blood blood of the sugar factory / and the pipe of the slave driver bragging to the sky ...[3]

They talk about Nancy Cunard, who after publishing *Negro Anthology* and denouncing Mussolini's invasion of Ethiopia, went to Spain to support the *republicanos.*

"Nancy wears Schiaparelli dresses and a whole jumble of bracelets, but she joins every struggle," says Damas's friend, who knows Henry Crowder, Nancy's Black lover.

In my hand, I held the pamphlet that Man kept in his desk drawer: *Black Man and White Ladyship.* The text is a scathing response written by Nancy to her mother's racism toward Crowder.

I look at Damas. I wonder what he thinks of me, seeing me with Man. *White Man and Black Ady. Old White Man and Young Black Lady.* Is our relationship horrifying to him? No, I think Damas is one to rise above prejudice.

A handsome young man with an ascetic face, Damas is barely older than me. He's from French Guiana. He gave up his studies in law to pursue his art and take up his bewitching pen. He says, "Paris is the center of the world and all artists flock to it!" He laughs at himself, a grating sound. His family has cut him off. No matter! He'd rather endure starving to death in Paname than join the ranks. He recounts his misery with a certain detachment and the elegance of a dandy: the bits of cardboard lodged in his shoes with holes in the soles, his empty stomach, the cold, the winters, neuralgia, the alcohol, the sleepless nights spent wandering around beneath the sinister streetlamps, filling incandescent pages with text and stoking his nausea in a dingy hotel room. He writes for magazines and newspapers here and there: *Esprit, La Revue du Monde noir, Les Cahiers du Sud.* He is an uncompromising poet

---

3 Léon Gontran Damas, "La complainte du nègre," in *Pigments – Névralgies* (Paris: Présence africaine, 1972 [2005]), p. 47 (translated by Mehdi Étienne Chalmers).

and a proponent of Négritude. I listen to Damas and gaze at him admiringly, thinking he knows a lot about history, past and present. It feels like I'm related to him somehow, like he's a distant cousin. As he speaks, I can hear my dear uncle from Basse-Terre, sitting on the little bench in front of his *case*, recounting Africa, the lost country, and the epic tale of the *nègres marrons* in the days of slavery, in the *mornes* and woods clinging to the slopes of La Soufrière. I can see the stacks of sugar cane tossed into oxcarts lined up around the Darboussier factory. I think of the legions of women on the docks of Pointe-à-Pitre, carrying on their heads the heavy bundles of bananas bound for France. I also think of the desolate poverty and harsh solitude of the *nègres* in my country.

When Man and I take our leave, Damas whispers to me, "You're from Guadeloupe, aren't you? My mother was from Martinique, you know. Ady, promise me something: don't ever let anyone break your spirit ...." Then he kisses me and hugs me, like a brother.

Alas, the civil war in Spain is still in full swing. With Hitler's support, Franco's repression has intensified. On April 26, 1937, we are in Paris when the Nazi planes of the Condor Legion bomb the small Basque town of Guernica. Furious hordes come to bolster the Italian fleet. The aerial attack is an act of genocide.

Deep down, I'm very scared.

My stomach hurts.

There's no doubt about it, war is going to spread across the land like weeds in an untended garden.

I already know that the good times are over.

War is about to sweep through France, more devastating than the 1928 hurricane.

Our days of loving one another are numbered ...

Having set himself up in the gigantic attic of a former convent at 7 Rue des Grands-Augustins, Pablo paints his anger and powerlessness. Dora found the place for him. The place is dark, the canvas enormous: eight meters by three and a half. He paints under Dora's watchful eye, she is utterly devoted to him. She's hanging on, Dora. She's so eager to exist in Pablo's eyes. Wants to rise to the same level as the master. He actually encouraged her to take up painting: the highest art form. He paints his rage to dazzle and fascinate Dora. He shows her his creative force, the full scope of his genius, against which she, too, is poised to measure herself. Will she be capable of joining him in this dance? But Dora is already under his thumb. The great photographer fights tooth and nail. She thinks she's good enough, maybe even his equal. So, dressed in a man's shirt and pants, she circles him and shoots. She's the one running the show for the time being. The artist is her subject. He's at work, looking like a bricklayer toiling away on a construction site. As the hours and days go by, the canvas gives birth to characters and animals. With broad brushstrokes, life and death gradually take shape. Dora's shots are stacking up. He is exhausted. And now he has finished it. The masterpiece is right there in front of them: the color of barbarism, of pain and hope, reduced to the flame of a lantern, the sublime monstrosity of the world, life in its decay, agony, and death. All too admiring, her eyes wet with emotion, Dora is lost, but she doesn't know it yet – or at least she pretends she doesn't. Their fate is already sealed. As far as Picasso, the Minotaur, is concerned, there is no other end in sight: Dora is *La Mujer que llora*, the *Weeping Woman*.

Man has wrapped up a new book. *La photographie n'est pas l'art* has just been published by GLM. He spent several nights working on the text and choosing the photographs. Breton wrote the preface in his surrealist style, sprinkled with a few boisterous words. Man dotted his i's and crossed his t's. He's had just about enough of being asked whether he's a photographer or a painter. He reveals the essence of his thinking, which may change, of course.

Who's going to stop him?

Man hates being put in a box. But people feel the need to be reassured, to catalog things and people definitively. Where is the freedom in this idiotic mania? Man does what he wants. He paints his ideas. He draws his dreams. Or rather: his hands dream. He looks at me; he's overcome with the urge to photograph me, with a basket of fruit, my stuffed animals, in an apron, naked, wearing a washboard, reading, on the phone, trapped in hoops …

One afternoon, he finds me peeling an orange. Instead of cutting the orange into quarters the way he does, I do what my manman taught me: make a long strand of orange peel. Is this a surrealist creation? Man immediately sees the hidden beauty of a work of art. He takes out his notebook and draws the peel. You never know, it might be part of a future composition …

I explain. In the Caribbean, we hang orange peels. When they're completely dry, we put them in a jar filled with rum. Add cane sugar, a vanilla pod, a cinnamon stick, and an ounce of nutmeg. Put in the cork. Place the flask in the sun. We wait. After a while, we open it. It releases a fragrance that always makes you smile and lick your lips. Inside, there's no longer that blend of rum, peel, and spices. We've created something new: Shrubb, an amber liqueur. Lucette would murmur, "With golden reflections, like a sunset in Marie-Galante." We drink Shrubb at Christmas with friends, telling ourselves that we've managed to trap a little of that damn sun and that life is beautiful after all.

As I talk, I can picture manman standing in front of her oranges. I can picture the kitchen again, the red terracotta tiles. I can picture Lucette with her dry savannah look. I can picture the colors of the sky, and our house on Rue Condé.

My sisters and I find ourselves increasingly succumbing to this kind of nostalgia. It catches us by surprise, but the mere mention of certain words can instantly transport us back to those moments. Creole whispers fill the air. The sound of drums beckons and the smell of sweet memories brings tears to our eyes. It's as if sorrow were lying in wait, always ready to invite itself into our conversations.

Reading his newspaper one day, my brother-in-law Narcisse tells us that Félix Éboué has been appointed Governor of Guadeloupe. "This is wonderful news for the country! A man of color at last in charge in the colonies!" Raymonde starts to cry. Why? The news reminds her of Uncle Adrien who was mayor of Pointe-à-Pitre until 1933. She forgets her resentment and declares that her children must grow up in the Caribbean. "Enough is enough! France! Good God! All day long, all we hear about is war! War! War! Hitler! Hitler! Hitler! I'd rather have the wrath of heaven than the wickedness of men ... In the end, people from Guadeloupe are no worse than the rest. At least over there they don't see us as foreigners ... The other morning, in front of school, someone called the kids dirty negros! All the white people were laughing. I was so ashamed ...."

I love spending time at our house in Saint-Germain-en-Laye. Man bought me a beautiful bronze-colored bicycle. It's the countryside out there. I go into the village and to the market. I ride among the tall trees to the château. Sometimes, I pedal at full speed to feel the caress of the wind on my face. When Man is away for work, I take my brother and my nieces and nephew there. They spend the day with me. I show them the plans Man has drawn up for the future extension. They're astonished, "You're going to live in a beautiful palace, Auntie Ady!" In the afternoon, we bake a cake and drink soda. I tell them not to worry about the bad guys who see the world in black and white. Sometimes I tell them stories about *diablesses* and *volants*. They laugh themselves silly. Afterwards, we take the train back to the Gare Saint-Lazare. I take them home to the outer suburbs. I can't say I care much what they say to my sisters about it all.

It's true, my family knows very little about my life. All they know is that I live with an American man, a white photographer twice my age. Narcisse advised me to clean up my act. Raymonde sighed, as if to say that I was a hopeless case and that she'd given up trying to put me back on the straight and narrow. At any rate, she can see that I'm not unhappy. I'm always laughing. I'm never short of anything. I'm always well-dressed, with my hair and makeup done. Shoes, jewelry, and frills galore. Man is very generous with me.

I still go to the Bal Blomet. Alone or with Man. I haven't stopped touring with my troupe. I visit my family and friends whenever I want.

I have a lot of freedom with Man. He's always saying, "Enjoy yourself, Ady! Live your life, Ady!"

I pose for Wols, a German painter-photographer who has also chosen exile in Paris. We met him in February, at the Galerie de la Pléiade, where Man's photography was displayed alongside works by Cartier-Bresson, Miller, Brassaï, and many others.

And then I do a bit of film work. I act in *Les Secrets de la Mer Rouge*. The film is due for release in September. Oh, it's a very small role, really nothing at all! Some of the assistants on the set promised they'd think of me for future productions. I've got a chance to break through; they always need exotic characters to put in the background. We filmed in the studio, but the story takes place in North Africa. Gaby Basset, who plays Anita, is charming. We chat a little at mealtimes. A touch moved at the memory of her past loves, she tells me that she was once married to Jean Gabin. I don't want to stir the pot, but I remember that he starred alongside Joséphine in *Zouzou*. Too bad they're no longer together. I might have had the chance to meet the great Baker and the handsome Gabin ...

One evening, I come out of rehearsal to find Man at home on Rue Denfert-Rochereau, rummaging through his boxes. I'm beat. A kiss. We talk a little. I slip away to run myself a bath. He calls me back over. "Come and look at this, Ady!" His voice is hollow.

Sometimes, he gets sad thoughts, my little Man. They come on suddenly and then pass. I want to hold him in my arms, coddle him like a baby.

He stops me.

"It was raining that evening in Montparnasse. It was a grim October night in 1932. I was walking alone, desperate. I was carrying a revolver. I wanted to kill one of my rivals. I'd had so much to drink ... I was sick as a dog. I was ashamed of myself, you know? Suicide! That one word kept popping into my head. Suicide! Suicide! Suicide! I thought back to the artists and painters who had committed suicide. Van Gogh, Pascin, Rigault, Nerval, Maïakovski ...."

"No, my little Manou," I say. "Please! Don't talk about suicide."

He continues. "I run into Jacqueline Goddard. She modeled for me, you know. No, never went to bed with me ... Freezing cold, we head inside the Brasserie du Dôme. We drink. A lot of liquor. I tell her about my romantic troubles with Lee Miller. I wish I were dead. I put the gun on the table. Jacqueline listens, a little frightened, pity in her eyes, probably wondering if I'm going to end it all. Then, the Dôme closes its doors. All around us the chairs are already on the tables, legs in the air. They've dimmed the lights. The last servers glare at us. We head out, walk through the Montparnasse cemetery. We drag ourselves to Rue Victor-Considérant. This is as grim as it gets. Then we go back to the studio. And this is what came of it ...."

He tosses several photos on his desk.

How sad!

Man, shirtless, sitting at a table, wild-eyed. A real zombie! A rope around his neck. Revolver in his hand. A bottle in front of him, a funnel in a glass possibly filled with poison, an alarm clock showing 5:05 a.m., a lighter with his name on it, cigarettes. Jacqueline Goddard struck the same pose, with the rope, the gun, the funnel, the glass ... the whole kit and caboodle to end it all ...

"I hear she's coming back," says Man. "She'll be at the Rochas sisters' costume ball next week. All of Montparnasse knows about it. It's been five years since she left and they're raring to go because 'Miss Elizabeth Miller is back'!"

I nod my head and ask him, "Do you still love her?"

He stays silent for a moment and replies, "I don't know ...."

I go back to the bathroom, feeling dejected. The bathtub is half-full. I pour in the salts and foaming soaps. I want to sink into scented bubbles and big white clouds. To disappear ...

Sometimes, I speak to Man in Creole, just as he occasionally speaks to me in English. Whichever language comes out is the language of the heart. I'm frightened. I don't want to lose my little Man. We get on so well ... I start singing "Asi paré" ... by Léona Gabriel.

Asi paré mwen pa bèl anko
Asi paré ou vlé kité mwen
Asi paré mwen fèw on kèkchoz ...

Ou ka kité mwen pou an kannay ...

Alé missieu

Sa ou fèla pa kay poté bonè Alé engra ...
Alé bouwo ...

Am I afraid of Miss Lee Miller? Of course I am!

I know she turns men's heads in the twinkle of an eye. Aziz, her Egyptian prince, had a wife, Nimet. Considered one of the five most beautiful women in the world. Man had photographed her in the early thirties. And what do you know! Nimet lost in no time. When she discovered that Lee had her sights set on Aziz, the poor woman drank herself to death in a hotel, leaving the field wide open for her rival. The redoubtable blonde queen brought down the princess of *One Thousand and One Nights* in a heartbeat.

Lee is thirty, I'm twenty-two. But that's not the point.

She's married. Pfff! That's a minor detail in the surrealist world.

She's American, like Man ... They speak the same language.

Both share the same passion for photography.

She's white and I'm Black; but I've declared that I don't feel inferior to any white women.

The evening of the costume ball arrives. Man and I are dressed up, as we should be. He's sporting a turban. The only clothing he's wearing is a pair of baggy pants and some Moroccan babouches he found who knows where. He's a harem guard, but that doesn't mean he's a eunuch. As for me, I've decided to flaunt my feminine charms. I'll be surrounded by white people and probably the only Black woman there. I've got a big chain around my neck and I'm wearing a very short loincloth. I can play the African woman escaped from the wilderness – Joséphine Baker plays the Caribbean woman well … The two of us are bare-chested, stripped of our coats. This is the couple knocking on the door of the grand bourgeois Rochas.

The surrealists are out in force. *Tout-Paris* too, in exotic, futuristic, provocative, hideous, shimmering outfits … I remember Max Ernst, his dyed-blue hair, his chest covered with painted eyes. Roland Penrose, shaggy, dressed as a beggar, his pants and hands daubed with paint …

By the fireplace in the gigantic salon, decorated with works of art of all kinds, I spot a tall blonde woman with a bob cut. She's not wearing a costume, just posing like a diva in a long navy-blue evening gown. I can tell it's her. Lee Miller, the Dangerous Woman returning from the desert. People have gathered around. Laughter. Hugs. A stream of English words I don't understand. Then snippets of French. A crowd of men shower her with questions. Her life in the sands of the Sahara? The Nile, the Pyramids? How does one survive in Cairo? Why would an American woman choose to wander those arid lands? She smiles, dips her red lips in her champagne, recounts, enchants … She captivates and bewitches them. She's the Scheherazade of the evening, the kind of magnetic woman whose company everybody craves. She's funny, witty, whimsical. She laughs wildly with a kind of ferocity. She has a little gap between her front teeth.

There's music and champagne aplenty. A pantagruel buffet. I dance. I drink. I get dizzy. No, I'm not going to drink myself to death like Nimet of Egypt. I'm very frightened, but I don't want to be intimidated by Lee Miller. I show off my smile and my little breasts. I dance, telling myself that Man and I love each other and that nothing can ever tear us apart.

Man loves to dance, and yet he's not dancing. With a glass of champagne in hand, he chats with Paul Éluard, René Char, and

Michel Leiris. From time to time, I see him glance in the direction of the fireplace. The gallery owner Julien Levy and the blue-handed tramp are presently in conversation with Lee. They all look like courtiers. Now it's Man's turn to pay his respects to the Queen. They talk for a moment, then kiss, giggling like good old friends. Man hails me from across the room. "Ady! Ady!" He beckons me to join him and introduces me to Lee Miller. She smiles, looks me up and down, lingers on my erect Black nipples. She kisses me as she takes me in her long arms.

All my mistrust deflates like a botched soufflé.

No shadows around her eyes.

Nusch and Paul are smiling broadly.

Man laughs, "Well, Ady? No more little fits of jealousy!"

Two days later, we learn that Max Ernst organized a dinner party the very next day after the costume ball, at Roland's request. He has fallen madly in love with Lee. It's a spectacular case of love at first sight. The lovebirds are apparently inseparable. Lee has more or less left her suite at the Hôtel Prince de Galles. She spends her nights with Roland Penrose, in a cramped room at the Hôtel de la Paix. We see them laughing, smoking, and smooching on the terraces of Montparnasse brasseries. Joined at the hip, they also rush to theaters, social evenings, and surrealist meetings.

Miracles do sometimes happen in life.

A few weeks later, Man and I join Lee on a trip to Southampton. We're the best of friends. She's shown no hint of a claim to Man. No, we're not rivals in a vaudeville act. I have to say that Man quite likes finding himself in this kind of slightly ambiguous and kooky situation, caught between two lovers, two somewhat irate friends, detractors, and worshippers of his works ... What turn will things take? A mystery! We shall see ...

Roland Penrose and Max Ernst have already left Paris for London. The exhibition devoted to Max will run for at least three weeks at the Mayor Gallery.

When we arrive in Plymouth, Roland is waiting for us in his Ford V8. Lee falls into his arms. A languid kiss ensues, for all to see. Off to Cornwall, to the sprawling Lambe Creek House, with its towering centuries-old trees. There are already a few surrealists on site. We reunite with Nusch and Paul. Max is accompanied by Leonora Carrington, a young painter barely twenty years old whom he has just met in London. Roland introduces his friend

E.L.T. Menses, sculptor and pianist. Everyone is very comfortable. We wait for Eileen Agar and Joseph Bard; she paints, he writes. Finally, Henry Spencer Moore, a sculptor, arrives with his wife Irina Radetsky, a painter of Russian origin, like Man.

The memories I have of Cornwall ...

Leonora and I are the youngest. Two girls in love with old gentlemen born in the nineteenth century. Max Ernst is forty-six, Man forty-seven ... It gets worse: Picasso, whom we'll be joining in Mougins, is already fifty-six in 1937, Dora is about to turn thirty.

I'm the only Black person in this clan.

I'm the only one who's not an artist. But I tell myself that dance is an art, too, like painting or poetry; a means of expressing your feelings, of releasing anxiety, helpless rage, and fits of anger.

The old walls of Lambe Creek tremble under the frivolity of the surrealists.

The manor house owned by Roland's brother is a gigantic building cut off from the rest of the world. Our rooms overlook a splendid wooded park. All around is a tranquil tableau of lush green plains, gentle rolling hills, and dense forest with a flowing river. In the distance, on a clear day, you can see the three spires of Truro Cathedral. All is quiet outside.

Inside, behind the stone walls, there's the kind of wild effervescence that surrealists are capable of creating in an instant. Bared chests dart back and forth in the hallways of the manor house under the gaze of ancestors looking on unperturbed in their precious frames. Collective baths are taken in the early hours of the morning. Frenzied races run in unlikely disguises. They've brought bottles along, and French wine is drunk at all hours. Old scotch is unearthed from the cupboards; the empty bottles start piling up. A party every night. Menses takes to the piano without being asked. Nusch sings Marlene Dietrich songs and I sing Baker. Unforgettable outings to the Heron, the village pub nearby, where we drink bottomless glasses of whisky and pints of beer. In the living room, we meet for somewhat "serious" conversations, sometimes heated, always passionate, about painting and creation, interspersed with bursts of laughter, ramblings, and ample swearing. Then there are the charming strolls through Land's End and along the banks of the River Truro. Suddenly, someone has an idea: "Let's swap partners and identities for a day!" Not everyone is thrilled with the idea. The most fervent agree and immediately get down to business, led by Lee Miller and Roland Penrose. "I'll be you, you be me." Sleeping sessions. Questions about sexuality. Dares to undress. Lovemaking, wild embraces, casual caresses ... Madness! Penrose is quite the rascal. No holds barred during this English interlude. It's a great bonfire of taboos and prohibitions. The photographers are on the prowl. Penrose loves Lee. Man loves Ady. Paul loves Nusch. And everyone loves each other.

There's a wonderful photo from that stay in Cornwall, very chaste, well known. Nusch, Lee, Leonora, and I, sitting on deckchairs on a terrace, eyes closed. Four drowsy women, dressed from head to toe, Sleeping Beauties. Roland is behind the lens. Lee is sitting on my lap. Like Nusch, she has a cup and saucer in her hand. Leonora seems to be asleep, searching for the sun. Her head is resting on Nusch's lap. With a ribbon in our hair, Lee, Nusch, and I are literally falling asleep. A night of madness, making love ... We are the muses of the surrealists.

On the other side of the Rhine, the "Degenerate Art" exhibition opens in Munich on July 19, 1937. Works seized from German museums were presented as the work of Jewish artists or Bolsheviks. Nazi propaganda proposed slogans such as "The Jewish longing for the wilderness reveals itself – in Germany, the *nègre* becomes the racial ideal of a degenerate art." Visitors flocking to the gallery are invited to resolutely shun these paintings and instead admire the Nazi-endorsed "heroic art" on display at the highly reputable House of German Art.

One evening, at Lambe Creek ...

"Who remembers that Hitler wanted to be a painter in his youth?" quips one of the surrealists. "The fool flunked the entrance exam to the Vienna Academy of Fine Arts twice. He persevered, I can assure you. He kept his tubes of paint, his palette, and his little brushes all neat and tidy. The damned schmuck painted and sold his silly pictures so he could afford to eat ...."

"Revolting! Who bought those?"

"A failed artist!" a voice chides. "And now he's the master of Europe!"

"This is what the world gets for upsetting an artist!" They laugh. I laugh with them.

Late July marks the opening of Buchenwald camp.

In August, we head for Mougins and the Vaste Horizon. Dora and Picasso have already taken up residence there. Picasso's love

Four women asleep [Lee Miller, Ady Fidelin, Nusch Eluard and Leonora Carrington,], Lambe
Creek, Cornwall, England 1937 by Roland Penrose. Roland Penrose ©
Lee Miller Archives, England 2023. All rights reserved. leemiller.co.uk

affair with Dora has given him wings. Dora's Rolleiflex is always
at the ready. She immortalizes the Minotaur, his face masked by
an ox skull found on the beach.

They speak of Paris, the first days of the Exposition Internationale
des Arts et Techniques dans la Vie Moderne and the Spanish
pavilion where Pablo presented *Guernica* and Miró *El Segador.*
The reviews of *Guernica* are quite poor, but Picasso doesn't care.
He makes jewelry for Dora, swims, goes for walks with his dog,
and he paints.

I'm pleased to be back in Mougins.

The sea, the beach, the sun, the warm sand. Just like back home,
in the Caribbean.

The view from the hotel still fills me with wonder. On the surrounding hills, cypress and olive trees sing with cicadas. In the distance, we can see the Massif des Maures, and even the peaks of the Alps, wearing a white cap in the middle of summer. At the foot of the hills, the Bay of Cannes beckons.

We resume our usual little routine and our sweet retreat.

La Garoupe beach, swimming in the sea, photos, making love all over the place – even on the rocks. Wine, poetry, drawings, painting, discussions about surrealism and war, love, always and forever …

Picnics on Île Sainte-Marguerite, boat excursions, and secret, sensual beaches.

Visits to friends in the region.

Marie and Paul Cuttoli … Marie produces tapestries that replicate the works of artists. She's very warm and takes me under her wing.

We push on to Nice to meet Matisse at his residence in Cimiez. Among the books in his collection, I come across John-Antoine Nau's *Poésies antillaises*. Matisse's white coat, little beard, and round glasses make him look like a professor. He informs me that Nau won the Prix Goncourt in 1903 for his science-fiction novel *Force ennemie*. Matisse is a fascinating man. He has traveled the world, Algeria, Morocco … Spent time in New York and painted Black women in Harlem. One day, if he finds the right inspiration, he tells me, he'll illustrate Nau's *Poésies antillaises*. Man asks him about his son Pierre, who runs an art gallery in New York, perched on the seventeenth floor of a skyscraper on Madison Avenue. As we take our seats in the salon, Matisse wistfully reminisces about Tahiti and the Tuamotu Archipelago. Pacific islands that never cease to haunt him. Picasso had known the old master since 1906. They respectfully exchange works, sizing them up surreptitiously. For both of them, an artist bears witness to their work.

For several months, Paul has been working on a book with Man: *Les Mains libres*. Drawings and texts. Paul's poems illustrate Man's drawings. Some sketches are inspired by old photos. Man likes to reinvent works based on his own creations, paintings, and photos. It's true, he draws what he can't capture on film.

On Pablo's advice, Nusch took up collage. Last winter, she suffered from insomnia and depression. She tells me that her psychoanalyst advised her that the best way to chase away dark thoughts was to devote herself to an artistic activity. Her husband is a poet, so she wasn't going to start competing with him; especially given that Nusch isn't particularly proficient in French. She didn't attend school for very long in her childhood in Alsace. She's feeling better now; the depression has passed. I sit next to her and watch her fine hands carve out silhouettes of naked women.

This year, Man rented an apartment with a terrace in Antibes. He really needs a workshop to paint in. I spend time with him. He photographs me. He paints. He paints my portrait, *Le Rire de rêve*, inspired by the photo *Four Women Asleep* that Roland took during our stay in Cornwall. And on the canvas, Man writes in Creole *"Maime quand i qua domi i qua ri."* Which means "Even when she sleeps, she smiles." He's proud to be able to speak Creole with his American accent.

Picasso paints anywhere and everywhere, at any time. I've seen him draw Nusch's face on a paper tablecloth with wine, coffee, lipstick, and a pencil. That summer, he paints our portraits. No, we don't pose. Pablo doesn't need a model seized by cramps to sit still in front of him to be able to paint. He has an image of us in his head. That's enough for him. Dora, Lee, Nusch, and I all have the same face on his canvases, both front and side.

Delighted, Roland buys Lee's portrait for fifty pounds sterling. He gives it to his sweetheart, who is going back to Egypt. Roland has promised to wait for her. After the madness of Cornwall and the joy of bodies in Mougins, she's made the sensible decision to head home to Aziz, her kind husband. Lee is thrilled. In Pablo's painting, her face is yellow and her hair is green.

Nusch is strangely beautiful on Pablo's canvases. Big, soft eyes, a pink-and-blue face in a yellow halo.

Picasso paints my portrait. Is that me? Very Black and blue, with strange eyes, looking evil … I don't recognize myself at all. I think he was inspired by one of Man's photos: *Adrienne Fidelin with Washboard*. I make a face. I'm a little upset, and for good reason! Man assures me that it really is me. He reasons with me, insisting that paintings are no longer meant to be faithful reproductions of the original. "Listen, Ady! Nowadays, there are machines that can do that kind of thing very well. It didn't used to be like that. Painting has evolved. And today's painters have understood this. The artists of the twentieth century are men sentenced to a colossal challenge. The context is a dramatic one, they are caught between two wars. Yet art must rise up and survive ... They have no choice, Ady ... It's either that or perish."

Yes, I understand all that ... But I still prefer Man's works. Picasso never painted my face again, no doubt offended by the face I made.

The portraits he paints of Dora frighten me. It looks like he's casting a spell on her. I think Pablo wants her to become this tortured weeping woman. Canvas after canvas, his paintings get crueler and crueler. It's as if he were lacerating her face with a penknife, then sticking pins into it. It strikes me that the Dora I met in 1936 is gradually disappearing behind *La Mujer que llora* ... Poor Dora, inhabited and possessed by this creature of gouache and canvas. The real Dora thinks a lot, her eyes empty, her mouth closed. Although, unlike Nusch, she hasn't yet had a breakdown, she seems extinguished, broken from the inside out. I feel sorry for Dora. I don't say anything, but I observe.

Man and I are under the impression that these are the last happy days we'll enjoy together in Mougins. It's the end of the good times for the happy family, with Nusch and Paul, Dora and Pablo. Everyone senses that it will all soon be over. With a heavy heart, we say goodbye to Mougins, goodbye to the Vaste Horizon, goodbye to happiness and *free hands* ...

It's already time to return to Paris.

Late August, summer is still hanging on a little.

I visit the Exposition Internationale des Arts et Techniques held on the Champ-de-Mars, at the foot of the Eiffel Tower and in the Trocadero gardens. Of course, it reminds me of the one held in the Bois de Vincennes in 1931. The pavilions of Guadeloupe and Martinique are on the Île aux Cygnes. Stellio's orchestra sets the mood. Roger Fanfant scores a smash hit with Al Lirvat's new song, "Loulou mi touloulou a ou la" ... Everyone sings along to the chorus, even the white people who don't understand the words. I can't help dancing and singing louder than everyone else ...

Loulou mi touloulou a ou la
An ba ti pié mango a ou la
Loulou mi touloulou a ou la
An ba ti pié zikak a ou la

Loulou mi touloulou a ou la I ka kouri asi koté
Loulou mi touloulou a ou la ...

No, really, there's nothing like the *biguine* to help you forget your worries and reconnect with your homeland. With your eyes closed, picture the Place de la Victoire in Pointe-à-Pitre, coconut sorbet vendors, lovers, kids armed with sticks running after a barrel, childminders, maids ...

Loulou mi touloulou a ou la ...

I wonder what happened to Lucette. Did she go back to Marie-Galante? Does she still read the colors of the sky? Does she still understand the language of dogs? Does she have children? A husband? After all this time, almost ten years ... Would she recognize me? Have I really changed that much?

Loulou mi touloulou a ou la ...

How about that! French bananas from the tropics are being showcased at the Martinique stand. People crowd around to taste the spotted bananas presented by beautiful Creole *doudous*. I want a banana, too. Want to feel the taste of the Caribbean in my mouth. Gorge myself on old images of times gone by.

All the French colonies are represented. Scattered fragments of African and Asian folklore. Even a Haitian village with its *cases* made of wood and straw and its dirt roads. But what scares me are the two enormous buildings facing each other on either side of the Eiffel Tower: the gigantic pavilion of the Third Reich, topped by an eagle holding a swastika in its claws; and the equally monumental pavilion of the USSR, on which a man and woman are proudly brandishing a sickle and hammer. I go to the Spanish pavilion to see *Guernica* and *El Segador.* I wander the aisles. I contemplate the Algerian minaret. I swing my hips with the dancers from the Maghreb. Then I head back home, with two images in my head: a sickle and hammer, and an eagle and a swastika. A bitter taste in my mouth ...

A week later, I find my sisters distressed by the news that my brother-in-law is constantly relaying as he reads his political newspapers. "The world is in trouble! War is inevitable ...." This is his mantra.

My nephew and one of his schoolmates are playing soldiers with cardboard rifles and old tin cans. One has declared himself a Senegalese Tirailleur, the other a Teutonic Knight. My little niece is crying because there's a war on the way. My brother repeats that he won't die for France on any battlefield.

Back on Rue Denfert-Rochereau, I am in the little love nest I share with Man. The two of us talk very little about the war. Nor about Black people or Jewish people ... Manou asked me to read Damas to him. I skipped the page where he poeticizes Hitler, *nègres*, and Jewish people ...

While Nancy Cunard and Pablo Neruda publish *The Poets of the World Defend the Spanish People*, Man and his friends work on a big project for the following year, 1938: the International Surrealist Exhibition in Paris.

The location has not yet been finalized. Aragon, Éluard, and Duchamp are on board. They draw up lists of artists to invite. This exhibition will demonstrate that surrealism is not just a flash in the pan or a case of carrying water to the sea. It's a state of mind, it's great art. Visitors will be treated to a journey into the world of surrealism. As usual, Breton and the others meet in cafés and debate, dividing up tasks and roles. Breton and Éluard plan to write *Le Dictionnaire abrégé du surréalisme*. Tanguy is asked to design the cover. Man selects his photos.

Marcel is currently living in Paris. His partner, Mary Reynolds, is an artist and bookbinder. These days, we mostly see them at our place. We dine together from time to time. As the snow falls outside, we discuss the forthcoming exhibition, which promises to be one of the highlights of 1938. Then Man and Marcel play a game of chess. In the kitchen, I chat while preparing dinner. Mary peels the vegetables. The surrealists are men like any other, and their muses Jills of all trades.

We meet up with Nusch and Paul from time to time. We go to Luna Park together, a big amusement park just outside Porte Maillot. It's all *joyfulness*, *playfulness*, *pleasure* at Luna Park. We have the time of our lives. Luna Park has everything you need to fill you with wonder, to laugh, have a ball, travel in your mind. We eat cotton candy and grilled sausages, drink wine by the pitcher. We dress up as cardboard plane pilots. Ride the merry-go-round. Have our fortune told. Dance, watch the show ... Smiles and balloons everywhere. We get our portrait taken pointing a gun at a target. If the bullet hits the bull's-eye, you win your photo. Naturally, Man loves the photo shooting. "Go for it, Ady! Focus! Take your time, but keep a sharp aim!" We stick our heads in the funny board holes, just like in Mougins. We scare ourselves silly in the bumper cars, splash around in the Water-Chute, ride the roller-coaster, and even climb to the moon …

In mid-September, the Galerie Ratton displays a series of headdresses brought back from the Belgian Congo. The American magazine *Harper's Bazaar* is very interested. Two pages will be devoted to African headdresses. Paul Éluard is already working on the text on his end. On Rue de Marignan, Man has set up an appointment with two of his model friends. I'm free, so I accompany him, just to see, and to help him carry his gear and a chessboard.

William Randolph Hearst, owner of *Harper's Bazaar*, is an American press mogul. I know that some Yankies don't like Black people. I've come across a few at the Bal Tabarin. They climb off their coaches and look down their noses at people of color.

On the way there, Man tells me that Hearst has banned pictures of *niggers* from his magazines. He drives quickly, irritated, mumbling to himself, and casting me a wrathful look from time to time.

I tell him, "Hey, watch the road, Man! Why are you so angry?"

"*Fashion in Congo*, pfft! Hearst wants to see African headdresses on Parisian women's heads … You're going to pose too, Ady!"

I laugh.

He zooms past bicycles and cars and skids to a halt in front of the Galerie Ratton. I know Man. When he gets an idea in his head, no one can stop him. The models arrive: two beautiful brunettes.

Man introduces us. "Ady, this is Consuelo, a friend of mine. She's the wife of a famous French writer and an exceptional aviator, Antoine de Saint-Exupéry. And this is Alice Rahon, who has just returned from an *ashram* in India. They're both artists, poets, and painters, close friends of the surrealists. You may give each other a kiss …."

Following Man's recommendations to the letter, they have to change clothes several times. Wear various hats. Slip on wooden and ivory bracelets. Adorn themselves with brooches and necklaces. Move a piece on the chessboard. While one poses, the other changes outfits behind an improvised screen. Charles Ratton's collection is impressive. There are all kinds of little headdresses made from natural fibers, shells, feathers, and pearls. I close my eyes. I imagine the Black peasant women in their loincloths. In Africa, in villages, sitting on mats laid on the red stone floor. Around them, baobabs and mud huts similar to those at the 1931 Colonial Exhibition. Monkeys, lions, and giraffes, like at the zoo, but in the wild. Naked children run around and play, stirring up a fine dust of red dirt. The women stay silent. They watch the work of their dry, black hands, nimble and steady. Each work they produce with their hands is unique, delicate, original. I stroke the weaving and stitching with my fingertips. I travel through the colors of an imaginary Africa. Bibi hats, checias, hardhats, pillbox hats and caps, berets, horned helmets ... Feathers all around, raffia fringes everywhere, tiny pearls, and enough rows of cowry shells to make you dizzy ...

The session is over. While I'm lost in thought, Consuelo, Alice, and Monsieur Ratton talk with Man. Their expressions are tinged with anger and disgust, and sometimes they look over at me with a kind of pity. After a while, his eyebrows furrowed, Man beckons me to join them.

"Everyone agrees with me, Ady. You have to be the star of this feature. I'm going to make Hearst buckle."

Man then asks me to take my turn at posing.

I say, "But I didn't bring anything to change into ...."

"No need."

Charles Ratton unhooks a loincloth from a display case.

"Yes, that will do just fine," says Man.

Alice and Consuelo choose jewelry. A necklace with tiger's teeth, thick bracelets.

Here I am, wearing a three-horned headdress decorated with cowry shells, my elbows resting on a chessboard, eyes closed, hands cupping my ears, my chest bared. That's me, in fashion from the Congo.

Here I am, all smiles, with a black feathered pillbox hat, my bracelets, the tiger-tooth necklace, my chest bared. "Look somewhere else, Ady! Think of Africa!" Man calls out.

Here I am again, sitting on a table, a bibi hat on my head, my bracelets, my necklace, bare-chested. I look elsewhere, pensive, happy because Man has his eyes on me. And I smile, to please him, telling myself that my ancestors may have come from the Congo, that this is a return to my roots, a voyage into the beloved Négritude of Damas and Césaire.

A few weeks later, the final photo appears as a full-page feature in the article for *Harper's Bazaar.* Man cropped the photo, of course; American readers can't see my little Black breasts brimming with arrogance. Consuelo and Alice share the other page with Paul's text titled, "The Bushongo of Africa sends his hats to Paris."

I know I'll always be a Black woman in the eyes of white people. And Picasso is right – because I'm the only one posing with my chest bared that day. With my café-au-lait skin, I alone embody Africa, the great continent of religious idols and primitive statues, the land of the man-animal that must be elevated toward more civilized living ... And Joséphine Baker is right: give them exotic images and maybe they'll be less afraid of *noirauds* ...

The magazine, freshly arrived from America, is lying on the table in the living room on Rue Denfert-Rochereau. Man is happy. Art is also about breaking down barriers.

One afternoon, my younger brother comes to visit me. He's passing through the neighborhood. Needs a little money. When I come out of the bathroom, I see him gawking at my portrait in *Harper's Bazaar.*

"Look, that's you, Ady!"

I nod, feeling very proud.

"You're a star, then! *Han han!*"

When he leaves, I look for the magazine everywhere.

The trees begin to shed their leaves, carpeting the boulevard's sidewalks. The Jardin du Luxembourg is now merely a place where Parisians walk past each other in the alleys without making eye contact. October heralds the onset of winter, with its bitter cold, perhaps frost and ice. I'm reluctant to go out. I don't even go to the Bal Blomet anymore. I've more or less given up on my dance troupe. I turn on the heaters and loiter around the apartment in my night robe. Man and I keep warm. He photographs me. He paints. We make love. I prepare curries for him, as good as those at La Coupole. The type of curry we call "colombo" in Guadeloupe and that originates from the Indians who arrived after the abolition of slavery. They needed extra hands to work in the cane fields with the *nègres* released from their chains. "So, there are Indians in Guadeloupe, too?" marvels Man, the first time I cook chicken colombo. "*Han han!*" I reply. "That's what it's like over there. People come from all over the place, just like in Paris ...."

Work is scarce this season. No commissions for *Vogue, Harper's*

La mode au Congo. Banque d'Images, ADAGP / Art Resource, NY ©
Man Ray 2015 Trust / Artists Rights Society (ARS), NY / ADAGP, Paris
2023.

Bazaar, Vanity Fair ... No *haute-couture* collections to photograph.
But Man is not bothered. Man paints. Man draws. Man writes.
Man prepares the next great surrealist exhibition. His mind is never
at rest. He builds objects, edits photos. Man has fun. I don't need
to chase after work, Man's not stingy. He takes good care of me.
I spoil him, too. I leave him to his art, which is no rival.

We see the Éluards again one evening. Paul is giving a lecture at
the Comédie des Champs-Élysées. Nusch arrives with a bad cold,
but she's always there for her husband. "The Future of Poetry" is
the topic of the day. We have dinner together. Then we part ways,
promising to meet again very soon. Seeing us bundled up in our
winter coats, no one would ever imagine what we do together in
the summer in Mougins, stripped of our clothes.

In November, Man is very happy. The collection *Les Mains libres*
has just been published by Jeanne Bucher. There's even a deluxe

limited-edition collection. Man asks me if I can see myself in the collection. I say, "Yes, of course, at the end, the portrait." Then he smiles. He tells me to take a good look and lights a little cigar. He waits. "You're all over *Les Mains libres*, Ady! Look closely at my drawings." He flips through the pages of the collection. *Fil et Aiguille, C'est Elle, Le Don, La Lecture, L'Arbre-rose, Des nuages dans les mains, Pouvoir, Avignon, La Couture …* Yes, we're all over *Les Mains libres*. He stops on the *La Couture* page and smiles softly. "*Couper,* remember … *Koupé* means to make love in Martinican Creole …." With his fingertips, he caresses the woman and the scissors drawn on the paper. "Who will understand? The mystery will remain intact. But, believe me, art critics will certainly find a very clever interpretation for this drawing. You'll see, Ady!"

Finally! Joséphine Baker is a French citizen. She has married Jean Lion and can now start saying "Je t'aime" to France again. Lion is a rich, refined sugar broker. He claims to be a politician, but his mother is apparently Jewish. The wedding took place at the end of November, in Crèvecœur-le-Grand, in the Oise *département*. Rumor has it that the entire town was invited.

In December, Man sets off for Belgium. His paintings are being exhibited at the Palais des Beaux-Arts in Brussels. Being invited as a painter is a source of real satisfaction for him. Of real recognition. He is among peers, alongside painters with well-established reputations: Yves Tanguy and René Magritte. I stay alone in Paris, nice and warm, on Rue Denfert-Rochereau.

A friend, Marcel perhaps, tells us that Ernest Hemingway was in Paris in late December. He had just returned from Spain, after covering the war for the American press. Man remembers the twenties. I love these moments. It's just the two of us, with no audience. He isn't putting on a performance. He tells me about the days when, on Rue de Fleurus, he kept company with the American Gertrude Stein, a great friend of artists and an art collector. He shows me his photos of Hemingway, then a promising young writer and boxing enthusiast. He digs out photos of Stein from his files. "Almost twenty years ago now, she called them the lost generation! Fitzgerald, Cummings, Hemingway, Dos Passos … We'd just come out of a war. We didn't think there would ever be another one in the world …."

1938

I can picture myself. Waiting for the worst.

That year, I know, I pose and smile as I always do in photos. I look frivolous, so far removed from the Nazi threat. But in my heart of hearts, sorrow is burrowing deep tunnels. I come and go everywhere with Man. Our love is intact. We never tire of each other. Every night, we sleep snugly next to each other. We make love. We cuddle, we kiss, we comfort each other without really identifying it for what it is. Our Parisian life is a whirlwind: dinners, exhibitions, conferences, events of the small surrealist world. I laugh, even though I see shadows and ghosts everywhere. Dark thoughts run through my head. I have nightmares full of hurricanes, *nègres* hanging from tree branches, dying horses, swastikas, sickles, and hammers ...

I dance and I smile. What good is there in moping?

What's meant to be will be. Man knows that, too. We don't talk about what's eating away at us. We don't talk about Hitler, about the persecution of Jewish people under the watchful eye of the League of Nations. Man builds himself a solid shell with his art. I'm holding on thanks to love.

Love is art. Great art, even!

Love is built on bricks and mortar, on primary colors, flesh, and spirit.

Love is a mix of ingredients, like Shrubb, like a surrealist work.

If you're looking for love, you'll find it, even in the midst of horror.

Being in love with life means traveling in your head through wars and storms.

It means dreaming at all costs.

It means inventing never-before-seen landscapes and images to brighten our days.

Being in love means offering your body up to desire, giving and experiencing pleasure with confidence. Always being grateful for the joy of caresses and kisses.

In January, I'm looking forward to exploring the famous Exposition Internationale des Surréalistes held on the Rive Droite, at the Galerie des Beaux-Arts, Rue du Faubourg-Saint-Honoré. Man and Paul are very excited. Nusch and I join them there on opening night. The chic venue has been transformed by the surrealist spirit. Over two hundred and fifty works are on display. Some sixty artists have poured out the treasures of their imagination and nuggets of creativity, mixing the burlesque with the eclectic, the improbable with the scabrous, the mysterious with the marvelous, the absurd with the ridiculous.

The exhibition was curated by Messieurs Breton and Éluard. Duchamp, who is not present, staged the paintings and objects. Man is the Master of Light, that goes without saying. At the entrance to the gallery, each visitor is given a flashlight. Which is logical, since the rooms are plunged into semi-darkness.

What a wild imagination these artists have! A thousand coal sacks dangling over our heads, stuffed with old newspapers. Looking like ominous clouds in a tragic battlefield sky. The sacks released a fine, sinister black dust that really made Man laugh. I said to him, "The sky is falling on us." He replied, "We're better off laughing about it now!"

I can picture the pond surrounded by extravagant plants, the big bed with its loose sheets and hydrophilic carpet, Dalí's lobster – Aphrodisiac Telephone – the brazier, the sky of coal sacks, the mannequins dressed up by the artists in all different ways … Man's mannequin *Adieu Foulard* in prime position, with clay pitch pipes and bubbles in its hair, tassels hanging from its armpits, glass tears.

I remember the ceiling of another room, adorned with a fantastical array of white skirts and plastic legs. I still remember feeling a sense of unease and claustrophobia. The dark grottos, the piercing beams of the flashlights, the eerie, pallid faces of the visitors as they brought the works out of the darkness. Duchamp once said, "It's the viewer that makes the work." And then we had to endure dismal sounds blared from a loudspeaker: the bugles and boots of a Nazi army parade, deranged laughter from a psychiatric asylum … It smelled strongly of coffee. We walked on sand and dead leaves.

The exhibition ran from January 18 to February 22. I did not go back. Man went every day. I let him enjoy his art with his friends. I told him their exhibition terrified me. At the time, it all made me think of hell, a world of desperate lunatics hailing misfortune … Man retorted that the horror was not in art but in the world, right next to us, within reach of the artist's eyes, just like beauty.

Images have a way of sticking. What my eyes saw, my memory locked in a corner of my mind. And, through no fault of my own, this exhibition profoundly affected me. Like the evidence of a world lost in absurdity and barbarism.

I remained haunted by these images during the Occupation through to the sixties. In the real world, everything took me back to the Galerie des Beaux-Arts. I could picture Dalí's *Rainy Taxi*. The rain falling on the mannequin-passenger-customer trapped in the back seat. In the street, Parisian women's legs reminded me of the mannequin legs in the exhibition. Mannequin table legs. Mannequin legs pedaling from the ceiling. I saw a mannequin behind every woman. Every coat rack. Hat rack and blonde curls. Woman corseted in morality. Woman subjected to the murderous madness of men. Woman tested by war, woman hampered, hindered. Devout wife, mother, daughter, sister, dancer, pleasure-seeker, an ever-malleable object in the hands of men ...

In '40, when he left for the United States, I wondered if our love would have lasted if it hadn't been for that nasty war.

I have often thought so.

Deep down, what was I in his eyes? A portable woman, a Black doll, an exotic puppet? And yet I know that, for all those years, I was his muse, his lover, his friend, his companion, his confidante. Yes, I consoled Man many times. Stood by his side like a rock. Comforted him in difficult times. We loved each other passionately. And no one can take that away from me. But all stories come to an end, don't they?

Adieu foulard, adieu madras
Adieu grain d'or, adieu collier-chou ...

I wait for spring. It'll be here soon, at attention. It's the law of the four seasons in France. A certainty written into the calendar that I can rely on. Even if it's hailing and snowing in March, we still welcome springtime. Even in times of war, we cry out, "Spring is here! March winds and April showers bring May flowers and June bugs."

I wait for the war. Even though I'm anxious, I'm gradually getting used to the idea. The more I hear about it, the more familiar war becomes, like a gentle madness filled with whispering voices. Madmen get used to madness. Poor people to poverty, like Black people to their Blackness.

March 4 is my birthday. Red roses, a bottle of Cordon Rouge, a seafood dinner at La Coupole, and a night of lovemaking. Fortunately, there are always ways to make love, even in times of war ...

On March 13, 1938, the Germany of the Third Reich annexes Austria, relentlessly pursuing its plan to reunify the German-speaking territories. The *Anschluss*. France and the United Kingdom protest by diplomatic voices that go unheard.

I remember my brother came to visit me that day, all excited, with a newspaper under his arm. The *Anschluss* was featured on the front page, but he was interested in the sports pages. They were reporting on the victory of Panama Al Brown at the Palais des Sports in Paris. The triumph of a Black boxer against a white man, the Spaniard Baltasar Sangchili. "You see, Ady! Panama has taken his revenge! At the age of thirty-five, can you believe it? He'd been cheated. Made fun of. Everyone was betting on Sangchili to win. They said Panama was smoking opium, spending his time in cabarets instead of training ... That he thought himself a poet with his dear Cocteau, and that poets' playthings don't climb into the ring ... Look! Fifteen rounds! *La perle noire* lasted fifteen rounds ...."

A few weeks later, my older sister tells me that our uncle Adrien has died, back in the Caribbean. She says the family has to stick together. She sends her love and wishes me all the best.

I have very few memories of the summer of '38.

Yes, we drove down to Mougins. We returned to our friends, our rituals, the sun, la Garoupe beach, Île Sainte-Marguerite, love and lovemaking ...

Alas, there was a sense of doom in the air. Like a permanent sand cloud. A feeling of defeat. The impression of a faded charm. The end of a state of grace ...

Man spent a lot of time in his Antibes studio, which he intended to hand over to Pablo. His days already seemed numbered. He had a pressing need to continue and complete his work. To fill the hours. To create again and again ... He'd wake up in the morning with a project in mind. He wouldn't go to bed until he'd examined his sketchbook. He was sleeping very little.

I didn't let any of my fears show. I kept them locked up inside me, in my guts. I already had a constant stomachache. I kept smiling, to avoid making the days any heavier.

At the end of September, the Sudetenland region of

Ady Fidelin, Lee Miller and Nusch Eluard, Lambe Creek, Cornwall, England 1937 by Roland Penrose. Roland Penrose © Lee Miller Archives, England 2023. All rights reserved. leemiller.co.uk

Czechoslovakia was ceded to Germany under the Munich Agreement between Germany, the UK, Italy, and France.

No comment …

1939

I'm not a historian. But I can't erase the sequence of events from my memory.

March 15, Germany invades Czechoslovakia.

April 1st, end of the Spanish Civil War, victory for the fascists.

Pablo introduces us to his protégé, Wifredo Lam, a young anti-Franco Cuban painter. He had to flee Franco's Spain and recently arrived in Montparnasse. Man photographs him.

July 2, two Caribbean men are thrown out of the Victoria, a Parisian dance hall. Guilty of being Black.

It's official! Dous married Édouard, her Frenchman. It was on July 17, in Saint-Paulet-de-Caisson, in the Gard region. I couldn't attend the wedding. We hadn't gone to the south that summer. The uncertainty and imminence of war were already turning our lives upside down. I sent Aimée a bouquet of white roses and a note, "We wish you all the happiness in the world," signed, Man and Ady.

Even if we had been in Mougins, I don't think we could have made it to the wedding. We would have had to drive three or four hours to get to Saint-Paulet-de-Caisson. We wouldn't have found the strength to leave our friends and the beach, I'm sure of it.

September 1st, Hitler invades Poland. Conscription begins in France and the United Kingdom.

September 3, France and the United Kingdom declare war on Germany.

That same month, at the wheel of his 402 Peugeot, Man sets off for Antibes to clear out the studio he left to Picasso; some of his personal belongings are still there. On his return, he places his works in our house in Saint-Germain-en-Laye. He tells me that something unexpected happened on the way. Soldiers stopped him several times, but he had a pass. Then he had an accident. He was driving fast. In the rain, the 402 skidded around a bend, executed a spectacular somersault and landed on its four wheels two meters below, between two trees, right in a turnip field. More scared than hurt. Not a scratch. Miraculously, the Peugeot was in perfect condition in its turnip patch. A local mortician hitched up a horse and towed the car to a garage in a neighboring village. Man had to compensate the farmer and pay the mechanic to check the engine.

Man clowns around. He laughs and makes fun of himself while telling me about his surreal mishaps. I laugh because he's alive.

I think he wants to spin the story in a comic way to see me smile, dispel my fear of war a little. We learn about our dear friend Max Ernst's arrest. He's German, once again declared an enemy. He is interned in the Milles camp, near Aix-en-Provence. The bird of prey in a cage.

Man's parents urge him to go back to the United States. What will he do in America? What will become of his artworks?

"My life is in France, Ady, you know that. If I have to leave, will you come with me?" I nod. And, at the same time, I see the tall trees of America with *nègres* hanging from the branches. I see white people standing around laughing. I say, "Yes, my little Man, I'll come with you."

When I think back to those years, I see a tanker crushing everything in its path, worse than the 1928 Hurricane in the Caribbean.

My memory is of general panic, haste, jittery fear, helplessness. France is cornered. "There's no escape – it's going to happen!" Narcisse, my brother-in-law, keeps repeating. "We're going to war."

At Raymonde's, I hear that Admiral Robert has just landed in Fort-de-France, appointed High Commissioner of the Republic to the Caribbean. He arrived with the *Jeanne-d'Arc* and *Émile-Bertin* (two cruisers belonging to the French navy), an aircraft carrier, an oil tanker, and hundreds of marines ... In Guadeloupe, people are saying that Hitler is going to win the war and will soon reimpose slavery.

"The war will spare no one ... It's not even worth going back home. The situation there will not be much better. It's better to stay in France," Narcisse declares.

One evening, a dancer tells me that some Jewish people she knew, from Austria and Poland, have gone to Haiti. They had taken refuge in Paris, but people were starting to look at them sideways. Apparently, in exchange for investing in the country, they became Haitian citizens.

A feeling of being shredded to pieces by history, which couldn't give a damn about Man and Ady's little love story. Couldn't care less about art and all the rest.

Desnos tells us that *Pigments*, Damas's poetry collection, has just been banned by the censors, deemed subversive and a threat to national security.

I remember *Notebook of a Return to the Native Land*, published in the periodical *Volontés*.

I remember the comical, ugly *nigger* in the *Notebook*. I remember the sneers of the white women on the streetcar. I remember struggling with difficult words and rereading each sentence in the *Notebook* over and over again without fully understanding the meaning. *And the tawer was Poverty. And the tawer was Poverty ... And the tawer was Poverty ...*[4]

I looked up words in the dictionary. *Taw*: to turn white, referring to animal hides. *Tawer*: a person whose trade is to taw animal hides.

---

4 Césaire, *Notebook of a Return to the Native Land*, p. 29.

I remember a lively conversation with my cousin and his student friends. In June, two Guadeloupean men were turned away at the Victoria, a dance hall on Boulevard Saint Michel. "Nice guys named Camprasse and Chalus. You haven't heard the news, Ady! Come down from your ivory tower! Other Caribbean people went to see if it was true ... And it is: now they refuse to serve Black people drinks in Paris. I'll spare you the racist and negrophobic comments, Ady ... Students were expelled, arrested by the police, and charged with inciting rebellion. The Union des travailleurs nègres took action. Satineau alerted Mandel, Minister of the Colonies, who called on the Minister of the Interior ...."

The next day, a dancer friend tells me that the Victoria is temporarily closed for safety works.

I tell myself that the good life in Paris is well and truly over. Like Césaire, I'm thinking of a return to my native land. Better to live through poverty, hurricanes, and earthquakes than a white man's war.

I remember Man painting *Le Beau Temps*, *Fair Weather*, on Rue Denfert-Rochereau. I pose in front of the painting, brush in hand. I smile. He photographs me. I'm accustomed to painting the backgrounds of Man's pictures. I help him, it's really not much work at all. While he prepares his colors, he tells me how to spread the paint.

On the *Fair Weather* canvas, there are two large mannequins that look a little like Giorgio De Chirico's, trees that resemble pitchforks, our house in Saint-Germain-en-Laye, Man and I as two shadows embracing behind the bay window; two monstrous beasts in a fight to the death on the roof. Two ruthless creatures escaped from a nightmare Man had one night when cannons thundered far away from our little paradise ...

VII

My body would like to kiss you in your sleep.

My body would like to be sleeping in the middle of the night and in that darkness be awoken because you kissed me.

My night knows no dream more beautiful nor more cruel today than this.

My night screams and tears its veils, my night collides with its own silence but your body is nowhere to be found.

I miss you so very much. And your words. And your color.

Day will soon dawn.

Frida Kahlo[1]

---

1 Quoted in Gérard de Cortanze, *Frida Kahlo. La beauté terrible* (Paris: Éditions Albin Michel, 2011), p. 123 (our translation).

1940 and beyond ...

On April 18, 1940, my sisters organized a lovely party for my niece's ninth birthday. It's just like back home: *chaudeau* and sweet bread, lemonade and little pastries filled with guava jam, which my brother-in-law gobbles down between glasses of Negrita rum. My niece is a real chatterbox, a true Parisienne. She gives me a big kiss when I hand her her present: a gold-plated chain with a crucifix on it, to protect her from Hitler. I spend the afternoon laughing and cuddling the children under Raymonde's blank stare. She's depressed about the war. I suppose she's also still angry at me for leading such a peculiar life. Naturally, she's heard about Man, the nude photos my younger brother saw on Rue Denfert-Rochereau. She can't fathom that it's all art. She's never met Man. No opportunities to ... It makes me sad.

Narcisse hasn't said a word all afternoon. But when I'm about to leave, he blurts out, reproachfully, "Do you still follow what's going on back home, Ady? Have you heard that Admiral Robert is ruling the Martiniquais with an iron fist? Do you know that Governor Sorin has arrived in Guadeloupe?"

I say, "Yes, sort of ...."

He glares at me, "No you don't, you're a Parisian now. You dance ... You pose in magazines for your American ... You've forgotten your roots."

I don't understand. I leave. The bitter look in my sister's husband's eyes hounds me as I hurry to get home before curfew.

Ever since France declared war on Germany, we've been waiting for the hostilities to begin. "Here it goes! Paname is dressed for battle," sighs Man. Walls of sandbags block the streets. Trenches are being dug all around Paris. We see bombardiers on guard duty stationed in various, perhaps strategic, locations. In the Jardin du Luxembourg, there's an anti-aircraft gun aimed at the sky – a cannon against a hateful tide. Under the blue lights that have appeared on street corners, the anguish is palpable on people's faces.

Fear and gloom abound. In the train stations and corridors of the *métro*, along the gray sidewalks, on the Boulevard du Montparnasse. Parisians walk with glum faces, hurried steps, and hunched backs, their gas masks slung over their shoulders in pewter cans. Sugar is rationed, as well as tobacco, coffee, and petrol. The black market kicks off. Lines stretch out in front of grocery stores. Every now and then, a siren wails. Time to find shelter, fast. The windows of stores, restaurants, and apartments are latticed with strips of adhesive paper. Rumors of imminent attack spread in conversations. On brasserie terraces, at café counters, in the lounges of Haussmann buildings, hatred of Jewish people spreads insidiously in fervent debates. And in the pale skies of Paris, the aerostats supposed to signal German invasion float high like friendly balloons.

The Nazi ogre is lurking in wait beyond the border. He's not yet satiated. After Poland, Czechoslovakia, Bohemia, and Moravia – all nations he made short work of – he's invaded the Netherlands, Belgium, and Luxembourg ... War is on Paris's doorstep.

In the spring of '40, Man photographs the latest fashions for *Harper's Bazaar*. Many of his American colleagues have arrived in Paris. That year, *haute couture* houses are competing fiercely in terms of creativity, seemingly determined to demonstrate their resilience in the face of Hitler's aggressive rhetoric, to show that while France may be populated by degenerates, the art and freedom of designers would not tremble behind the Maginot Line.

Photographing the models was no mean feat. Man works night and day, in a mad rush, for two weeks straight. Magazine editors and buyers are on edge. It's all unbridled cavalcades, shouts, and exhortations to go faster. Sinister sirens wail at all hours, signaling an enemy attack. Man has to interrupt his photo shoots immediately and turn off the lights. Dressed in their evening gowns, the panicked models run down the stairs to take refuge in the cellars. As for Man, he goes to the dressing rooms with a book or newspaper, waiting patiently for the alarm to pass.

Man is reluctant to go down to the air-raid shelters. He did once. Got stuck in the dark with crying kids and petrified women. Felt like a sheep in a docile flock being led to the slaughterhouse. He'll never be seen down there again. So, if he's outside when the siren sounds, he goes into a café or takes shelter under a *porte cochère*. If – by some miracle – he finds himself near a garden or park, he sits down to read or lies down on a bench. One day, a policeman asks him to explain his behavior, and Man replies that he's claustrophobic. What's bound to happen will happen. The officer leaves without any further questions.

On June 3, 1940, the sky darkens, suddenly laden with enemy Luftwaffe planes. Their mission: bomb the air bases of the Île-de-France region and the Citroën factories that had been repurposed for arms production. In a single afternoon, Messerschmitt, Junkers, and Henkeil planes claim the lives of over two hundred and fifty people, leaving almost seven hundred wounded, most of them civilians. Some Caribbeans were hit. Some died. I knew at least two of them. Dashing, joking *nègres* who used to sweep the ladies off their feet on Saturday nights at the Bal Blomet.

I have a constant stomachache. I pray that the war won't come. Like my mother, I pray for the living and the dead. I pray for peace in the world. I feel like I've walked into a nightmare I can't escape. I even go to Saint Sulpice to light candles and kneel.

The German army has spread out north of the Maginot Line. The British meet defeat at Dunkirk. Debacle! Normandy is invaded. The Nazis arrive. Their planes fly over Paris. The government is on the run.

And then, the fatal blow: Parisians are ordered to evacuate the capital within twenty-four hours.

Exodus, a biblical nightmare. Millions of refugees from the north have already headed south. Now it's time for the French to pack up and leave. In one fell swoop, leave everything as it is, without looking back. Flee in the face of the enemy, their swastikas, their Führer, their tanks ...

Even today, fifty years later, I wonder how this abomination ever began, how it ever continued unchecked.

Why did we stand by and do nothing?

Why did we allow this Nazi monster to gain traction in Germany?

I can picture us that morning, Man and me, on Rue Denfert-Rochereau, hastily gathering our things. We are on edge. Man paces around the studio. There are so many works we could take with us. Why bother? He tells me not to bother packing any frills, just to take a small suitcase of clothes. In the kitchen, we put a bottle of Cordon Rouge champagne and a few cans of sardines in a basket. We slam the door. We dash off to Man's mechanic, who agrees to sell us a few extra cans of petrol. Off to Saint-Germain-en-Laye. We flee Paris, like all the other Parisians. Like everyone else: the baker, the color merchant, the flustered families, the elderly, the hairdressers, the laborers, the railroad workers, the pimps, the harlots, the bourgeois from the nicer neighborhoods, the government ...

We drive west, while the flood of Parisians makes their getaway toward the south. Thousands of people on the streets. On foot, rushing, racing. Cars topped with mattresses and all manner of things, bicycles pulling trailers crammed with bundles, strollers, wheelbarrows, carts. Rickety carts, snotty-nosed kids in laceless shoes ... Haggard-looking cats and dogs. Bird cages ... More mattresses, trunks, cases from the last war, and suitcases, suitcases, suitcases ...

Helplessly, I hold my trembling hands together. My stomach hurts so much. This is war. This is war looming on the horizon. It's night falling in the middle of the day. It's the 1928 hurricane coming back to visit us. To wreak havoc once again. Killing, assassinating, ripping everything to shreds, with no regard for where the blows will land. Narcisse prophesized that war would spare no one, not even women or children. War is as blind as a hurricane.

I remember the day of the exodus ... a long and very dark tunnel with no exit in sight. I feel the weight of History in my bones, writhing in pain. I already know the horror to come. This is only the beginning ...

On the road, Man ridicules everything and anything while I smile at his jokes. He laughs at the people who have taken their birds with them in cages. It's a beautiful, sunny day. He tells me we look like we're going on a picnic, with our little basket, champagne, and cans of sardines in oil. How majestic! It's true, our car does seem quite empty compared to the others, overloaded with people, packages and objects, each more unlikely than the last.

Man laughs to keep from jumping up and down with rage. I smile to keep from collapsing.

Fewer people in the neighborhoods we pass through the west of Paris. Deserted streets. A policeman stops us. "Where are you going? The Germans are approaching from the west!" Man proclaims his American nationality and declares himself neutral. I, the Black woman, sink into my seat. The policeman lets us go. Man takes off at full speed. We drive through abandoned villages. Not a soul to be seen. Stores closed. Man races along.

I watch the landscape unfold, the abandoned fields, the plane trees that bear no fruit, and I think of the *niggers* hanging from tree branches over in Georgia.

On the Place du Château in Saint-Germain-en-Laye, we are surprised to find the restaurants open, terraces crowded with customers and beleaguered refugees. We take a seat. All around us, the tables are buzzing with speculation. "Peace, war, the Bosch, the defeated army, France's honor ...." Unanswered questions flow here and there: "Good Lord! What's going to happen now? What will become of us? When will this nightmare end?" At some tables, people are dejected. At others, they are restless and rancorous. Children run around, play, laugh, whimper in their mothers' arms.

I think of the bastard children in the Rhineland, and the sterilization program intended for them.

I wonder what I'm doing here, so far from my island. I feel so foreign. I'm a Caribbean girl, a Guadeloupean. What do I have to do with all this European mess? Germany wants to colonize the world. All this business is a notorious affliction of the Old Continent. They did the same thing in Africa, Asia, in the Americas.

I remember a friend of mine studying at the Sorbonne, who used to talk about the woes of the Herero people in Africa ...

At the beginning of the twentieth century, German settlers begin to realize that Namibia is a land of great wealth. Copper, diamonds, gold, uranium ... The Hereros are ordered to leave their land. Resistance fighters are exterminated, the wells in the bush are poisoned. They could revolt and die under cannon fire. Leave and die in the desert. Die either way. Over sixty thousand Hereros perish in this genocide. The survivors are herded into concentration camps surrounded by barbed wire. The conditions are appalling.

Forced labor, abuse, malnutrition, murder, hanging, rape, sterilization of the women.

I think of the *nègres marrons* from my old uncle's stories ... I think of the Nuremberg Laws, the Code noir ...

I think of the horrors human beings are capable of, the organized, legitimized, legalized barbarism, of the ...

Man has started whistling. He smiles at me. I return his smile. We're in the same boat and he finds the courage to smile.

Yes, I have to be like Man: not let myself be consumed by all this human misery. I'm just a little dancer from Guadeloupe. I can't change any of this calamity. I just want to keep a little of my joy alive inside me ... *Unconcerned but not indifferent.*

Then, gradually, the world outside slips away. The voices and clattering of cutlery become a peaceful, continuous murmur, similar to the wind that once blew through the reeds in Mougins; like a lullaby that rocks babies to sleep. Man and I are in our glass bubble, sheltered from the turmoil. We eat and drink as if it were our last meal, a feast for kings.

I remember the harsh taste of wine in my throat. I recall the lovely sunshine that hit my face that day, the way I looked at Man. Like a savior, a knight, a protector, an elegant and kind prince. I whisper to him, "I don't know how this is all going to end, my little Man ... But I want you to know that the years I've spent by your side have been wonderful. I'll never forget the happy days we shared together." He smiles again. Before furrowing his brow and looking into the distance, as if he can read our future in the blurry line drawn between the sky and the treetops in the distance. Then he takes my hand from the table and squeezes it tightly, without a word.

When we arrive at the house in Saint-Germain-en-Laye, Man hastily retrieves some of his works. He turns off the water, gas, and electricity. He checks every door and window meticulously. He leaves out money and a note for the cleaning lady who comes every day. He writes instructions for the workers. I have to give up my beautiful bicycle. I'd have liked to take it along too, hang it on the front of the car, as I've seen others do, but Man says no, out of the question. He himself is refraining from taking his infinitely more precious works with him. So, my bicycle ...

After that, we head south.

We drive at a snail's pace. The exodus route is so long and

exhausting, beneath the wrath of the sky dumping angry leaflets and the hum of hostile planes all set to strafe us. Two days and two nights before we reach Les Sables-d'Olonne. During the day, Man drives. At night, we sleep in the car, off the road. When fuel is running low, Man always manages to get some.

At last, we find a hotel in Les Sables-d'Olonne and a little room under the roof, the last available, with no windows. All the hotels are fully booked, filled with refugees: Belgians, Dutch, French. A night's rest in a real bed ...

The next morning, we go downstairs for breakfast. The atmosphere in the dining room is bleak and anxious. We get funny looks. At some tables, people chatter away. Others seem to be plotting something. "Quiet! The Marshal is about to speak!" the boss suddenly shouts as he turns up the radio. Immediate silence. Pétain presents us with a *fait accompli*: the armistice has been signed. The Germans have taken over Paris – now declared an open city. No, the ceasefire obtained from the Germans is not a disgrace for the country. The parties have agreed on a demarcation line separating France into occupied and free zones. Refugees are requested to wait for new instructions before moving, to allow the victorious troops to circulate. "The war is over," he concludes. Then the Marseillaise sounds. Everyone stands up, stunned. The moment is solemn. We cry, we hug. With wet eyes, we sing the verses of the national anthem.

I don't know if they are tears of joy or dismay. Man murmurs that we would have been better off not leaving Paris. "All this fuss for nothing! Back to square one. Except that now we're in the occupied zone ... The Krauts won't be long."

Days go by as we wait for the Nazis. In the hotel restaurant, rations are dwindling on our plates. We drink coffee water for breakfast. The milk runs out. Our meals are frugal. They serve us a bland potato soup, white beans, and, at best, a thin slice of cold ham. Anyone unhappy about paying full board can either go elsewhere or complain to the Bosch.

The first cars of the German General Staff landed on the eleventh day after our arrival in Les Sables-d'Olonne, followed by ominous trucks and tanks. The Marshal urged the French to put on a brave face against the invaders. Astonished, people flocked to see the bellicose war machines go by. A burlesque parade, like a Mardi Gras in the heart of Pointe-à-Pitre. Every window overlooking the main square is crowded. No one flinches when the soldiers emerge from the trucks and rush toward the bank and the town hall. The doors are closed. The Germans draw their pistols and blow the locks, just like in the movies. Fortunately, the bank vaults were emptied earlier. A pack of soldiers rush into the building, machine guns in hand. A minute later, they're on the rooftops, holding us at gunpoint.

I pinch myself. No, I'm not dreaming. This is actually the real world.

They are here, flesh and bone. Armed to the teeth.

All around, the compact crowd clench their fists and ruminate on their misfortune. One old geezer casts an unkind glance at my little Man. And he sputters his bitterness, "Oh! In my day, we wouldn't have given in so easily!" I feel like cursing at him in Creole. Man pulls me by the sleeve and we walk away.

Years later, on television, I saw June 14, 1940, in Paris. Restored images, frozen and crackling, from footage taken at the time, with commentary in a nasal voice. There were horses when the German troops marched down the Champs-Élysées. Horses ridden by proud cavalrymen trotted ahead of hundreds of Nazi foot soldiers. They were goose-stepping, determined and implacable. Like real robots! It was in 1970, I think. I was already married to André Art. He remembered the tanks, the cannons, the Nazi salute, the military band, the bugles, and bass drums ... He remembered the petrified faces of Parisians in the face of this display of force and intimidation. The tears and the white handkerchiefs ... As I watched the horses in harness, their coats shiny, I thought again of Paul, of his poetry.

> *Lonely horse, lost horse,*
> *Sick from rainfall ...*
> *And, loyal to the stones,*
> *Lonely horse waits for nightfall*
> *So he does not have to*
> *See clearly and flee ...*[2]

In Les Sables, the Nazis occupy the area like masters and lords. Houses and cars are requisitioned. Everyone has to report

---

2 Éluard, "Cheval," in *Les animaux*, p. 18 (our translation).

to headquarters with their identity papers. Cunning Man keeps his car from being seized. I think he removed a plug that stops the engine from starting. He talks nonsense to one of the officers, presents himself as American, and thus neutral. He is left alone.

The Germans allow us to leave Les Sables-d'Olonne after three weeks. We are forbidden to go south and to cross the demarcation line between the free and occupied zones.

Alas, our plan was to join Picasso and Dora in Royan. Man was also planning to reach Bordeaux, the Atlantic coast. He'd heard that American ships were moored there, waiting to collect and repatriate American nationals, as well as potential exiles ... He'd thought of driving to Arcachon, where Duchamp and Mary Reynolds were expecting us. Maybe get to Spain ... I wanted to go and see Aimée and her husband Édouard in Saint-Paulet-de-Caisson, in the Gard ...

Under no circumstances does Man want to return to Nazi-infested Paris. But without a pass, we must accept it.

I don't remember much about our trip back to Paris. I think I'm stunned. The whole thing makes no sense. The situation is comical and pitiful. I feel like one of the dogs circling the Place de la Victoire in Pointe-à-Pitre the night before the 1928 hurricane. Like them, I can sense a great misfortune coming, but there's no way to escape, nowhere to take refuge. Without saying much, I watch Man drive straight ahead, scrounging for petrol here and there. Lost in thought, I watch the names of towns and villages roll by, the monotonous road, the enchanted woods and clearings, the spring in the surrounding fields, the sweet France of Charles Trenet. Nantes, the long lines at the gas pumps. Angers, Le Mans ... Everywhere, people on the run who, like us, are looking for an escape.

Along the roads, prisoners of war from the French army. Columns of bewildered young men led by German soldiers who don't look much older. And these defeated men embody a demoralized France, heading for disaster. France fallen from its pedestal. The mother country colonized, like the land of the Herero people. An entire country unceremoniously cast adrift ...

After this absurd interlude in Les Sables-d'Olonne, we are back in Saint-Germain-en-Laye at the end of June. Thankfully, the house escaped requisition. But the garage door has been smashed in. My beautiful bicycle is gone. I start sobbing like a baby. It's the first time I've cried this much since my parents died, since I arrived in France. The first time Man has seen the color of my despair. I'm crying over a bicycle … So, baffled, not knowing how to console me, my little Manichou promises to buy me a solid gold bicycle bedecked with mink. It's the kind of magic pirouette only he knows how to perform. We laugh, of course. He gives me a long kiss, then starts tickling me.

What else can we do in such a mess?

Laugh in the face of sorrow. Hold each other. Whisper untrue words. And go through the everyday motions that offer reassurance in the darkness.

Give our days meaning.

Take a bath, change the sheets, make love, prepare dinner …

Wait for the worst without wincing in pain.

Keep a brave face, no matter what.

Off to Paris, back to Rue Denfert-Rochereau, to see how the Germans have disfigured our Paname.

We find many stores closed. The German military, all-powerful in their gray-green uniforms. Very few cars. Limousines and other requisitioned luxury automobiles carry the Führer's henchmen on their dirty business, along the streets to the Hôtel Crillon, where the Third Reich has established its headquarters for the next thousand years. A sinister Nazi flag flies from the balcony, a way of marking their territory. On the rooftops, machine guns keep watch day and night. On the Place de la Concorde, laborers demolish balustrades and dismantle bronze statues. In the Saint-Germain-des-Prés district, the Hôtel Lutetia now houses the German intelligence and counter-espionage service. The occupied zone is placed under the strict control of the Bosch's military administration, who have appropriated the Hôtel Majestic. The names on Parisian street signs are in German, to make it easier for the enemy forces to get around. New notices appear in cafés and brasseries, stating that the premises are reserved exclusively for Aryans. And there are all the posters plastered on the walls, showing the German as a friendly invader. We are now on Teutonic time. All clocks have been set forward an hour. Paname and Berlin beat in unison.

The swastika casts its shadow over Paris. I feel like vomiting.

On June 18, speaking from London over the BBC, General de Gaulle issued an appeal to the people of France. "Nothing is lost … France is not alone … She has a vast empire behind her …

This war is a worldwide war ... In the universe, there are all the necessary means to one day crush our enemies ... the flame of the French resistance must not be extinguished and will not be extinguished ...."

The Appeal of June 18 is on everyone's lips. But, for the time being, Paris is occupied, and the flame of resistance is burning like a small candle in a breeze. Man is seriously considering returning to the United States. Yet Parisian life seems to be picking up again. We've got to entertain the Bosch! Theaters and cinemas have been instructed to reopen, and artists told to report immediately for work, to dance and sing, act and what have you ... And among the new occupants wining and dining in restaurants, regular customers return, jaded, forced to smile in the face of despair.

Radio Paris tells us that the French government and parliament are entrenched in Vichy. On July 10, the National Assembly votes to give full powers to Marshal Pétain.

Man has no commissions. No one comes to the studio to be photographed anymore. When he went to the American embassy, he was told that the ambassador, declared *persona non grata* by the victors, was in Washington. He paints despair, the fair weather having disappeared.

In August, General de Gaulle is sentenced to death for treason and desertion abroad in time of war.

German soldiers are everywhere. With their weapons, their war machines, their malevolent landmines.

I seldom dare go out anymore. One day, on my way back from my sister's place, German officers, lounging like lords in a big black convertible, start driving slowly alongside me. I pick up the pace on the sidewalk. They want me to hop in with them. They offer me money, furs, and jewelry, even a luxury car and villa, if I like. I pretend I can't hear them. But they insist. So, I ask them if they can't see that I'm the wrong color. They say they don't care. They just want to have a good time with me. "It's all just politics. Germans love all things exotic ...."

The atmosphere in Montparnasse is strange. Some Parisians keep a low profile and walk with their heads down. Then there are those who openly collude with the enemy. They sit happily on brasserie terraces, thick as thieves with the Bosch. The receptionist at a hotel that Man frequented before the Occupation acts like he doesn't recognize him. He sports a Nazi uniform and captain's stripes. The hotel lobby is swarming with Germans. Man doesn't flinch. He's American, first and foremost, not Jewish …

A week later, Man finally gets both our travel passes from the German headquarters. "We'll start by heading to the free zone," he tells me. "And then we'll see what to do next."

Man prepares to leave for America. Return to his native land. He puts his papers and belongings in order. He takes down his large paintings and rolls up the canvases in protective cases. Lefebvre-Foinet, his paint merchant, agrees to keep them safe until things get back to normal. Man also gives him proxy for his possessions. Lefebvre-Foinet is a man he can trust.

I'm in a kind of haze this whole time. I see him coming and going, scrambling around, making phone calls left and right. He tells me he's going to leave the car in the garage in Saint-Germain-en-Laye. "Yes, Man," I say. "OK, Man." He says he'll be right back. "OK!" I say, "See you later, Man."

One morning, I get up. I prepare breakfast. I do everything robotically. I put on makeup. I get all dolled up without really knowing why. I ask Man to bring me some silk stockings. Out of habit, I want to make myself beautiful for him, to stave off misfortune. And then the war catches up with us. He comes back, his face defeated. He tells me that the Bosch have bought all the stockings in the store. I feel like I've fallen into a black hole.

Another day, he talks about a train to Portugal. The train leaves in the evening. I have to pack. He says we'll probably be back in a few months. "*Han han!*" I reply. "Pack your bags, Ady," he says. "And go easy on the frills!"

"*Han han!*" Haze.

Pain in my stomach.

My heart drowned in tears.

"The Éluards are going to join Joël Bousquet in Carcassonne," he says. "Dora and Pablo have sent news. They're still in Royan …." He talks and talks … "Breton and Jacqueline arrived in Salon-de-Provence. Dalí and Gala hope to set sail for America …."

"*Han han!*"

He talks and fidgets. I hear nothing. I sink into myself.

I stay in bed. I watch him pack suitcases and put away his beautiful rayographs, drawings, objects, clay pipes, the *Minotauromachy* etching that Picasso gave him as a thanks for the portrait of Dora. He takes his tuxedo, his patent leather shoes, a few shirts and pants, a camera.

"Get up, Ady!" he says, trying to pull me out of bed.

"No, no, Man," I say.

"What? No? What's the matter with you, Ady?"

I look at the rectangle left on the wall by the last painting Man has taken down. The white of the rectangle is slightly brighter than the rest of the wallpaper.

I still think about that white rectangle some days. Years later ...

I tell myself that, if I'd been a painter, this is how I could have painted Man's absence from my life: a silent white rectangle in a whiter shade on a white wall. It's a perfect, understated geometric figure that you wouldn't have expected, hidden behind the canvas. Also, the memory of something that has been and will be no more. The mystery of vanished colors. The mark of passing time. An insignificant trace that tells a forgotten story.

"No, Manou. I'm not leaving this time. I'm staying in Paris. I can't leave my family ...."

He gets worked up. "*What!* Your family! That's an excuse, Ady. There's something else ... I have been assured that, from Spain, we can reach Portugal. Then set sail for the United States. We'll be safe there ...."

I shake my head.

He gets angry for the first time since we met. His black eyes are two big glass beads, quizzical and confused. He mixes English with French. He paces back and forth. He lights a cigarette and I watch the ashes fly all over the place.

Then his anger subsides suddenly, like a winter wind in the wrong season. He sits on the edge of the bed. His face is sad. He says, "You're abandoning me, Ady ...."

I wish I could console him, but I can't. I feel all limp and weak.

Man leaves in the afternoon. He needs to bid farewell to his beloved Montparnasse before leaving Paris. During this pilgrimage, he revisits his early years, the places he lived and created his art. The Val-de-Grâce workshop, the Hôtel Lenox on Rue Delambre, the studio on Rue Campagne-Première, the Hôtel Istria ...

I don't eat anything at all that day. I talk to Man's head sculpted in plaster. With my eyes closed, to take a trip through our love affair, I caress the sculpture's face with my fingertips. The hair, the nose, the lips ... Afterwards, I wander in my robe from the kitchen to the living room, from the photo studio to the bathroom. From the bedroom to Man's office. I traipse around in Man's robe. In his scent.

And then I decide to call my little brother on the phone. "Man has no choice but to return to America, because of the Nazis. Someone will have to go with him to Gare Saint-Lazare. You're going to help him with his two suitcases. Come on! Don't let me down, you hear ...."

When Man returns from his walk, he declares that Montparnasse is gray-green, foul-smelling, worse than a nightmare.

Haze.

He signs blank checks for me and tells me to empty his accounts. We kiss. He promises to write, to send news.

Adieu foulard, adieu madras …
Adieu grain d'or, adieu collier-chou …
Doudou an mwen i ka pati
Hélas, hélas, sé pou toujou.

Adieu, dear Man …

He writes to me at the beginning of August. Tells of his trek from Paris to Hendaye, German and Spanish soldiers on both sides of the border, weapons and uniforms everywhere. Finally, Portugal! Lisbon, from where he sends me a wire. He waits. There are countless refugees trying to register at the American embassy. The administrative formalities are tedious.

Finally, Man boards an American Export Line passenger ship, the *Excambion*, on August 6, 1940.

The war got the better of our love.

Man once told me that he had been given a prediction a long time ago. He could expect to change his life every ten years. He couldn't wait to see what fate had in store for him. He looked like a kid in front of a bag of candy …

The two of us only stayed together for five years, because of the war. The fault lies with Hitler and all those who let him get away with it.

I haven't believed in predictions since. No, we know nothing about the future. We only know that we're going to die one day.

With Man gone, my life changed, that's for sure.

I picked myself up. Had no choice but to ...

So many years have passed since I lived in this poor, disfigured Paris.

I shudder at the memory of the swastika flying from the Eiffel Tower, from the pediments of the requisitioned hotels and beautiful Haussmann buildings.

I can picture all the signs written in German. Yes, we are well and truly on German time. Everywhere, German propaganda posters remind us of this, along with the old, withered figure of the Marshal. WORK, FAMILY, HOMELAND ... Marianne statues are packed away in cupboards in the town halls. There was talk of national revolution and collaboration with the enemy. The mail is censored. On every street corner, feldgrau uniforms, armed Nazi soldiers, untrustworthy French policemen.

What else could he have done but leave ...

Finding enough to eat. That's what's on people's minds from morning till night during the Occupation. You have to have your ration coupons if you don't want to starve to death. An adult is entitled to 275 grams of bread a day. 300 grams of meat per week, 100 grams of fat, and 70 grams of cheese. 500 grams of sugar, 200 grams of rice, and 250 grams of pasta per month. The franc has lost all value. Prices everywhere seem exorbitant. Of course, the black market is thriving. Some people are fattening up, others are starving. At Les Halles, kids rummage through the garbage cans. People fight for a lump of butter, kidneys, a pound of rancid tripe, stale bread ... People grow vegetables in the Tuileries gardens. It's the only topic of conversation: ersatz goods, ration cards, supply notes. Food is an obsession that colonizes our thoughts and drains all our energy. There's a general shortage. Chocolate has disappeared from the shelves. We eat rutabaga and Jerusalem artichokes. We drink coffee made with chickpeas, roasted acorns, chicory. We grow accustomed to margarine. Jam becomes a luxury. We find cigarettes made from sunflower leaves. For want of leather, I see people wearing shoes with wooden or cork soles. Bartering is the name of the game: a ham for a gold watch, a rabbit for a small bag of coal ...

It's also difficult to keep warm in those years. Coal and electricity are in short supply. I freeze in the apartment on Rue Denfert-Rochereau, which I soon give up for a room under the roof. I can no longer afford the rent. Together with my brother and cousins, I move all of Man's works to Saint-Germain-en-Laye.

No more black cabs. Bicycle cabs have invaded Paris. I can no longer afford a cab anyhow. I take the *métro*, walk for hours to avoid spending money.

No, he had no choice ...

What else could he have done?

So sweet. He wanted to take me with him.

In September '40, a series of Nazi orders are issued, aiming to stipulate the criteria for qualifying as Jewish. Jewish people are required to register with prefectural authorities. They are then excluded from certain professions and dispossessed of their property as part of the Aryanization process. Jewish civil servants are dismissed. Foreign Jews lose their French citizenship.

I tell myself that, yes, Man did do the right thing by leaving before it was too late.

My brother-in-law Narcisse predicts that Black people will soon face the same fate. They'll have to register. They'll be banned from certain professions ... Raymonde retorts that Black people can't hide the fact that they're Black. They give themselves up automatically. There's no need to register. Two-person conversation.

What else could Man have done?

During the Occupation, I often wondered whether, at some point, Parisians felt that they too had been colonized. A poor defeated people stripped of their identity, cornered, obliged to collaborate with the terrorizer. Dispossessed of their land. Worth less than cattle in the eyes and ledgers of the invaders.

I don't know ...

On the Islands, it's *Vichy in the tropics*! Work, Family, Homeland. Admiral Robert and Governor Sorin keep the Black people in line. The regime is racist and makes no secret of it. Most Black mayors are dismissed and replaced by *békés*. Political parties and trade unions are dissolved. The press is muzzled, and postal mail routinely scoured. At school, on empty stomachs, children sing the Marshal's praises and salute the flag of the bitter mother country. In classrooms, the crucifix hangs above the chalkboards. Gatherings, balls, and carnivals are forbidden. Drinking rum is a criminal offense.

We Caribbean Parisians talk about what's going on back there. It seems like the population is under surveillance day and night by armed sailors from the *Jeanne* cruiser. They roam the streets like lords and barge into *cases* unannounced. You have to keep a low profile. They conduct a census of Jewish people, like in Paris. Opponents of the Vichy regime are hunted down, arrested and tortured, thrown in jail, shackled, condemned *in absentia* like de Gaulle, even exiled to the penal colony of French Guiana, on the Salvation Islands with no way back. And then, from 1942 onwards, following the American blockade, hardship falls even more ferociously on Guadeloupe and Martinique. People go hungry. There's a famine. No more flour from France, no more oil, no more salt or soap. Meat is scarce. People get by as best they can. Children are stunted. A return to slavery lingers in everyone's mind.

In the waters of the Caribbean Sea, the *Jeanne*'s patrol boats survey the coastline and track down potential exiles. Neighboring English lands – Dominica, Antigua, and St. Lucia – see French fishing canoes rolling ashore at all hours. On board, young dissidents ready to join *General Microphone*'s Free French Forces. Ready to escape once again, listen to de Gaulle and help France, die for freedom ... Above all, never return to the days of slavery.

The deathly years go by.
Scattered memories of this wretched time.
News from friends ...
Mary Reynolds remained in Paris, in her apartment on Rue Hallé, until '42. She took part in the Resistance from the very start of the Occupation. Threatened with arrest by the Gestapo, she found time to pick up *Les Amoureux* from Lefebvre-Foinet, before joining Duchamp and Man in America.

At the start of the war, Lee Miller returned to London and to Roland. Then she started working for *Vogue*, where she moved heaven and earth to be appointed war correspondent for the US Army. In June '44, she photographed nurses and wounded patients at American surgical units in Normandy. She was in Saint-Malo and Omaha Beach, right in the middle of the D-Day landings. Then she hitchhiked to Paname to be there for the grand day of the Liberation. No, when she returned to Paris in August '44, I didn't see Lee. Nusch told me that she had undergone a metamorphosis. So long, evening gowns and glamor. Henceforth, Lee sports big combat boots, military pants, and shirts. Toward the end of the war, in '45, she pushed on to the Buchenwald and Dachau concentration camps. Her photos appeared in *Vogue*: liberating Soviet and American soldiers, Nazi guards, gaunt prisoners in striped uniforms, trucks filled with emaciated corpses. A ransacked Europe … Ruins everywhere, gutted cities, haggard refugees, hunger, destitution … For *Life*, she posed naked in Hitler's bathtub.

Max Ernst, Peggy Guggenheim, André Breton, and Jacqueline Lamba managed to make their way to New York via Martinique – thanks to the American journalist Varian Fry, who, from 1940 onwards, was constantly raising funds to arrange repatriation by boat for Americans and artists of all kinds.

Pablo and Dora have returned to Paris, but I barely see them. Picasso is somewhat protected as an internationally renowned artist. Dora is increasingly gloomy and withdrawn, Paul tells me. In '43, Pablo fell in love with a certain Françoise. Dora withers and loses her soul in the shadow of genius.

Leonora Carrington fled to Spain, then to Mexico in 1942, where she met up with Alice Rahon.

Robert Desnos joined the Resistance and was denounced and arrested at his home by the Gestapo in the winter of '44. I later learned that he had been deported to Auschwitz, carted from Buchenwald to Floha and Flossenburg, eventually winding up in the Theresienstadt concentration camp. My dear Robert Desnos … The poet died of typhus in June '45. On June 8, '45. When his ashes were returned to Paris in October, Paul gave a beautiful speech paying tribute to our friend.

Yes, Man was right to leave Paname during the Occupation.

During those war years, I often found myself standing in worried lines outside squalid grocery stores. Hours of waiting for a little oil, three green-eyed potatoes, bread, sugar …

Alone in Kraut-ridden Paris.

Adrift in the streets where Nazi Germany marks its territory, day after day. Lost in the *métro*, dazed, a leaflet in my hand: "Resist. Down with the Vichy traitors. Down with collaboration. Long live de Gaulle, Savior of France."

So sad to see the persecuted Jews around me, hounded by the French police and the Gestapo. Murdered, denounced, dispossessed, scorned by the French, thrown into cattle trains bound for who knows where ... So powerless ...

In '42, May '42, along the sidewalks, we start seeing Jews wearing the yellow star. They look like zombies, poor things. People look at them with disdain and suspicion.

I remember that Jews are forbidden to enter restaurants, cafés, and cinemas. No longer allowed to go to concerts, music halls, museums, or libraries. Unwelcome in parks, fairs, campsites, swimming pools ...

People have already become accustomed to informing. Collaboration is well underway. The French police and the Gestapo burst into buildings, escorted by Nazi soldiers. They climb the stairs, kick down doors, and evict everyone. No mercy, that's the law. Before long, these poor people's homes are being raided and occupied by the informers.

Things go from bad to worse for the Jews. In mid-July '42, the big Vél' d'Hiv round-up takes place. The Jews are herded in like animals. Nothing to drink. Nothing to eat for days. Or very little ... Nothing even that could pass as a toilet. Old people, children, infants, the infirm, whole families in despair. People spoke of suicide, of surprise killings ... Then they were taken away in Régie Parisienne buses. They were dropped off on station platforms under the watchful eye of armed soldiers and French police. They were pushed onto trains. I heard about internment in Pithiviers and Drancy ... I later learned that they were deported to concentration camps: Auschwitz, Birkenau, Dachau, Mauthausen, Buchenwald ...

Man was right to leave.

They certainly worried me, all those yellow stars.

I have a lot of nightmares during the German Occupation ... One night, I'm standing in an all-white landscape. It's white, but it's not snow. I can't really describe it ... It could have been big Styrofoam panels all around me, above and below, like a Duchamp installation. The silence is white too, oppressive. Then, all of a sudden, a big black horse galloping along throws me to the ground. A trapdoor opens above my head at the same time. Hundreds of yellow stars fall from the sky. I wake up with a start. I shout, "Man! Man! Where are you?" And then I remember he's gone ...

He did the right thing in leaving, my little Man.

Black people were deported, too. Members of the Resistance. French people suspected of hiding Jews or helping them reach the free zone ... Sédar Senghor spent two years in a camp in France. Almost got shot. He wrote poems during his internment, just like Robert Desnos ...

Joséphine Baker had taken refuge in Morocco. She toured extensively, singing and dancing for Allied troops stationed in North Africa and the Middle East. She also supported the Red Cross. La Baker belonged to Free France's secret services. Sneaked messages into her musical scores. Hid microfilms in her bra ... At the end of the war, de Gaulle awarded the Black Venus a medal. No, Joséphine wasn't just a brainless dancer.

I saw Paul and Nusch from time to time during those terrible years. They helped me as best they could. We sometimes ate soup together. We kept hope alive by warming ourselves with our memories. In '42, Paul sold deluxe copies of *Les Mains libres* and some works that Man had entrusted to him before leaving. I sent Man 2,500 francs. Paul had gone underground and joined the Communist Party. In the middle of the war, he was writing leaflets and still finding inspiration for his poetry. Nusch would ride her bike and cart the leaflets around in candy boxes. Nusch was getting thinner and thinner, but kept her big, beautiful smile. She never complained about anything. Yet, in '45, I could already see death circling around her.

I remember writing four-page letters to Man. I keep going, watching out for the mailman. I write desperate words of love. I send him photos of me. Identity photos ... I tell him I love him and I'm waiting for him. I smile in the photos. I put flowers in my hair and smile like I used to ...

In '46, I write, "What are you up to, Man? Have you fallen in love with a pretty girl from your homeland? Are you working a lot? Tell me everything, Man. You know, Man, I have met an honest boy who wants to marry me. I know his parents, they are very nice. All for me. I speak about you all the time. Naturally, I don't tell them that you were my lover, but that I adore you like a best friend. You know, Man, I don't want to get married if you come back, because I'd like to live with you again. You're the best time of my life, Man, and, above all, I love you, Man. I love you so much ...."

Yes, one night at the Bal Blomet, I bumped into a guy who looked vaguely like Man. Except taller and much younger. His name is André Art. He's got the same wavy black hair. The gift of the gab ... He sort of helps me to get organized, to survive. His family has adopted me. I really like his parents. They're not racist or antisemitic. André is a spirited young man. A dreamer. He makes plans, imagines a life for himself after the war. André is the reason I can stay on my feet. He draws me into his dreams, and I forget about reality. It does me good not to look too closely at what's going on around me. André tells me that one day he'll be a millionaire. He truly believes it. He distracts me from Man's absence. He numbs my pain. I love him very much, but I was frank with him. He knows I'll leave him in a heartbeat if Man ever returns and wants me back ... André has the sword of Damocles hanging over his head.

We make love, of course, and the earth stops spinning out of control. In the throes of lovemaking, I ascend to seventh heaven. And up there, I settle on a soft cloud. I feel sheltered, far from the storms, at a safe distance from the horrors that shape my day-to-day life. I cling to my cloud as long as I can. When I'm dislodged by the wild forces blowing around in my mind, I float back down in slow motion, like a feather in the wind, moving this way and that, until I land silently on the hard ground of the real world.

I'm five years older than André Art. This time, it's me who's old, and he's the youngster. He's like Man, says that the age difference doesn't matter. I teach him how to make love properly, how to reach orgasm beautifully, how to give yourself over to the other person and let yourself be carried away by the pleasure. We make love to forget the Bosch and the misery.

The days and nights drag on under the German Occupation. In Paris, I feel like history is repeating itself.

Misfortune, just like in 1928 in Guadeloupe.

People lining up in front of grocery stores.

Occasionally, I go to the soup kitchen.

I go to the pawnshop to sell my jewelry ...

I also sell my watches, my shoes ...

The house in Saint-Germain-en-Laye was broken into. Fortunately, they didn't take much. I let it to a reliable friend for the rent money.

Ady, passport photo attached to an April 14, 1945 letter addressed
to Man Ray.

I moved several times between '41 and '45. Little rooms under
the roof with the toilet on the landing. Then, after the Liberation,
a cheap one-bedroom apartment on Rue de Wurtz in the thirteenth
arrondissement. In '46, a tiny apartment on Rue du Commandant-
Guilbaud, in the sixteenth, not far from the Longchamp racecourse.
That year, I turned thirty-one. André and I settled down together,
for better or for worse, him with his dreams of riches, me with
my ghosts.

André's passion in life is turf racing. Putting on three-way bets
is his hobby. We live just a stone's throw from the racetracks.
Gambling is his guilty pleasure. He's an obliging, easygoing
person. I can ask him anything. André and I moved Man's works
several times, eventually storing them in the attic of a neighboring
house in Saint-Germain-en-Laye. Paintings, books, and drawings,
notebooks, and index cards, objects, large quantities of film and
photographs, chess sets, and African masks ...

A haunting memory …

I'm standing among the people pounding the pavement outside local grocery stores. That's me, freezing, worried, in a funk. Paris is liberated, but the misery is still there.

In these lines, I see all kinds of women, from season to season. Worn-out mothers, pregnant to their eyeballs, silent women constantly feeling for the ration coupons in their pockets, talkative ruffians ready to rip into grocers, knitters who keep their hands busy to avoid thinking. Jokers, too, who find a way to laugh and entertain the crowd.

It always took me back to 1928, to Guadeloupe …

The patience of rotten water. Words to deceive death. Laughter to numb anguish.

In Pointe-à-Pitre, many long days after the hurricane, there were these *négresses* who smiled at the memory of their ancestors sold to the white people by their brothers, in exchange for trinkets, knick-knacks, guns, glassware. They laughed about the men who knocked them up and abandoned them. They knew that they were powerless to change the course of history, since their entire lives had been written on the pages of this colony, and there was no other way forward, there was nothing else to do but live. And laughing warmed the heart. It was a way of keeping a little candle of hope lit somewhere in the heart. Laughing for laughter's sake, to stop hurting. Laughing to forget the pain. Laughing to forget the sky that fell on their heads on September 12, 1928.

All through the Occupation, I dance. Initially to be able to eat. Then, to forget the livid, bile-filled hatred running through Paris. Hatred of Jewish people. Hatred of *métèques*. Black people are no longer in fashion, Aryans are. I pray for peace in France and in the world. I pray for Man to come back to me …

I rarely see my sisters. They think Man has abandoned me.

André and his parents are supportive. But it's the hope of seeing Man again that feeds my soul every day. I smile to myself when I think of him; his jokes, his touch.

As time goes by, I get it into my head that I have some kind of mission. I'm responsible for the works he left behind. I have to watch over his paintings and photographs, the chessboards, the pipes, all the objects …

Every day, I tell myself that the war will soon be over, and that my little Man will come back. With his joy, his laughter, his love …

I tell myself that this war is just a dream. Just another nightmare. I'll wake up and everything will be as it was before. Man will be by my side, naked under the sheets, and he'll take me in his arms ...

Alas.

No, war doesn't just leave a trail of death, of widows, and orphans.

War separates people who love each other.

I wrote letters to Man at his sister's address. I didn't hear from him often, except via Lefebvre-Foinet, the color merchant, and Nusch and Paul Éluard. Many of my letters got lost or were sent back to me ...

Then came the Liberation. The joy of the Parisians.

Liberté by Paul Éluard on everyone's lips: *I write your name ... On the gilded images ... On all my azure cloths ...On the wings of birds ... On the foam of clouds ... I write your name ... On every hand reaching out ... On hope without memory I write your name And by the power of one word I begin my life anew I was born to know you To name you Liberty.*

When the Liberation is announced, Man has only one thought in mind: return to Paris. Together with Duchamp and Breton, he celebrated peace in New York, in a German restaurant ... Peace decreed in devastation, cities wiped off the map, mined landscapes, millions of dead all over Europe, mass graves, refugees wandering the roads ... Misery lies at the heart of the restored freedom.

In this dirty war, millions fell in defense of freedom – civilians and soldiers, people of all faiths and colors ...

On November 28, 1946, Nusch died of a stroke. Paul was distraught, inconsolable, I was told. Dead at forty, my dear friend, my sister.

I was sick, hospitalized in Cannes, with André's mother at my bedside. I couldn't go to the funeral at Père-Lachaise cemetery. I still had this stomachache tearing away at my guts. I underwent many operations. I had a gallbladder stone, a liver abscess, and suppurating pleurisy. I pulled through, thanks to André and his family, thanks to God ...

Man returned to Paris in the summer of '47, having married Juliet a year earlier. He was so grateful to me for saving his work.

"You and Lefebvre-Foinet have been the custodians of my possessions!" he said, pulling me into a tight hug.

Me, Ady, guardian of Man Ray's treasure. It warmed my heart.

Man was now fifty-seven. He would have liked to arrive in France on a liner in Le Havre, as he had in the past. But the city was devastated … He took the plane. He got on well with André. We laughed, talked about our lives, and told stories … We had lunch in a bar. He was happy, excited to be back in Paname … Juliet and I posed for photos …

His marriage to Juliet, he confided to me, had come about quite naturally, in a wholly unforeseeable way. Max Ernst and a certain Dorothea Tanning were visiting him in Hollywood. They were getting married. They wanted Juliet and Man to be their witnesses. So, on a whim, Man said, "We can too!" Double surrealist wedding in Beverly Hills, over in California.

I was happy for him. But angry deep down. I thought that if it hadn't been for the war …

Man and Juliet went back to the United States. We continued to correspond. A page had been turned, even if there was still love between us. André and Juliet knew it. But nothing would ever be the same again. The war had damaged us. Ady and Man, that was a thing of the past …

Man loved Paris too much to stay away, despite all the honors and tributes. In 1951, he was back again with Juliet. Of course, André and I were happy to host them in our home on Rue Guilbaud until they found a place of their own.

Paul Éluard died in Charenton-le-Pont on November 18, 1952. He was fifty-six years old. He joined Nusch in Père-Lachaise.

André and I got married in Paris in '58. Always one for dreams and grand plans, André was intent on starting a real estate agency in the south. He was due to join his partner in Albi. The business was supposed to yield a lot of money in next to no time. Alas, the poor fellow had a car accident. Died on the spot. Unluckily, no papers had been signed between the two associates. André had put all our money into the agency. It was a massive failure that left us completely cleaned out.

We still settled near Albi with André's parents. In an apartment in a small housing estate on the outskirts of town. We lived frugally. To keep the kettle boiling, I had to sell some photos of the "Happy Family" that Man had given me as mementos of our happy years.

1940 and beyond ...

When Man wrote his *Self-Portrait*, at the very beginning of the sixties, I asked him not to go into too much detail, for André and Juliet's sake. "We had a good time, Man. We were in love, but maybe it's best not to tell the whole story ...." He smiled into the phone. Said softly, "I'll leave some stories between the lines."

In 1968, I heard on the radio that Marcel Duchamp had died. I gave Man a call to comfort him. We reminisced about old times. We laughed with *joyfulness, playfulness, pleasure.*

Before it was too late, Man celebrated the women he had met and loved: assistants, muses, friends, lovers, wives, mistresses ... Kiki, Lee, Juliet, Natasha, Sheila, Irina, Alice, Nusch, Dora, Gema, Adon, Sonia ... and me, Ady. In '70 or '71, he drew us all and gathered the drawings in a book entitled *La Ballade des femmes hors du temps ...*

Man died in Paris in 1976, on Rue Férou.

I went to Guadeloupe that year, to see my country again before I died. Rue Condé, Place de la Victoire, Pointe-à-Pitre, my childhood, the *mornes* and woods of Trois-Rivières ...

I was sixty-one years old. More than forty-five years since I had seen my island ...

La Soufrière volcano was threatening to erupt. People were saying that Guadeloupe was in danger of disappearing beneath the ashes, and that hundreds of people would die. Access to Basse-Terre was forbidden, blocked off by gendarmes. From a distance, I could see a little flameless smoke rising into the sky. Then nothing. I brought many things back to Albi: lobsters, seafood, images of beaches and landscapes superimposed on those of the South of France, Antibes, Golfe-Juan, Mougins ...

The Man of Light died on November 18, 1976, at the age of eighty-six.

I'm sure he kept his young man's soul to the end.

I like to think that the Paname of the interwar years remained intact in his mind, in his heart.

Paris, love, art, freedom, friends, painting, and poetry ... Good times and *Fair Weather.*

Man Ray and Ady Fidelin, Mougins, France 1937 by Lee Miller.
© Lee Miller Archives, England
2023. All rights reserved. leemiller.co.uk

Sources for the Original French Text

Augé, Marc. *Paris, années 30: Roger-Viollet* (Paris: Hazan, 1997).

Bangou, Henri, *La Guadeloupe*. *Tome 3: La Nécessaire Décolonisation, 1939 à nos jours* (Paris: L'Harmattan, 1977).

Bilé, Serge. *Noirs dans les camps nazis* (Monaco: Éditions du Rocher-Poche, 2016).

Blanchard, Pascal, Éric Deroo, and Gilles Manceron. *Paris noir* (Paris: Hazan, 2001).

Bonini, Emmanuel. *La Véritable Joséphine Baker* (Paris: Pygmalion/Gérard Watelet, 2000).

Bourgeoisat, Jérôme. *Paris d'antan. Paris à travers la carte postale ancienne* (Paris: HC Éditions, 2004).

Champeaux, Antoine and Éric Deroo. *La Force noire. Gloire et infortune d'une légende coloniale* (Paris: Tallandier, 2006).

Chopin, Anne and Hervé. *Guadeloupe d'antan* (Paris: HC Éditions, 1998).

Collectif Atelier Man Ray: Unconcerned But Not Indifferent (La Fabrica Editorial/ Pinacothèque de Paris, 2008).

Collectif Images Mémoire de Coco Chanel à Maurice Chevalier (Paris: Larousse, 1996).

Collectif, Paris Années folles (Paris: Parigramme, 2014).

Cortanze, Gérard de. *Frida Kahlo, la beauté terrible* (Paris: Albin Michel, 2011; Le Livre de Poche, 2013).

Digne, Stéphanie Suffren Jean (ed.). "Montparnasse noir 1906-1966 amours en contre-jour." *Catalogue d'exposition présentée au musée du Montparnasse* (Marseille: Éditions Transbordeurs, 2006).

l'Écotais, Emmanuelle de, Manfred Heiting, and Katherine Ware. *Man Ray* (Cologne: Taschen, 2020).

Éluard, Paul and Man Ray. *Les Mains libres* (Paris: Gallimard, 1947).

Grossman, Wendy A. and Sala E. Patterson. "Ady Fidelin." *Le Modèle noir de Géricault à Matisse* (Paris: musée d'Orsay/Flammarion, 2019).

Penrose, Antony. *Les Vies de Lee Miller*, translated by Claro (Paris: Arléa/ Seuil, 1994).

Ray, Man. *Autoportrait*, translated by Anne Guérin (Paris: Seghers, 1964; Paris: Actes Sud, 1998).

—. *Correspondance avec Ady et André Fidelin*. Centre Pompidou/MNAM-CCI/ Bibliothèque Kandinsky, fonds Man Ray.

Renault, Olivier. *Montparnasse entre bohème et Années folles* (Paris: Parigramme, 2018).

Sanchez, Serge. *Man Ray* (Paris: Gallimard, 2014).

Tardieu, Marc. *Les Antillais à Paris d'hier et d'aujourd'hui* (Monaco: Éditions du Rocher, 2005).

Vignas, Agnès. "Man Ray/Paul Éluard – Les Mains libres." *Les lettres volées*. www.lettresvolees.fr

Bibliography for the Translated Text

Anonymous. "Complainte de Violette Nozière" (1933).*

Baudelaire, Charles. "Un Fantôme. Le Parfum." *Flowers of Evil*, translated by Lewis Piaget Shanks (New York: Ives Washburn, 1931), pp. 32–33.

Césaire, Aimé. *The Original 1939 Notebook of a Return to the Native Land.* Bilingual edition, translated and edited by A. James Arnold and Clayton Eshleman (Middletown: Wesleyan University Press, 2013).

Chevalier, Maurice. "Dans la vie faut pas s'en faire" (Paris: Pathé 2030/2031, 1921).*

Cortanze, Gérard de. *Frida Kahlo, la beauté terrible* (Paris: Albin Michel, 2011; Le Livre de Poche, 2013).*

Damas, Léon-Gontran. *Black-Label et autres poèmes* (Paris: Gallimard, 1956 [2011]).*

—. *Pigments* – Névralgies (Paris: Présence africaine, 1972 [2005]).

Éluard, Paul. *Les animaux et leurs hommes, les hommes et leurs animaux* (Paris: Au Sens Pareil, 1920).*

—. *Capitale de la douleur* (Paris: Gallimard, 1926).*

—. *Poésie et vérité* (Paris: Éditions de la main à plume, 1942).*

Éluard, Paul and Man Ray. *Les Mains libres* (Paris: Gallimard, 1947).*

Georgel, Thérèse. "L'oiseau de nuit." *Contes et légendes des Antilles* (Paris: Éditions Nathan, 1957 [1994]), pp. 95–99.*

Nau, John-Antoine. *Hiers bleus* (Paris: Librairie Léon Vanier, 1904).*

Perse, Saint-John. *Éloges* (Paris: Gallimard, 1911 [1960]).*

Ray, Man. *Self Portrait* (Boston: Atlantic Monthly Press, 1963).

Thaly, Daniel. "Le jardin des Tropiques." *La Nouvelle Revue Française*, n. 32, 1911, p. 246.*

Villon, François. "Ballade des dames du temps jadis." *Poems (1870)*, trans. by Dante Gabriel Rossetti, 6th ed. (London: Strangeways and Walden, 1872), p. 179.

* These texts were translated specifically for this translation. The translators are credited in the footnote on the page where the text appears.

Author's Acknowledgements

To the fans of the wonderful Ady Fidelin: Philippe Rey, Pierre Coquelet, Wendy Grossman, Sala Patterson.

To my friends, for their unfailing support and encouragement: Alex Foggéa, Gerty Duplain, Joëlle Etzol, Max and Marie-Cécile Rippon.

To my friend Sophie Carayon, who accompanied me on my adventure following Ady's footsteps in Albi, and Man Ray's tracks in Montparnasse.

To André Art's family: Nicolas Beaumont, Catherine Noviel, Irène Beaumont.

To the kind people who guided me along the way: Nathalie Julan, Louis Dessout, Rose-Lee Raqui, France-Yan Fidelin.

To my daughter Laure, to my sisters near and far.

Photo Credits

Page ix: FIG. 1
Ady, 1937. Banque d'Images, ADAGP / Art Resource, NY © Man Ray
2015 Trust / Artists
Rights Society (ARS), NY / ADAGP, Paris 2023.

Page 23: FIG. 2
Ady, 1937. Banque d'Images, ADAGP / Art Resource, NY © Man Ray
2015 Trust / Artists
Rights Society (ARS), NY / ADAGP, Paris 2023.

Page 40: FIG. 3
Picnic, Île Sainte-Marguerite, Cannes, France 1937 by Lee Miller. © Lee
Miller Archives,
England 2023. All rights reserved. leemiller.co.uk

Page 59: FIG. 4
Paul et Marie Cuttoli, Dora Maar, Pablo Picasso, Ady Fidelin et Man Ray.
Banque d'Images,
ADAGP / Art Resource, NY © Man Ray 2015 Trust / Artists Rights
Society (ARS), NY /
ADAGP, Paris 2023.

Page 76: FIG. 5
Ady Fidelin, Roland Penrose and Nusch Éluard, Mougins, France 1937 by Lee
Miller. © Lee
Miller Archives, England 2023. All rights reserved. leemiller.co.uk

Page 100: FIG. 6
Man Ray and Ady Fidelin, Mougins, France 1937 by Lee Miller. © Lee Miller
Archives, England
2023. All rights reserved. leemiller.co.uk

Page 125: FIG. 7
Ady Fidelin et Nusch Éluard, 1937. Banque d'Images, ADAGP / Art Resource, NY © Man Ray
2015 Trust / Artists Rights Society (ARS), NY / ADAGP, Paris 2023.

Page 127: FIG. 8
Roland Penrose, Ady Fidelin, Picasso and Dora Maar, Cote d'Azur, France 1937 by Lee Miller.
© Lee Miller Archives, England 2023. All rights reserved. leemiller.co.uk

Page 144: FIG. 9
Four Women Asleep [Lee Miller, Ady Fidelin, Nusch Éluard and Leonora Carrington,], Lambe
Creek, Cornwall, England 1937 by Roland Penrose. Roland Penrose © Lee Miller Archives,
England 2023. All rights reserved. leemiller.co.uk

Page 153: FIG. 10
La mode au Congo. Banque d'Images, ADAGP / Art Resource, NY © Man Ray 2015 Trust /
Artists Rights Society (ARS), NY / ADAGP, Paris 2023.

Page 159: FIG. 11
Ady Fidelin, Lee Miller and Nusch Eluard, Lambe Creek, Cornwall, England 1937 by Roland
Penrose. Roland Penrose © Lee Miller Archives, England 2023. All rights reserved.
leemiller.co.uk

Page 185: FIG. 12
"Ady, passport photo attached to a 14 April 1945 letter addressed to Man Ray." There is no copyright claim on this image.

Page 190: FIG. 13
Man Ray and Ady Fidelin, Mougins, France 1937 by Lee Miller. © Lee Miller Archives, England
2023. All rights reserved. leemiller.co.uk

Glossary

In addition to the translators' personal knowledge of the terms that appear here, this glossary was compiled with the use of the online dictionary created by Centre National de Ressources Textuelles et Lexicales, and Danièle Bernini-Montbrand, Ralph Ludwig, Hector Poullet, and Sylviane Telchid's *Dictionnaire Créole-Français (Guadeloupe)* (Saint-Denis: Orphie, 2013).

Art nègre:
African art.

Bamboche:
A social gathering at which food is served. *Cf. bamboula.*

Bamboula:
1. A drum used in certain African and Afrodiasporic cultures.
2. A dance or a party.
3. (pejorative) A term for Senegalese Tirailleurs.

Béké:
A Creole word originating from Martinique to describe the Creole population, Creole here meaning those born on the islands, descended from the white European colonizers. Although a minority in the French Caribbean, this population controls much of its industry. In Guadeloupean Creole, *blan-péyi.*

Biguine:
A dance that originates from nineteenth-century Martinique.

Boucan:
A wooden grill used by people from the Americas and the Caribbean to smoke meat and fish.

Boudin (noir):
A sausage made with the blood and fat of pigs (or other animals) and various herbs.

Bougnoule:
(pejorative) A racialized term used for a Black or mixed-raced person. It has roots in North African indigenous communities.

Bridé:
Shortening of "yeux bridés" which are eyes whose lids appear to be stretched laterally and whose opening is narrow. In this context, it appears to be a pejorative term to refer to people from the French colonies in Asia.

Bwana:
(pejorative) A loanword from Swahili, meaning "master." *Oui, bwana* is used as a collective noun to describe subservient Black people.

Cabritt-bois:
A Frenchified form of the Creole term *kabrit-bwa*, a type of cricket common in the Caribbean.

Case:
A Caribbean and African word for house.

Chaudeau:
A Frenchified form of the Creole term *chodo*, a custard dessert prepared with rum.

Compè Lapin, Roi Lion:
Two figures in traditional Caribbean and Creole folk-tales: Compè Lapin is a mischievous rabbit who uses his cunning to ridicule the people in power (often Enslavers or Plantation Owners), while Roi Lion is a lion that represents supreme authority, often the figure with whom Compè Lapin is at odds and on whom he plays tricks.

Diablesses:
A mythological creature in Guadeloupean folklore, the Diablesse is a beautiful, finely dressed, young woman who lures men into madness, danger, or both.

Doudou:
A nickname for a Caribbean woman. It derives from the French adjective *doux*. Cf. *Dous*.

Dous:
In the French text, Ady's sister Aimée is given the nickname *la Douce*. *La Douce* is a nominalized form of *douce*, in the feminine, an adjective used to describe a female who is sweet, soft, gentle, and pleasant, and roughly translates to "sweet one." The nominal phrase *ma douce* is incidentally an affectionate term of address, meaning "sweetie," "sweetheart." Aimée's nickname has been creolized in this translation. Firstly, because the use of nicknames over real names is a common practice in the Caribbean. Secondly, because *douce* is a polysemic word with several possible translations into English, and Creole, as a phonetic language, is readable by English speakers. Cf. *Wòz*.

Fatou:
A common given name for females in West Africa.

Fè dyèz:
A term in Guadeloupean Creole which means "to show off."

Grabiot:
A Frenchified form of the Creole term *grabyo*, which is a confection common in the Caribbean made from grated and caramelized coconut.

Han han:
An onomatopoeia and interjection used in Creole, mostly as a form of acknowledgement, which roughly translates to "mm-hmm."

Haut-et-bas:
Haut-et-bas houses are the homes of those with lesser financial means. They are stone buildings where the ground floor is used as a shop and the upper floor as living quarters. The ground floor is sometimes surrounded by a passageway or balcony supported by metal pillars.

Indigène:
The French word used to speak about people born in the colonies.

Marrade:
A nominalized form of the French verb *se marrer*, meaning "to have fun," which roughly translates to "great times."

Masque de poix:
Literally, a mask made of tar. A reference to a line of the poem "Narcisse" by Paul Éluard, which appears in the collection *Les Mains libres*, accompanied by a drawing by Man Ray.

Métèque:
(pejorative) A person, often a foreigner, whose exotic appearance, allure, and behavior do not inspire confidence.

Métis (m.) and Métisse (f.):
A person born of parents of two different races or from two people of the same race but of different skin tones. Cf. *Mulâtre and Mulâtresse*.

Métropole:
A state, or the territory of a state, considered in relation to its colonies (or its mandated countries, its protectorates) or its overseas territories. In France, people often refer to the mainland as the *Hexagone* or the *Métropole*. Despite the fact that islands such as Guadeloupe and Martinique and French Guiana are also all considered part of France, they are excluded when the terms *Métropole* or *Hexagone* are used.

Morne:
A word for "hill" or "mountain" that is particular to island formations.

Mulâtre (m.) and Mulâtresse (f.):
A person who has one white parent and one Black parent and who has a darker skin tone. Cf. *Métis and* Métisse.

Nègre (m.) and Négresse (f.):
1. In the French Caribbean and in some places in French-speaking Africa, *nègre* is used to mean "man," "person," or even "human." It was reappropriated by Afro-Caribbean intellectuals in the 1930s and 1940s and lent itself to the neologism "Négritude." The term *nèg* in Guadeloupean, Guianese, Haitian, and Martinican Creole is indissociable from "man" and "human." Thus, the term carries a different and more nuanced meaning in French than any potential equivalents in English, which carry different cultural connotations, given the distinct contexts of their use in both languages.
2. (pejorative) Black person.
N.B. Usually, the context of the word can help the reader understand if its use is related to definition 1 or 2.

(Nègres) marrons:
Enslaved people who fled slavery for the mountains and formed independent communities away from the enslavers.

Noiraud:
(pejorative) A term used to describe Black people with a dark skin tone.

Paname:
A nickname for the city of Paris, originating in the 19th century. The origins of the nickname are unknown.

Soucougnans:
Female shape-shifting spirits present in Caribbean folklore that appear as old women by day, but sheds their skin and transform into a firebird at night to catch individuals and drain them of their blood. Cf. *Volant.*

Toucouleur:
A racial term that refers to the Peul ethnic group of West African origin.

Tout-Paris:
All the personalities of the French capital who, because of their notoriety, their social position, and their importance in any field (political, literary, artistic, commercial, etc.), regularly appear in the social events of Parisian life.

Volants:
Flying shape-shifting spirits present in Caribbean folklore. Cf. *soucougnan.*

Wòz:
In the French text, Rose is called *la Rose*, "the Rose." Her nickname has been creolized in this translation. Firstly, because the use of nicknames over real names is a common practice in the Caribbean. Secondly, while *rose* does have a direct translation in English, the name has been creolized to maintain consistency in how Ady would have spoken about her sisters. Furthermore, Creole, as a phonetic language, is readable by English speakers. Cf. *Dous.*

Y'a bon (Banania):
(pejorative) A term for Black people. It is a reference to the caricatural depiction of a Senegalese Tirailleur used in advertisements for the chocolate drink Banania.